D1526533

Cover Design and Interior Format

FORTUNE'S
BRIDES
BOOK
FOUR

# Never Vie for a Viscount

# REGINA SCOTT

*To all the scientists and engineers who have inspired me over the years, and to the Lord, the author of all inspiration*

# CHAPTER ONE

*London, England, late April, 1812*

A townhouse had never looked so daunting.
Lydia Villers stood on the pavement gazing up at
the four-story white row house situated on fashionable
Clarendon Square. Her muslin dress had seemed light and
airy when she'd donned it that morning, her pink velvet
Spencer hardly needed for the warm spring day. Now she
felt perspiration trickling down her back.

"It is the best situation for your goals," Meredith Thorn
reminded her.

Lydia glanced at her companion. Oh, for an ounce of that
confidence! Meredith, owner of the Fortune Employment
Agency, always looked in complete control of herself.
Perhaps it was the sleek black hair, so unlike Lydia's pale
ringlets. Or the depth of her lavender eyes, the color so
much more compelling than Lydia's misty green.

Or maybe it was the grey cat in her arms, gazing serenely
at Lydia as if she didn't doubt Lydia could win over anyone
who stood against her.

Lydia drew in a breath. Her family and friends had
consistently commented on her sunny smile, her optimism
and enthusiasm. She should not allow her regrets over one
man to dim her light.

"You're right," she told Meredith. "Let's go."

Meredith nodded in satisfaction. Her cat, Fortune, stood tall in her arms, tail waving like a cavalry flag as they moved forward.

A man answered their knock on the green-lacquered door, and Lydia could only marvel at his size in his sturdy brown coat and breeches. She was used to strapping footmen in white powered wigs. His hair was brown and thick and short-cropped. He took the card Meredith held out in one massive ungloved fist.

"We'd like to call on Miss Worthington, if you please," Meredith said. "We've come about a position."

His gaze, brown like his hair and clothing, traveled over Meredith and Lydia and lit on Fortune in Meredith's arms. A smile tilted up, making him suddenly approachable. "Come in and wait. I'll ask Miss Worthington if she wants to see you."

Rather direct for a footman as well. As he ambled off, Meredith and Lydia stepped into the entry hall. It was not the most remarkable place, for all the work in this house had the chance to change her life. The painting of a ship in full sail still graced one of the light-blue walls as it had when she'd last visited a year ago. Like it, she felt the wind pushing her to new horizons. The gilt-framed mirror and half-moon table still stood opposite, the reflection in the oval glass showing her a bit paler than usual, her eyes luminous. The only thing to give her pause was the gentleman's tall hat and ebony walking stick on the polished wood surface. She swallowed.

She would not be working for him. Not directly. She had to remember that. If she never saw Frederick, Viscount Worthington, again, it would be too soon.

The manservant returned and tipped his head to the corridor on the right of the stairs. "This way, if you please."

She knew the layout of the house. He was no doubt taking them to the withdrawing room at the back. It had been a pleasant space, done in shades of rose and blue, with a settee in front of the wood-wrapped hearth and a few chairs scattered about. The Worthingtons entertained rarely. Far too busy with more important matters.

Charlotte Worthington was sitting at the walnut secretary along one silk-draped wall when they entered. Setting down her quill, she smiled at them. Lydia had always admired her. Like Meredith, she was cool, confident. She tended to speak her mind, even if she knew how to coat vinegar with honey. Only her auburn hair, coiled in a bun at the back of her head with tendrils escaping along her sculpted cheeks, was at odds with her polished demeanor.

"That will be all, Beast," she said.

Beast? The manservant didn't show any sign of resenting the rough name. He nodded and withdrew, leaving the door open behind him. Charlotte rose and swept toward them, grey lustring gown glinting in the sunlight coming through one velvet-draped window. Fortune leaned forward as if ready to welcome her.

"Miss Thorn," she acknowledged. "And Miss Villers. What an unexpected pleasure."

Another time, in another situation, it might have been a pleasure to see Charlotte again. She'd been polite, even friendly, the one other time they had met since Lydia had returned from her sojourn in Essex. Why? Charlotte's brother could have made no good report of Lydia. He'd been the one to sever all acquaintance, as if she'd developed some dread disease.

She shook off the thought and dipped a curtsey. "Miss Worthington. Thank you for receiving us."

"Of course. You are always welcome in this house."

She was? Straightening, she gazed at Charlotte in wonder, but those deep grey eyes did not suggest a lie. Still, Lydia could not embrace that truth.

"Please, join me," Charlotte said, going to sit on the settee. "Would your pet like a cushion?"

Meredith drew a hand along Fortune's back. "Fortune

prefers to stay with me. But I appreciate the offer." She took the closest chair and nodded Lydia into another nearby. "I won't keep you long. I understand you're looking to add a member to your team."

Charlotte glanced between the two of them as if she wasn't sure who was being offered. "I had just begun making inquiries. Do you know of someone?"

Meredith glanced at Lydia.

"Yes," Lydia said, pausing to take a deep breath. "Me."

Charlotte's russet brows rose. "I wasn't aware you were interested in scientific pursuits, Miss Villers."

Few knew. She'd always loved learning about discoveries. When she was little, she used to sit on her father's knee in his study as he read aloud from *Philosophical Transactions*, the journal of the Royal Society. After he'd died, she'd made sure the subscription continued, devouring the latest advances in science, medicine, and industry. She thrilled to read how luminaries like Sir Humphrey Davy, Sir Nicholas Rotherford, and William Herschel were pushing back the boundaries of chemistry, peering into the recesses of space. She'd applauded the work of the Royal Institution, making such advances practical. She'd begged her brother to take her to one of the public lectures, but he'd been appalled by the very suggestion.

"Never speak of this unseemly fascination outside the house," Beau had ordered, glaring down his long nose at her. "They'll think you a bluestocking."

A bluestocking. A far too educated woman. The term conjured up spinsters gathered over tea, clucking like hens, dreams of husband and family supplanted by second-hand accounts of scientific advances. That wasn't her. She was destined to marry well. Beau had promised her parents before they'd died that he'd make sure of it.

And so she'd tried. She'd danced and flirted, sang at too many musicales, endured dozens of drives through the park. At Beau's insistence, she'd shoved herself at every titled gentleman on the *ton*. Several had shown interest. She knew how to dress and bat her lashes and smile winsomely, after all. She could play Society's game, appear more interested in the color of waistcoats than discussions of politics and natural philosophy. But no matter how much she flattered a gentleman's consequence, none had felt compelled to offer.

Even the one she'd prayed would offer.

Now she squared her shoulders. "I am very interested in scientific pursuits, Miss Worthington. I've spent the last six weeks working closely with Augusta Orwell as she developed a formulation to heal skin conditions. I understand the properties of various substances—animal, plant, and mineral. I am fluent in the actions of various change agents like heat, light, water, and air."

"Miss Orwell would be delighted to provide a reference," Meredith put in.

Charlotte leaned back, gaze uncompromising. "We work long hours. There's little time for Society."

Lydia smiled. "Excellent. I no longer need to spend time in Society."

"So you are off the marriage mart?" Charlotte challenged.

That was the one question she was thoroughly confident in answering. "Absolutely. I plan to devote myself to the furtherance of knowledge."

"Hogwash."

The male voice behind her sent a shiver through her. Her breath left with her confidence. Her body swiveled of its own volition to face the man in the doorway. Hair as smoldering as his sister's, cut long enough to brush the collar of his coat. Eyes as grey but brighter, suggesting a spark of starlight within. High cheekbones, firm chin. A lean physique shown to advantage in a simple navy coat and fawn trousers. Beau would have known the name for that fold in his cravat. The Mathematical? How suitable. Anyone looking at Lord Worthington would see a gentleman of the *ton*.

She knew better. She could not move, could not speak, as the viscount she'd once vied for strolled into the room.

Frederick, Viscount Worthington—Worth to his friends and family—stared at the vision of loveliness seated on the chair across from his sister. Those blond ringlets, the big green eyes, the curves outlined by her fashionable gown. Lydia Villers, in his home? He'd never thought to see it again.

But he couldn't believe the preposterous story any more than he'd believed she'd cared for him, not after he'd learned the truth about her.

"Worth," Charlotte said, an exasperated tone creeping into her voice. "I didn't realize you were home. This is Miss Thorn, of the Fortune Employment Agency."

The other woman, a regal raven-haired female in a lavender-colored gown, turned to meet his look. He inclined his head in greeting, and his gaze lit on the grey cat in her lap. A handsome creature. The blaze of white down its chest made it look as if it were wearing a cravat. He couldn't help his smile.

"Miss Thorn, a pleasure," he said. "And I'm delighted to meet your companion as well."

"Surely you remember Miss Villers," Charlotte chided.

"Of course I remember Miss Villers," Worth said, refusing to look at the woman who had broken his heart a year ago.

"I believe your brother is referring to my other companion," Miss Thorn said with a smile. "This is Fortune, my lord. Fortune, meet Viscount Worthington."

He bowed, straightening to find the cat regarding him with interest in her copper-colored eyes. Miss Thorn relaxed her hold, and her pet dropped to the carpet and padded up to him to twine herself around his boots.

"She likes you." Lydia sounded shocked.

No more shocked than he'd been to hear her proclaim a love for natural philosophy. But then, that was part of her charm—her unbridled enthusiasm for everything.

And everyone.

He'd let it sway him before, convinced himself what she felt was real, unique to him alone. He knew better now. He'd far sooner trust the cat. People were unpredictable. Nature—for all its eccentricities—followed knowable paths.

He squatted and put out his hand, allowing Fortune to sniff at his gloved fingers. She arched her back, inviting his touch, and Worth ran his hand gently along the fur. "I see that Fortune is a highly discriminating creature."

"She is," Miss Thorn agreed. "She approves of you almost as much as she approves of Miss Villers."

Perhaps not so discriminating after all. But then, deciphering the motives of the human heart was his downfall.

He straightened. "Nevertheless, I believe we are fully staffed at present."

Charlotte was frowning at him. "We need one more to achieve your timetable, and you know it. Miss Villers has been working with Augusta Orwell. She has experience."

"Alas, distilling concoctions for beauty preparations does not usually equate with experimental rigor," he said, trying to keep his voice and look kind.

Lydia swept to her feet and turned to face him fully, and he took a step back from the intensity blazing from her eyes.

"Our work," she said, moving toward him, "may look simple to a man of your letters, Lord Worthington, but we follow the scientific method laid down by Bacon. We observe that certain elements appear to affect healing. We hypothesize that a particular ingredient may be beneficial."

With each step in the process she described, she advanced,

and Worth could only retreat.

"We devise experiments to test its efficacy both alone and in combination with other ingredients. We measure response, attempt to replicate the experiment, and see if we gain similar results. We document our findings. Our work may never appear in *Philosophical Transactions*, but the formula we recently developed has been evaluated by other apothecaries and found to have merit. It is being sold on the market to help others. Can you say the same of your work?"

His back was to the wall, literally and figuratively. His best application, the result of years of painstaking experimentation and documentation, had been stolen by a colleague who had claimed all credit. That's when he'd first learned the pain of betrayal, even if hers had hurt more.

"Perhaps my brother questions your dedication rather than your credentials," Charlotte said. Over Lydia's head, he could see that a smirk had replaced his sister's frown. She was enjoying this, the brat!

"Six weeks is a short time to be involved in scientific pursuits," she qualified when he shot a glare in her direction.

Lydia drew herself up, until her pert nose was pointing at his chin and he could see deep into her eyes. "Six weeks laboring from breakfast until long past dinner. I'm not afraid of hard work, when it has a purpose."

Miss Thorn rose and came to collect her pet, who had retreated with Worth to the back wall. Fortune gazed up at him as if she expected him to make the right decision. Would that he knew what that decision should be.

Charlotte was right—their timetable was tight. He had promised the Prince Regent to have something to demonstrate by the end of May. He was so close! Another pair of hands, another mind focused on the task, might make the difference between success and failure. And if he accomplished what he'd set out to do, he could at last feel he had lived up to his family legacy and redeemed himself for his past mistakes.

"Miss Villers has already made significant sacrifices to pursue a career," Miss Thorn said, pet back in her arms. "She has left her position in Society, defied her brother."

Interesting. Beauford Villers had been instrumental in introducing Worth to Lydia. He had always thought the fellow would be over the moon had his sister and Worth married. Did Villers still insist that she wed?

"Most women of our class face persecution when stepping away from traditional roles," Charlotte acknowledged. She knew. After several Seasons on the *ton*, she had retired to their home and focused on helping him. The result had been unkind comments from Society's reining belles, slights from former friends. Charlotte had ignored them all to remain at his side and help him achieve. There wasn't much he wouldn't do for his sister.

Except, perhaps, hire Lydia Villers.

"I don't care," Lydia said, chin in the air. "I was ill-suited to the traditional role. I don't miss it."

Now, that he could not believe. Everything about Lydia Villers—from the artful ringlets framing her piquant face to her frilly muslin gowns and normal exuberance—was designed to appeal to a gentleman seeking a bride. She had certainly appealed to him. He was more than a little chagrined to find she still did.

"So, what do you want?" he asked.

She beamed up at him, the sun coming out after a storm, lifting his spirits despite his reservations.

"I want to learn more—how things work, why they function as they do." Her voice rang with determination. "I want to expand the boundaries of knowledge, discover great things that help others." She flung out her arms as if she would embrace the world. "I want to cure disease, double the food supply, soar beyond the stars."

She dropped her hands. "Surely that's not too much to ask."

Not in the slightest. The same longings pushed him. Indeed, they had been a hallmark of his family. As a military commander, his great-grandfather had earned the family its title and prestige. As a magistrate, his grandfather had helped establish civil liberties others now took for granted. In Parliament, his father had championed minimum wages for the poor.

From an early age, he'd been praised by his parents and tutors for his keen mind. That mind, he'd soon discovered, demanded challenges. He wasn't suited to be a fighter, a judge, or a politician. Those spheres were too narrow. How much better to embrace the grand challenge of advancing knowledge to improve lives?

Now he experimented, evaluated evidence, and calculated the chances of success. Until Lydia's declaration, he would have put her chance of joining his team at less than twenty percent. How had she known the one thing that might sway him? Was he that obvious? Was this a trick? Was he looking at the situation all wrong?

He glanced to his sister, once more unsettled and unsure of his answer.

As always, Charlotte knew his mind better than he did. She rose, serene in her grey gown.

"Well said, Miss Villers," she declared. "I believe you will get on famously with the rest of the team. When can you start?"

# CHAPTER TWO

Lydia started the next morning, precisely at eight. After negotiating a monthly stipend and a half-day off each week, Meredith had made her comfortable in her townhouse, just down the square from the Worthington home. Like so many of the others in the neighborhood, it was tall and elegant, but Lydia had been surprised to find most of the rooms empty.

"I'm still accustoming myself to the space," Meredith had said as if she noticed Lydia's look when they passed a bedchamber lacking bed or wardrobe. "And I allowed the family of the previous owner to take whatever pleased them in remembrance. They had a great number of remembrances. But never fear. I have one functioning guest room."

It was a warm, comforting room, with pale pink walls and a canopied bed hung with chintz curtains patterned with tulips of the same shade. Though simpler than the bedchambers in many of the homes Lydia had visited, it was far superior to some of the spaces Beau had been able to afford since their parents had died.

Now Lydia drew in a breath before climbing the stairs and rapping at the green door of the Worthington home. The same manservant answered, scowl on his face as if he sincerely doubted she had any ability to contribute to the inspirational work being conducted on the premises. She did not tell him she had the same doubts.

In truth, her encounter with Worth had shaken her more than she cared to admit. Since he had rejected her last year, she'd done her best to avoid him. It hadn't been difficult. He didn't frequent the many balls, routs, and soirees that made up the Season in London. He attended services at St. Mary's on Paddington Green while Beau preferred St. George's Hanover Square. So long as she did not convince anyone to take her to the Royal Institution lectures, she had every expectation they would not meet.

She'd thought herself prepared to brave him for the sake of her future. But one look from those grey eyes reminded her how they could gleam with appreciation. The curve of those lips brought back whispered endearments. And she could not forget how protected and cherished those large hands could make her feel when holding hers.

Until they had fallen away.

Enough! She had not taken this position to moon over her lost love. She was going to pursue natural philosophy, earn respect, make a difference.

"Good morning," she said to the manservant. "Beast, isn't it?"

Pink stained his cheeks. "Bateman will do. Miss Worthington is expecting you. This way." He turned and walked deeper into the house.

If Beast truly was his first name, small wonder he was sensitive about it. She could not imagine parents being so cruel. Odd that Charlotte had used the name, but she was mistress of the house.

Lydia found her new employer in a room that had likely once been a gentleman's study. Now the tall bookcases held tomes from chest-level to ceiling, but the lower shelves were crowded with all manner of instruments. She identified a compass, sextant, and astrolabe, but her fingers itched to pick up the others and learn their purpose. She forced herself to look instead to the large table in the center of the room, which was spread with diagrams, notes, open leather-bound journals of various sizes, quills, and an ink stand.

"She's here," Bateman announced.

Charlotte smiled at him, and the pink in his cheeks deepened. "Thank you, Beast."

He inclined his head and left.

Charlotte rose from her place at the table and came forward, hands extended. "Miss Villers, I'm so glad to see you."

Had she doubted too? Lydia pasted on a smile. "I'm glad to be here. Where shall I start?"

Charlotte took her hands and drew her over to a window seat, where sunlight streaked her russet hair with fire. "First, a few stipulations."

Lydia sat beside her and arranged her skirts. Since she'd been working with Gussie, she'd managed to acquire a few less frilly concoctions more suited to serious pursuits. This one had yellow-and-cream-striped skirts of an airy cotton with a high-necked cream bodice and an ecru lace ruff. "Oh?" she prompted Charlotte.

"First," her new employer said, holding up one finger, "each member of the team has a special focus of work. We do not interact much. This is by design."

Another oddity. She was used to working side by side with the mercurial Gussie, their ideas building one on another. Working alone sounded a bit daunting. Immediately she scolded herself. She'd wanted to grow, hadn't she? Working alone was no different than moving from a groom-led pony to her own horse, and she'd managed that by age six.

"Very well," she said.

"Second," Charlotte continued, holding up another finger, "I will generally be the one directing your work. You will have little to no interaction with Worth."

"Oh, good." The words were out before she could think better of them.

Charlotte dropped her hand. "So you do harbor a grudge against my brother."

"No, no," Lydia hurried to assure her. "I wish him only the best. He's simply made it clear that he would prefer not to associate with me."

"Perhaps," Charlotte said, leaving the word hanging in the air, as tangible as the lamp on the table. "But I'm glad you'll have no trouble following our procedures."

"None at all," Lydia promised.

"Good. There is one more. Only Worth knows what we're attempting to accomplish."

Lydia cocked her head, sure she must have misunderstood. "You mean he determines the direction of each person's experiments?"

"Yes," Charlotte allowed, "but more than that, he's the only one who knows to what our experiments contribute."

Lydia blinked, straightening. "None of you knows the end goal of all this?"

"Only me," Charlotte said with a carefree smile. "We must learn to be content with that."

How? Was she merely to trust he had some higher aim in mind? Once, perhaps, but her viscount had proven fickle. She wanted to be taken seriously, not fritter away her time in another pointless activity.

"Surely if we knew the overall hypothesis, we could direct our efforts more efficiently," she told Charlotte. "We could pursue one approach and eschew another."

"That is why Worth is aware of all the work," Charlotte explained patiently. "We present him with a plan of study, and he approves or revises as necessary to achieve his goals."

It certainly wasn't her place to argue, but it seemed a strange path to success. Still, she'd only worked with Gussie, who was an Original. For all Lydia knew, most natural philosophers worked as Worth did.

"Very well," she said. "Anything else?"

"That should be sufficient for now." Charlotte rose, and

Lydia stood as well. "Come with me. I'll introduce you to the others."

A door in the far wall led to a short corridor that slopped down just the slightest.

"Worth purchased the adjacent townhouse to use for his work," Charlotte explained as their skirts brushed the tilted floor. "We didn't realize until we'd broken through the walls that the floors were slightly offset. That required a little accommodation." She paused and tapped at the first paneled door on the plain white wall. A muffled voice bid them enter. Charlotte opened the door.

The ornate carving on the white-and-grey marbled fireplace said this had been had likely been the withdrawing room. The space had been stripped down to hardwood floors and the same white-plastered walls as the corridor. Scattered around were stacks of reeds, bundles of straw, and spools of twine, with stripped saplings, fresh cut by the scent in the air, leaning against the far wall. In the center on a tall stool sat a sturdy-looking woman with dull blond hair braided around her wide-cheeked face. Her navy poplin skirts were speckled with chaff.

"Miss Janssen," Charlotte said, "allow me to present the newest member of our team, Miss Villers."

Miss Janssen glanced up only briefly, thick fingers busy weaving reeds together. "Miss Villers. Welcome."

"Miss Janssen." Lydia ventured closer. "How quickly you work. What are you making?"

"I know nothing," she said, voice hinting of German. She stopped and met Lydia's gaze with a frown. "Did no one explain the rules?"

Charlotte put her hands on Lydia's shoulders and steered her toward the door. "She's learning. Forgive the intrusion."

Glancing back, Lydia saw the lady was already back at work.

"I beg your pardon," she told Charlotte as Worth's sister closed the door behind them. "I didn't realize the restriction was so stringent. What research plan is she following?"

"At the moment, she is determining the optimal way to weave a basket that will support a minimum of three hundred pounds yet remain highly flexible against sudden impacts. Worth provided the tolerances." She started down the corridor once more.

Basket weaving? How did that advance knowledge? Lydia shook herself. Truly, was she no better than Worth? He'd all but sneered at her and Gussie's work, and they had done something splendid with the stillroom. Perhaps Miss Janssen's strong basket had some great use as well.

The next door had been removed from its hinges, showing narrow stairs leading down. This must have been the servants' stair to the kitchen. Muttered words floated up, followed by a crash.

Charlotte paused. "Worth?"

"Not metal," he called up. "The weight is wrong, and we could easily slice the ropes. I believe cedar our next best material. Make a note of that, Charlotte."

"Noted," Charlotte called.

"What is he pursuing?" Lydia asked, angling her head to try to see to the bottom of the stairs.

"I have no idea," Charlotte said. "Apparently, it has something to do with cedar. This way."

Lydia could only follow.

Charlotte stopped at the final door along the corridor and knocked.

"Come in." This voice was high and piping.

Charlotte opened the door.

This had likely been the dining room, for the far wall held a sideboard that would have been graced with silver and plate. Instead, the mint-colored shelves carried bolts of fabric—canvas and cotton and silk—along with skeins of thread, plump little cushions studded with pins and needles, and several types of shears. The oval table in the center was draped in scarlet silk, which spilled off one end into the lap of a diminutive woman with brown hair tightly curled around her narrow face.

"Miss Pankhurst," Charlotte said, "this is Miss Villers, who will be joining us."

Miss Pankhurst glanced up, tiny mouth pursed in a smile. "We've met. You will not remember me, but we attended a few balls together the year your brother introduced you to Society."

"But I do remember you," Lydia said, beaming. "I saw you most recently at the Duke of Wey's wedding."

She looked pleased. "Miss Worthington was so kind as to request an invitation for me to accompany her. Such an interesting event. Imagine, a footman attempting to steal from the guests."

Lydia knew the story. Mr. Mayes, a friend of her brother's, had put it about to hide the truth. What the others thought was a footman had been a French spy, come to capture Lydia's friend, Yvette de Maupassant, and return her to France for trial. Now, there was a lady of courage. After spying on Napoleon's court for years, Yvette wouldn't have been put off at meeting the man she'd once hoped to wed. Then again, Yvette was engaged now to the Earl of Carrolton, and the earl's sister was set to marry Beau, so Lydia supposed that meant they were related in some strange way.

"Yes, quite the scandal," Charlotte said before turning to Lydia. "This morning, I'd like you to take your direction from Miss Pankhurst. After she explains her expectations, you will be working in the room at the end of the corridor. We meet for tea at two in the afternoon in my study and end our day at half past five. Any questions?"

Dozens, but she merely smiled. "I'll be fine."

With a nod, Charlotte glided out the door.

Miss Pankhurst sighed. "How nice to be so self-assured. The burden she carries would melt many women under the strain."

Lydia went to join her at the table. "What burden could Charlotte Worthington carry? She has all this."

"Why the burden we all carry," Miss Pankhurst said. "You, me, Miss Janssen, Miss Worthington. Some bear it better than most."

When Lydia frowned at her, she gave her a patronizing smile. "Spinsterhood, dear. Now, have a seat, and let me show you how you too can be of use."

Propulsion. A simple calculation of motive force, wind speed, angle, and circumference coupled with human capability. The latter was the most variable, but since he would be the first human to try the device, he had some assurance he could estimate that portion correctly. But copper had thwarted him, and iron was too heavy. So were most woods. The cedar couldn't arrive fast enough. He was losing focus.

And he couldn't forget that Lydia Villers was working just upstairs.

He tossed aside the last hammered copper blade, the clang echoing about the old kitchen, which he'd appropriated for his laboratory. It had access to water and fire and had been somewhat hardened against both. The heavy plank table in the center held room for the various materials he was attempting to apply as well as his tools and journals. And the rear door gave easy access to the yard if he needed fresh air or to dispose of something noxious.

Now the space felt too full, but it wasn't the bits of copper flung about. His memories of Lydia crowded him.

He'd been attracted to her from the moment they'd met. Her brother, Beau, had made something of a nuisance of himself the last few years. The gentlemen of the *ton* joked that if he hadn't thrown his sister at you, you must have no title or no wealth or no expectation of either. Blessed with both, it had only been a matter of time before Worth came to Villers's notice.

But unlike his peers, who had run from the idea of marrying the sister of such a grasping fellow, Worth had found himself captivated. Lydia threw herself with enthusiasm into whatever she attempted, from dancing at a ball to listening to his explanations of what he was pursuing. He could rant, change his mind, change the topic as his thoughts veered, and Lydia would smile and nod with rapt attention. Used to those who, at best, tolerated his foibles, her ready acceptance had been amazing, tremendous.

Until he'd learned it had all been a lie.

He shoved back from the table. The light in those big green eyes, the joy in that winsome smile, had once convinced him she cared. He was proof against her wiles now. Charlotte had requested her help with the heat experiments, but he refused to trust Lydia with anything that critical. If he showed her the discipline required in their work, he'd reasoned, she would turn tail and leave him alone again.

It had seemed a logical plan. If she was sincere, which he doubted, she would persevere. If not, he saw no reason to keep her on staff. Everyone was working too hard.

Perhaps he should check on her. From time to time he visited each of his team members, discussed their progress. He would make the rounds, see how Lydia fared. It was all completely aboveboard.

So why did he feel as if he were indulging himself?

The work side of the house was Spartan by design—unpolished hardwood floors, no paintings on the walls. In part, this was for safety—less fabric to collect spills or vapors, less fuel for a fire. In part it proved one less distraction. He was too easily distracted some days. Every new theory, every advance, opened his mind to others. Yet here he was, going to meet the biggest distraction of his life.

His footsteps sounded unreasonably loud as he followed the corridor. His heart seemed to be beating in time. He clasped his hands behind his back as he approached the door to the room in which Lydia was to be working. It had been the butler's pantry, a tiny space more like a cell than a room. Functional, at best. Far less than she was used to. The door was open. Swallowing, he dared a glance inside.

She was the picture of domesticity. Scarlet fabric flowed across her lap to pool on the floor on either side of the spindle-backed chair. Head bowed so the glow from the lamp on the table beside her glinted on pale curls, she took careful, even stitches. Something inside him unfurled, warmed, as if he'd come to the hearth after a long time in the snow.

She inserted her needle in the pin cushion on the table, smoothed her hands over the fabric, picked it up, and...

RIP!

He took a step back, and she must have noticed the movement, for she glanced up with her usual sweet smile.

"Experiment number twelve," she announced.

He ventured into the room, feeling as if the walls leaned too near on either side. Now that he looked closer, he could see any number of holes in the fabric, thread hanging.

"Unsuccessful?" he asked.

"I suspect it depends on your measure of success," she said, voice cheerful. "Miss Pankhurst advised me to attempt a stronger bond between two panels. I have attempted several lengths of stitches and now width, as in rows set side by side. So far, none has prevented the fabric from tearing on a good tug."

"Perhaps you should test the strength of your thread," he suggested.

She held up the spool. "I was only given one strength. Perhaps you could remedy that."

"I'll speak to Charlotte."

She nodded. "Nothing coarse, I think. Silk, three-ply at

least, undyed."

Here less than a day and already she was dictating. "Rather specific. Your reasoning?"

"A hypothesis, if you will." The world sounded strange on those rosy lips. "Miss Pankhurst reports that the more tightly woven fabric best meets the criteria you provided her, which she is, apparently, not at liberty to tell me. The combing and dying process must provide some stress on the thread. Therefore, tightly woven, undyed thread might also meet your criteria."

Flawless. He bowed to her. "Madam, you impress me."

She picked up her needle and drove it into the fabric. "I also hypothesize that you are too easily impressed."

Worth straightened. "Based on what evidence?"

She began sewing again. "You must have accepted Beau's word before pursuing me, though I'm certain you could have found evidence to suggest it wasn't your best course. You accepted my word initially, with insufficient evidence in the end to sustain it. You obviously accepted someone else's word against mine. I can vouch for my brother's insincerity, and my own sincerity. Of course, I don't know who commented against me or perhaps you simply realized your mistake."

His heart was pounding again, as if each thrust of her needle pierced it. "Lydia, I…"

RIP!

She sighed. "Thirteen. I really could use that thread. Perhaps you could find some."

As soon as he found his dignity again.

# CHAPTER THREE

L ydia wasn't sure why she'd brought up their past when she'd been so determined to avoid it. Perhaps it was because his bizarre rules kept her isolated. Perhaps it was the task Miss Pankhurst had set her—attempting to sew the silken panels together with cotton thread as if she was apprenticing to be a seamstress and not a natural philosopher, as those who studied scientific matters were known. She could not complain that the work was hard. She was an accomplished embroiderer—what young lady on the *ton* wasn't? But she had left Gussie's employ because she'd wanted more, and sitting alone in a closet sewing did not suffice.

Now he inclined his head and left her. She'd pushed him away. At least this time she knew how.

She sighed, setting down the fabric lest she mangle it. She still remembered the night Beau had introduced them. She had become accustomed to her brother trotting her out to meet eligible bachelors—at the many balls they attended, during intermission at the theatre and opera, between races at the Royal Ascot and other sporting events. Beau wanted to see her well wed, but she'd noticed he favored the wealthy and titled, not necessarily men she might admire for their character or accomplishments. She'd also heard the whispers behind the painted and lace-covered fans.

*Hunting a title.*
*Feathering his own nest.*
*Reaching above his station.*

Most whisperers, she was glad to note, put the blame on her brother, but a few thought she was the one grasping at glory. To their minds, she wasn't pretty enough, clever enough, accomplished enough, rich enough, or prestigious enough to win a titled, wealthy gentlemen's hand.

She'd tried her best nonetheless. She'd learned to smile at every unkind or ridiculous thing her suitors might say, overlooking their foibles and finding reasons to compliment them. The only time she'd stood her ground was when one attempted liberties. Her brother might have let on she was for sale, but she would not come cheap.

Then, one night, at a ball to celebrate the prince's birthday, Beau had steered her across the room to introduce her to Lord Worthington. She'd heard of his exploits from Lord Stanhope and other natural philosophers she cornered whenever she could. He studied the qualities of the airs, both breathable and noxious. He'd been the first to propose how air changed with altitude, the second to confirm its expansion in various forms. It had been no effort to look admiring.

And a thrill had gone through her when she'd realized her admiring look was being returned.

She had welcomed him to call, done all she could to encourage him. He was not what she had imagined of a natural philosopher. Instead of slow, methodical investigation and pedantic conversation, his mind moved in leaps, like a deer bounding over streams and rocks others would have paused to consider. When she was with him, her mind seemed as agile, the future limitless. She'd begun to hope, to pray, he'd offer for her.

Then, one day, a letter had arrived. She'd found it among the various invitations. Recognizing the sprawling hand, she'd hurried to open it.

"Miss Villers," it had read. "It has been drawn to my attention that I may have raised expectations of a match between us. My apologies. I could never align myself with a lady of your interests. I will endeavor to ensure we do not meet again."

The paper had fallen to the table, and she'd swayed on her feet. She hadn't questioned what he'd meant by interests. He'd heard the rumors that she was after a title, and he'd preferred to believe in the story instead of in her. Her hopes were as thin as the air he studied.

Damp spots darkened the fabric in her lap now. She wiped at the material and blinked away her tears. She'd cried enough over Worth. She had a different path before her now, and she intended to make the most of it. She would not allow him to come between her and her dreams again. She seized the two halves she'd sewed together and pulled.

Nothing happened.

Lydia frowned, peering closer. She'd tried triple rows this time, her tiniest stitches, and she could see where the material strained against them. But the stitches themselves held.

Why?

She considered variables in material and construction, factored in conditions, timing. She could reach only one logical conclusion. Shoving the material from her lap, she gathered her skirts and ran to Miss Pankhurst's room.

Charlotte and Worth were conferring with the other lady, and all looked up as Lydia skidded to a stop on the wood floor.

"I have a hypothesis," she declared. "Cotton thread is stronger when it's wet. If someone would fetch water, I'll prove it."

Worth had never seen Lydia like this—determined,

confident, glowing with an idea. He rather thought he might look the same when a new thought beckoned. Her animation only made her more attractive, and that was dangerous.

"Your enthusiasm is noted, dear," Miss Pankhurst said with a titter. "But I don't believe we should pursue that line of inquiry." The look she shot Worth was all apology, as if her prize pug had chewed on his boot.

His first reaction was umbrage. How dare she belittle Lydia's hypothesis? Such thoughts were meant to be questioned. Lydia had every right to request a test, even though he doubted the results would help his current course of study.

Charlotte seemed to be of the same mind. "On the contrary," she said. "My brother encourages innovative thinking, isn't that right, Worth?"

The decision would always have been his. That was one of the stipulations of their employment, that he direct the course of all research. If Miss Pankhurst or Miss Janssen had approached him with the request, he would have considered it and given a reasoned response. Why, then, did every part of him demand that he allow Lydia her moment, with no further consideration, simply because she was Lydia?

"Science is built on innovation," Worth allowed. "Tell me more about this hypothesis, Miss Villers. What made you suspect that water would improve the strength of the thread? I would have thought the opposite."

"I was working on attempt number fourteen," she said, eyes still shining, "a triple row of tight stitches. They did not give."

"Then perhaps the stitches are the key," Charlotte said with a look to Worth.

Miss Pankhurst hitched herself higher on her stool. "I have ever said so, my lord. You know this to be true."

Indeed. The woman's requested course of study was

myopically focused. Perhaps that was why Lydia, as a newcomer, had come across something more original.

Lydia shook her head. "I highly doubt it was the stitching. Triple stitches had failed before. I did not expect any difference even with a shorter length. It was the addition of water."

Worth frowned. "What did you use for water? I saw none in the room."

Rosy pink the color of heated helium brightened her face. "It was a limited source."

Miss Pankhurst pressed a hand to her chest. "I do hope you're not one to spit on her thread."

"Certainly not!" Lydia wrinkled her nose. "If you must know, I shed a tear. I'm sure it was only from frustration."

Her lashes did appear damp, for they were a darker shade than her brows and spikier. She had never been the sort to tear up easily. He could not believe the work could have caused her to cry now.

Had he?

Decision made. He had no right to concern her, and she had every right to test her hypothesis, regardless of the utility.

"Charlotte," he declared, "ring for Bateman and have him bring as much water as Miss Villers desires."

Miss Pankhurst clucked her tongue as if she could not condone such an extravagant waste of time, but Charlotte went to the bell pull and summoned his man.

"You want what?" he demanded when Worth ordered him to bring in a bathing tub and fill it with water. He glanced around at the women in the room, then turned to Worth, heavy brown brows down.

"It's not for my brother, Beast," Charlotte explained, clearly amused. "Miss Villers has a hypothesis she'd like tested."

He turned to Lydia, and his brows lowered further. "And she can't test it herself? Lord Worthington has an appointment."

One of standing duration, with Bateman himself. Worth had never allowed other matters to interfere before. His life, and Charlotte's, might depend on it.

"It can be postponed," he said now. "If you'd be so kind, sir?"

With a nod, his man left.

Miss Pankhurst shivered. "Such a difficult fellow. I don't know why you keep him on, my lord."

For good reason. Bateman might not have been trained for service, but he had other skills Worth found indispensable.

Before he could defend the man who had become a friend, however, Charlotte rounded on the woman.

"Mr. Bateman is an asset to this household and my brother's work," she informed Miss Pankhurst. "I will not have him denigrated."

Miss Pankhurst pleated the fabric in her lap. "How commendable that you will so readily defend the fellow, Miss Worthington. It speaks for your heart."

Charlotte's cheeks darkened.

Worth stepped between them to hide her from Miss Pankhurst's inquisitive gaze as she gathered her normal composure. His sister offered him a grateful smile.

"Still, I cannot advise dumping all my thread in water," Miss Pankhurst maintained. "It could take days to dry out sufficiently. Surely that would affect your schedule, my lord."

"We have a schedule?" Lydia asked, glancing around.

Worth turned to meet her gaze. "One that brooks no delay, I fear. But I shouldn't think you'd need to dunk all of the thread."

Lydia shook her head. "Only a few pieces of the fabric with some stitching attached. We'd only proceed further if the effect proves useful."

That part was doubtful, but he wanted to see what she'd do either way. She claimed she wanted to study. Natural philosophers must accept that some hypotheses did not end well.

Bateman banged through the door to thump a copper bathing tub on the floor. He straightened and glanced at Charlotte. "Hot or cold?"

"Excellent question," she said. "Miss Villers?"

"Cold," Lydia said without hesitation. "But please begin heating some in case that doesn't work."

With a nod, he left. Lydia excused herself to fetch her fabric and hurried out.

"Such initiative," Miss Pankhurst said. "I can see why you hired her, my lord."

Something more than admiration simmered under the words. Did she know about his history with Lydia? He had made no secret of his admiration a year ago, and a year ago Miss Pankhurst had been serving as companion to another lady. She could easily have seen them together and question his altruism now.

Charlotte gave no indication that she had heard the same tone to the words, for she merely smiled. "In all actuality, I hired Miss Villers," she said. "And she is every bit as clever as I'd hoped. We have been behind on the fabric task for some time. Perhaps this will give us the advantage."

Lydia was back before Miss Pankhurst could comment. Her fingers held threaded needles, and fabric trailed in her wake.

"If you would each take two panels and stitch them together," she said, holding out the needles. "It doesn't matter how wide or long the stitches. Variety would be appreciated."

Charlotte and Miss Pankhurst took up a needle. Lydia turned to Worth. "You too, my lord."

Worth glanced up from the needle she offered in surprise. "I've never sewed in my life."

"High time you learned," she said. "You never know when a button will come undone, a hem snag, and there you are with no valet to help."

Had she had to learn that lesson? There'd been rumors her brother was hunting a title for more than the increased prestige it would offer him to be related to a great house. He was punting on the River Tick, with debts mounting. Had circumstances forced her to be her own maid?

"Quickly," she urged him. "We don't want Bateman's efforts to be in vain."

He took the needle gingerly from her, picked up the fabric and began sewing, mimicking the way Charlotte held the needle and pushing it into the fabric.

He immediately pricked himself.

Sucking his wounded thumb, he glanced up. Lydia and Charlotte had their heads down, needles flying along the silk. Miss Pankhurst was watching him, blue eyes bright. He bent once more to the task.

He managed a credible set of stitches without maiming himself before Bateman reappeared, bucket of water in each grip. He dumped them into the bathing tub.

"That enough?" he asked Lydia.

"Yes, thank you," she said, knotting off the thread. She snipped it from the fabric, then stuck her needle in Miss Pankhurst's pincushion and handed the plump ball around for the others to do the same. Setting aside the cushion, she gathered up the fabric pieces from each of them, then dumped all but one of them into the water and pushed them down.

"Bateman," she said, and he stood taller. "I suspect you're the strongest among us. Would you concur, my lord?"

Vanity ordered him to claim otherwise, but he knew she was right. "Yes."

Bateman shot him an amused look. He'd make him work the next time they sparred together.

"If you would be so kind," she said to his manservant, "take each piece and attempt to rip it apart at the seams, starting with this one." She handed him the dry piece. By the neat, orderly stitches in triple rows, Worth assumed it was her own.

Bateman tore it apart without so much as a ripple of muscle.

Charlotte gasped. Miss Pankhurst tutted as if she knew Lydia's stitches wouldn't survive such a test. Worth was more interested in how the wetted stitches would fare.

Bateman chose a wet piece next, and Worth recognized his own ungainly stitches. They popped like dried corn under the man's hold.

Charlotte's was next. Worth knew because her head came up, and she leaned forward eagerly. Bateman had to work at her more-accomplished stitches, sweat trickling down one side of his face, but her piece finally gave. He offered her a commiserating smile before turning to the last piece, the one Miss Pankhurst had sewn, and yanking hard.

It didn't budge.

He tried again, until muscle stood out like cords on his neck. Still Miss Pankhurst's stitches held.

"Imagine that," she said. "And it wasn't even my best work."

"You see?" Lydia turned to the others as Bateman dropped the fabric back into the water. "It worked. There is your answer, my lord. If you want the stitches to remain tight, you must keep the cotton thread wet."

It was an intriguing discovery. She had every right to be pleased. She'd developed a hypothesis, seen it tested. Normally he would have called for repeated testing, under different conditions. Her tear would have been composed of more than water. What additions to the liquid they had used would improve the strength? Which would lessen it?

Unfortunately, time was tight, and he could not afford to spend any more of it on a line of questioning that could have little bearing on his plans.

"Thank you, Miss Villers," he said. "I will take it under advisement."

She blinked. "Under advisement? What more proof do you need?"

"None," he assured her. "Your hypothesis seems sound. Unfortunately, the application I have in mind cannot be kept wet."

"Oh." Miss Pankhurst deflated. "Pity. And here I thought we'd found something useful."

"Let me understand," Lydia said, and there was a tone in her voice he hadn't heard before. "You went through with all this knowing it had no possible use to you?"

He had meant it as a compliment to her ingenuity, a way to reward her efforts. Every natural philosopher had a right to test, to advance. And he had wondered whether she would exhibit a less-than-logical response should the effort prove fruitless.

Now he was aware of a distinct sinking feeling, as if the floor was at a greater incline than usual. It appeared he had been wrong, a rarity to which he still could not accustom himself.

Worse? Lydia knew it.

# CHAPTER FOUR

L ydia's hands were shaking as she gathered up the needles and thread. She'd had jealous young ladies spill punch on her gown more than once, had a gentleman step on her hem and rip the flounce, and heard dowagers complain about her forward nature or her brother's financial woes. But of all the unkind things people had done to her over the years, this was the worst. He'd placated her, treating her like a well-meaning child. She expected better.

"I'm certain my brother had a reason to allow all this," Charlotte said, glancing at Worth as if she expected better too. "Theories must be tested."

"There are dozens of theories," Lydia said, picking up the dry, torn panels. "Some can be ruled out immediately." She turned to the manservant. Bateman was regarding her with brows knit, a typical stance for him, but there was a light in his brown eyes, as if he hadn't seen her clearly before.

"Thank you, Bateman," she said. "I'm sorry we wasted your time."

"So am I," he said, but his look was directed at Worth.

"I believe that's sufficient for today," Charlotte put in. "Miss Pankhurst, we will continue along a similar line tomorrow. Miss Villers has given us a clue. Water may be infeasible, but perhaps another coating may prove more efficacious. Please give that some thought."

Miss Pankhurst nodded agreeably.

Lydia knew she should take solace in the fact that she might have helped after all. Amazing how little comfort it provided at the moment.

"What shall I do with all this?" Bateman demanded.

Charlotte eyed her brother as if she would very much like to see the contents of the tub dumped on his head. "Have Nella hang the fabric to dry and put the tub where we can find it easily tomorrow if needed."

With a nod, he hoisted the tub and carried it from the room, water sloshing only the slightest.

"Good afternoon, Miss Worthington, my lord," Miss Pankhurst said, offering a curtsey. "Until tomorrow."

As they murmured their goodbyes, Lydia went to set the pincushion on the shelves. Irritating, impossible man. How was she to learn anything when he set her at meaningless tasks? Was he trying to force her to leave?

She gasped, whirling. "You are! You want me gone."

Charlotte frowned. "I'm sure I never said any such thing."

Worth had his hands behind his back, as if intent on hiding something. "If the work displeases you, Miss Villers, we will not hold you to your agreement of employment."

Charlotte stared at him. Lydia raised her chin and looked him in the eye. The grey seemed darker, as if his thoughts were as dismal.

"I came here to learn more about natural philosophy," she told him. "Nothing you have done, nothing you can do, will change that, my lord."

She thought he might look disappointed, perhaps chagrined that she had caught him at his game. Instead, he stepped forward and offered her his arm.

"In that case," he said, "may I see you home, Miss Villers?"

She wanted to refuse. He had disappointed her too many times. But he obviously had a hypothesis about her. She should let him test it, offer him evidence that she was more capable than he knew. If he spent time with her, learned more about her, perhaps he would come to understand why she was here and be more inclined to let her help.

She put her arm on his. "Very well, my lord."

He escorted her to where she'd left her things in her tiny room, then led her back through the house and out the front door.

"I apologize," he said as they walked along the pavement at the edge of Clarendon Square.

"For humoring me or for failing to accept the results of my experiment?" Lydia asked, voice pleasant from long practice.

"For upsetting you," he said. "I dislike seeing you unhappy."

Lydia stopped, forcing him to stop as well. "How extraordinary. Do you dislike seeing Miss Pankhurst unhappy?"

He cocked his head as if considering the matter. "I would like to think so."

"Then you would allow her to commandeer your time with useless experiments."

"No."

He had always seemed so open, so obvious in his thoughts, until he had sent that horrid note dismissing her. Could she believe him now? How could she continue to work in that house if she didn't?

"Then why," she asked, "did you do that for me?"

Again, his answer was swift. "Every natural philosopher has a right to test a theory. My approval, the application to my research, appeared immaterial in that moment. I wanted to know how you would go about testing it, your response to the testing."

"So, you did have a hypothesis about me," Lydia said, "and you were testing it too. What was your hypothesis, my lord?"

He colored. Truly, it was an amazing sight. The red climbed in his cheeks until it clashed with his auburn hair.

"I'm not entirely sure. Perhaps I was merely curious."

Curious, or wondering whether she'd behave logically? Of course, on hearing what he'd done, she'd all but stomped her feet and called him names, so there was that.

"Apology accepted," she said, starting forward at a brisk pace.

He hurried to fall into step beside her. "Thank you."

"However," Lydia said, skirts sweeping the pavement, "I believe reparations are in order."

"I see." He nodded thoughtfully. "Flowers perhaps?"

Lydia clucked her tongue. "Nothing so common, sir. You wounded me deeply."

"Should I apologize again?"

He sounded so perplexed, hands going behind his back once more. Was that what he did when he was uncertain? She could not doubt that she had disquieted him.

But she did not intend to encourage him.

"No," she said. "But you could give me a greater part in the work."

She glanced at him to find his head down, his gaze on the stone at their feet. "Alas, it would be unfair to Miss Janssen and Miss Pankhurst to take their work from them."

Lydia stopped at the bottom of the stairs leading up to Meredith's door. "Surely there must be something. Perhaps if you told me what we are working toward, I might be able to propose a role."

His face closed, and he took a step back from her. "I'm afraid that must remain quiet for now. Good afternoon, Miss Villers."

He turned and strode back the way they had come, for all the world as if she were chasing him.

Meredith poured Julian Mayes his second cup of tea for the afternoon. His hand reached out to steady the pot, fingers brushing hers, and a tingle went up her arm. His smile as he leaned back assured her he knew it and had been similarly affected.

She still could not credit that her childhood sweetheart was interested in taking up where they had left off. So much had happened since he had first proposed marriage—her mother's death, her cousin's interference to prevent Julian from hearing Meredith needed his help, her forced employment as a companion to a cruel mistress, her surprising inheritance from that lady and then being accused of her murder. She was a different person from the girl he'd once loved.

But then, he was no longer the same young man, fresh from Eton and eager to make his mark on the world. Julian had been instrumental in protecting her former client and friend Yvette de Maupassant from a French spy intent on harming her, but only after Meredith had protested that her friend was being used as bait. He had defied his superiors to honor Meredith's wishes.

Still, how he had gained such easy access to highly placed individuals in government and the peerage remained a bit of a mystery. He had been raised in the quiet of the Surrey countryside near her family, after all. She could only conclude that friendships made at Eton and in London where he served as a solicitor now had gained him this entre. Then again, it never hurt a gentleman to be handsome and charming, and he was easily both. Even Fortune agreed, winding her way around his boots for the third time in as many minutes.

He also appeared to be in no hurry to further his courtship with Meredith. He had been coming around for tea nearly every day. While his attentions were laudable, they were only slightly warmer than companionable, and she was aware of a decided disappointment. Where were the impassioned words, the sweet longing looks? Where the desire to take her out, introduce her to his friends? Was he merely doing what he thought she might enjoy, or was he unsure of her?

A sound came from the front door. He raised his head from studying his tea. "Were you expecting company?"

"No," she said. "But I do receive the occasional caller."

He glanced at the door as if waiting for Napoleon to come striding in, saber flashing. Instead, Lydia traipsed into the room. She stopped short on seeing Julian.

"Oh, I beg your pardon. Work finished early today."

"Mr. Mayes," Meredith said, "you remember Miss Villers."

He rose and bowed. "Miss Villers. A pleasure to see you again."

Lydia smiled and ventured into the room. "And you, sir. Have you spoken with my brother recently?"

As she took a seat, Julian resumed his. Fortune padded over to have Lydia caress her back.

"Alas, no," he admitted, retrieving his teacup. "He appears consumed with wedding preparations."

Lydia's brother was to marry the Earl of Carrolton's sister soon. Until then, he had been helping Julian on some matters.

Lydia giggled, a happy, carefree sound. "Yes, Lady Lilith is determined that he do his part. I had no idea a groom was expected to advise on flowers and food and seating arrangements."

"Not all grooms are so interested," Meredith agreed with a look to Julian.

"I'm surprised she didn't enlist your services as well," Julian said. "What's this I hear about working?"

His tone was bland, conversational. Why did Meredith hear condemnation? She knew what most of the *ton* thought. A true lady did not sully her hands with work, an easy sentiment when one had never known privation.

"I'm helping Miss Worthington and her brother with their scientific pursuits," Lydia explained, smile bright, as if she had no concerns for censure.

"Interesting," Julian said. "And what are you pursuing?"

"I have no idea." She rose. "Forgive me. I should change before dinner. Good afternoon, Mr. Mayes."

He rose, but she had already turned her back and left the room, Fortune scampering at her heels. He sank onto his seat and sent Meredith an amused glance. "No idea what she's working on, eh?"

"Not from lack of trying, I'm certain," Meredith assured him. "Lord Worthington may not wish to be forthcoming."

He sipped his tea before responding. "I haven't spoken to Worth since the Duke of Wey's wedding. I wonder why he decided to keep things so close."

"It seems a male trait," Meredith said, watching him.

He arched red-gold brows. "If I have been less than forthcoming about my work, it is only because of client privilege. I would expect you to do the same with your clients."

She could not argue with him there. She also could not feel comfortable demanding to know his intentions.

Yet.

"You're late," Bateman said when Worth joined him after walking Lydia home. He hadn't realized she was staying so close. He was certain the townhouse she'd entered had been inherited from Lady Winhaven only recently. Surely not by Lydia's family. And he'd give a twenty percent chance that her brother could afford the rent. Who was sheltering her, then?

"You're well paid to wait," Worth told his man as he pulled off his coat. He hung it on the hook beside the door and began to unbutton his waistcoat.

Bateman threw him his mufflers. "Not well enough."

Worth shook his head as he wound the protective padding around his fists. It was an old joke. Both knew why the former boxer remained in Worth's employ. After his last grueling bout, Bateman had been lost all stomach for the matches, retreating to his home, unwilling to venture out again. Gentleman Jackson, London's premiere boxer, had introduced Bateman to Worth. Like Worth, Bateman needed a challenge, albeit a physical one. Protecting Worth and Charlotte from an unknown enemy had given him the will to go on.

Bateman seemed to think he owed Worth a debt. Seeing how well he took care of them, Worth rather thought the debt went the other way.

Stripped to their shirts and trousers, hands wrapped, they took up their positions in the middle of the space now. One of the benefits of having purchased the neighboring townhouse was that Worth could use the rooms any way he liked. This had once been a schoolroom on the upper story, but he'd removed the shelving and replaced it with brass hooks and cupboards to hold the equipment needed for his physical regimen. His mind kept its rapid pace, he'd found, when his body moved on occasion as well.

Bateman set about circling, and Worth followed, fists raised and mind wary. That was the brilliance of boxing. Everything happened fast. No time to calculate, to second-guess himself. Action-reaction. Invigorating.

The boxer feinted. Worth blocked him.

"You made a mistake," Bateman said.

"You didn't land a punch," Worth replied.

Bateman swung.

Worth ducked away and struck his opponent's chest with a quick jab before dancing out of reach.

Bateman rolled his shoulder and began circling again. "Not in the fight. With her."

Worth watched for an opening in the big man's guard. "I apologized for my behavior this afternoon."

"It's not just this afternoon I'm worried about." Bateman lunged, and Worth stepped aside and let the man's momentum carry him, catching Bateman on the shoulder as he passed.

"Admit it," his man said, turning to face him once more. "You don't trust her."

"I don't trust most people." Worth swung. Bateman blocked him and slammed a fist into his ribs. Pain ricocheted up him.

"Why?" Bateman asked, stepping back as if to let Worth recover.

Worth rubbed at his sore ribs. "It's nothing that need concern you."

Bateman barked a laugh. "You hired me as bodyguard. Anything that threatens you concerns me."

Worth raised both fists and resumed the stance. Bateman fell in across from him with a lazy grin Worth tried not to find annoying.

"Miss Villers is less dangerous than your fists," he told his man.

Bateman swung, and Worth blocked, the strength of the blow reverberating up his arm.

"Most things are," Bateman allowed, dropping back. "Doesn't mean you shouldn't protect yourself against them."

"I'm sufficiently protected," Worth assured him. "She will not get under my guard."

"No?" Bateman lunged, fists pounding. Right block, left, left again. Worth retreated, but his friend kept coming.

"Enough!"

Bateman stopped, breathing hard.

Worth lowered his guard.

Bateman's fist shot out and connected with Worth's jaw. Down he went.

He lay on the floor a moment, staring up at the coffered ceiling. The painted cherubs on their fluffy white clouds eyed him back as if singularly unconcerned about his throbbing jaw.

Bateman began unwrapping his fists. "What have I told you?"

"Never let your guard down," Worth said, jaw protesting each syllable.

"Not with me and not with her," Bateman said. "I may have joined your household after she left you, but I saw the damage that was done. You think as fast as a flash of lightning, except when it comes to people. Then you dither like a senile old man. I can't protect you from that."

"No one can," Worth told the cherubs. One seemed to look commiserating, or maybe Bateman's blow had addled his wits as well as nearly broken his jaw.

Bateman offered him his hand, and Worth took it to rise.

"What did she do that was so awful?" the former boxer asked, releasing him.

Worth focused on unwrapping his fists. "Have you ever been in love, Bateman?"

His man paused, then turned away to hang the muffler on a hook. "Once. I wasn't good enough for her family."

The pain from their sparring felt like nothing. "I'm sorry."

Bateman shrugged, but he didn't meet Worth's gaze.

"I thought I was in love," Worth told him. "With a blithe spirit and a sweet smile that made me feel capable of anything. It was at a time when I had begun to question my abilities, my choices. I thought she was the answer, the proof that I had more insight than I expected. She was the proof all right. She proved that for all my intellect I know nothing about people, just as you surmised. The woman I thought I loved was a phantom contrived to lure me in. She cared only for the money and position I could offer."

Bateman smoothed the muffler on the hook, large hands now surprisingly gentle. "Isn't that why most of you lords marry? The lady might have money or land, the gentleman power or title."

"Some marry for those reasons," Worth allowed. "I never

intended to be one of them. I have money and position enough to satisfy me. I don't need to barter my well-being for more."

"Yet you allowed her to barter her time for pay," Bateman pointed out. "You have her at your side again, on important work. How can you trust she has your best interests at heart? For all you know, she's the one who's been sending those notes."

Worth paused. He'd hired a bodyguard because a series of notes had been arriving in the last year, each one threatening dire consequences if he didn't abandon his work. He suspected he knew the originator. For all his frustrations, he was at odds with only one person. Just in case he was wrong, he had let go most of his staff, closeted himself, encouraged Charlotte to hire only women she trusted. His approach seemed to be working. The notes had become less frequent, the last coming several months ago. Could he have been wrong again? Could Lydia be the culprit? He found it hard to imagine her so spiteful.

He tossed the mufflers on the hook. "I don't think Miss Villers sent those notes, but we would be wise to keep an eye on her, Bateman. I will not allow her to distract me from what's important again."

# CHAPTER FIVE

"Friction is the enemy."

Worth's voice echoed down the corridor, and Miss Pankhurst tsked where she and Lydia sat sewing. They had been sitting and sewing for the last two days since the test of the fabric. Lydia would arrive promptly at eight. Bateman would escort her to Charlotte, who would accompany her to Miss Pankhurst's room, as if afraid to allow her to so much as glimpse what was happening anywhere else in the house. Miss Pankhurst would assign Lydia some task that involved stitches that Miss Pankhurst would proclaim unsuitable before ripping them out and making Lydia do them over again. It was tedious, pointless work. It seemed Worth was still testing his hypothesis about her.

She refused to gratify him by complaining. She'd prove to them all that she had tenacity if she had to resew the seams eighty times.

She was fairly sure she was narrowing in on sixty at the moment.

"He is quite brilliant, you know," Miss Pankhurst said, taking another stitch.

Lydia merely smiled. Worth's commentary on his work floated up from below stairs from time to time, along with intriguing clanks and bangs. Once a cloud of smoke had drifted past the doorway. Lydia would have been alarmed if it hadn't smelled like cedar. More than anything, she wanted to sneak a peek, but her position might be compromised if she was caught.

And so, she sewed.

Tea was always a welcome break. They generally met in Charlotte's study. Today, Miss Janssen eased her bulk into an upholstered chair and picked at the chaff on her skirts, a ruddy brown without ornamentation that made her round cheeks look red. Miss Pankhurst had insisted that she and Lydia bring their work with them. Lydia bundled the fabric in her lap and sat on the sofa as she accepted a cup of tea from their employer. She could not help glancing at Worth, who was pacing back and forth along the bookshelves as if searching for knowledge no one else in the room had found.

"We will be ending early tomorrow," Charlotte announced as she served tea in the pretty violet-patterned cups. "We have been invited to attend Lady Baminger's annual ball. I encourage you all to take advantage of this opportunity."

Worth accepted his cup from his sister with a frown. "Why must we attend? We have work to do."

It seemed Lydia wasn't the only one who no longer saw any need to participate in the social whirl.

Charlotte was less forgiving. "Really, Worth," she chided, balancing her teacup above the journals, maps, and other papers on her work table. "Lady Baminger has been supportive of our efforts for years. She used her influence to locate that German altimeter you wanted last year. The least we can do is attend her annual ball."

"Lady Baminger has been helpful," Worth conceded, positively vibrating with energy so that she was surprised the tea didn't slosh from the cup. "But we cannot repay her kindness by ignoring the work she supported."

Logical. But then, he usually was.

Charlotte set down her tea. "So you ignore her instead." When Worth shrugged, she sat taller. "If you will not think of her, think of your staff. You cannot begrudge them this opportunity."

Miss Janssen blinked her brown eyes, which were as round as the rest of her, as she glanced between Charlotte and Worth. "What opportunities could a lady find at a ball?"

"I suspect Miss Villers could educate us," Miss Pankhurst said with a titter before sipping from her cup.

"Happy to help in any way I can," Lydia said, avoiding Worth's gaze. "Though I have attended quite enough balls for my lifetime."

"Indeed."

She couldn't tell if Worth's agreement stemmed from his dislike of the event or his judgement of her. She continued doggedly. "As for opportunities, Miss Janssen, many of the preeminent natural philosophers of our day attend Lady Baminger's ball. In the past, I've had the honor of conversing with Sir Joseph Banks, the president of the Royal Society; Sir Humphrey Davy, who discovered the properties of laughing gas; and that wonderful inventor, Lord Stanhope. I'd be happy to introduce you."

"Oh, my yes," Miss Janssen said, blushing. "Thank you."

She allowed her gaze to reach Worth. He appeared to be studying the amber-colored liquid in his cup as if it might hold the answers to all his scientific questions. Why did that disappoint her?

"And will you join us as well, Miss Pankhurst?" Charlotte asked.

"Certainly," Miss Pankhurst assured her. "I wouldn't leave you alone, dear Miss Worthington."

Hardly alone. The attendees at Lady Baminger's ball frequently numbered in the hundreds. She had to rent a ballroom to hold them all.

Charlotte, however, merely nodded. "It's settled, then. We will all attend. To minimize the disruption to our work, please bring your finery with you tomorrow. We can all dress and leave from here."

Worth nodded as if accepting his fate. He downed his tea.

"Lovely," Miss Pankhurst said, and she reached across to take Lydia's fabric and began ripping out the stitches again.

Conversation moved to other topics then—Miss Janssen's quandary over the relative merits of willow or ash branches for weaving a sturdy basket, Miss Pankhurst's assertion that silk thread was far superior to cotton, all coating aside. Lydia refused to flinch at the reminder of her earlier test. She knew better now. If Worth could keep things close, so could she.

He had returned to pacing the bookshelves, but he had a suggestion for every problem, his mind moving easily from one discipline to another. Yet he never demanded, never criticized. That, she supposed, could be considered commendable.

As they all prepared to depart for their various tasks, Charlotte beckoned to Lydia. "Miss Villers, I could use your assistance this afternoon."

Miss Pankhurst hesitated on the way to the door. "But my new research plan clearly lays out the role Miss Villers is to play."

Worth turned from the bookcases and started toward the door as well. "I have the utmost confidence in you, Miss Pankhurst. All your advances came before Miss Villers arrived. I'm certain you will move forward without her." With a nod to Lydia, he left the room.

Miss Pankhurst cast Lydia a considering look. "Very likely."

"That's settled then," Charlotte said brightly.

Lydia handed Miss Pankhurst the fabric, careful not to let the needle prick the lady, tempting though that thought was, and watched as she and Miss Janssen left for their work.

"How are you and the others getting along?" Charlotte

asked, coming to join her on the sofa.

"I hardly see Miss Janssen except at tea," Lydia said. "Miss Pankhurst has high standards, but I shall persevere until I meet them."

"Commendable." Charlotte smoothed her skirts, a deep green today. "Until then, I'd like your opinion on a matter."

Lydia swallowed her sigh. Very likely Charlotte would ask her advice on which gown to wear to the ball or how to arrange her auburn tresses. Certainly no one in this house expected her to know about more weighty matters.

"As I said," she told her employer, "I'm happy to help."

Charlotte met her gaze. "How would you transport fire without combusting the container?"

Lydia stared at her. Immediately her mind began sorting through all the bits of information she'd squirreled away over the years. "How long must it be transported?"

"Hours. Perhaps days. And weight is at a premium, so cast iron will not do."

No cast iron? "What about brass?" Lydia pressed. "Glass?"

"Brass is likely too malleable; glass too breakable."

"What other requirements must we meet?" Lydia asked.

Charlotte tapped her chin with one finger. "The container must retain its integrity through changes in elevation over thousands of feet and in temperatures approaching zero degrees by Mr. Fahrenheit's scale. The space to store fuel is also limited, so we settled on coal. And there must be a way to introduce additional fuel and control the temperature of the flame."

"Fascinating." Lydia wiggled on the sofa as thoughts careened through her mind. "I believe I read about a nomadic tribe in Africa that carries fire in hardened leather platters, but I don't know how long the leather maintains its integrity."

"Hardened leather," Charlotte murmured. She rose for her work table, dipped a quill in ink, and noted something in a journal. "Would the change in elevation cause it to shrink, do you think?"

"I don't believe cows shrink in the Alps," Lydia said.

Someone coughed at the door, the sound suspiciously like a laugh. Charlotte glanced up. "Worth? Was there something you needed?"

A thousand tingles ran through her. Politeness required that she acknowledge his presence. She glanced his way with her usual smile and saw only interest on his lean face.

"Miss Pankhurst reports that she has completed her immediate course of study," he said.

Lydia frowned. "But she hadn't found a stitch she liked."

"Apparently she found it shortly after she began working without you," he said.

His voice was bland. Miss Pankhurst's wouldn't have been. Lydia could almost hear her.

*I'm sure it was the distraction of Miss Villers's presence that kept me from the discovery, my lord.* And she would titter. Of course she would titter.

"How surprising," Charlotte said. "But I'm glad she found success after all her struggles."

"She requested the rest of the day off," Worth said. "Frivolous waste of time. I asked her to formulate her next course."

Charlotte's mouth tightened. "I would have preferred she address the matter with me. Everyone needs time away, Worth."

He frowned. "Why?"

Charlotte glanced at Lydia as if for support.

"I suppose," Lydia allowed, "some people grow weary of the work."

"Interesting hypothesis," Worth said, frown still evident. "I could imagine it of someone forced into labor he found abhorrent. But the scope of imagination required in natural philosophy alone makes the effort worthwhile."

She felt the same way. "Yet the tedium of each task, the lack of vision on what we are creating, must exact a price."

"So does the concentration required," Charlotte put in before Worth could argue. "We are mere mortals, Worth. We tire on occasion."

Was that why Charlotte had insisted on accepting the invitation to the ball? Was she tired of helping Worth with his studies? Miss Pankhurst, Miss Janssen, and Lydia left every evening. Charlotte would be here, ready to note whatever he liked, from the moment she woke until the moment she fell into bed.

Lydia rose to go to Charlotte's side. "Perhaps an afternoon off would do us all good."

"Agreed." Charlotte stood and met her brother's gaze. "We will continue in the morning, Worth. I'll speak to Miss Janssen and Miss Pankhurst."

Lydia thought Worth might protest further, but he inclined his head and stepped aside to allow his sister to pass him. Lydia started to follow, but he moved into her path.

"Shall I escort you home, Miss Villers?"

He was smiling pleasantly, as if her company was all he needed in that moment. He didn't escort any of the others home. She'd been told both Miss Pankhurst and Miss Janssen lived in ladies' boarding houses an easy walk from Clarendon Square. As Meredith's home was even closer, and it was still early afternoon, she hardly required protection. Why was he making this offer today? He had no need to apologize again.

"I am capable of walking home, my lord," she said.

His frown returned. "Of course you are. I merely thought to continue discussing the work."

Once again she was aware of a distinct disappointment. How silly. The work was why she was here in the first place.

"Happy to help," Lydia said. She went to collect her things and allowed Worth to walk her out of the house.

"Interesting discussion you were having with Charlotte,"

he said as they strolled along. The day was beautiful, the sun sparkling through the trees at the center of the square set leaf shadow patterns dancing across the pavement. Another time, and she would have spent her afternoon under one of those trees with a good scientific treatise. Now she couldn't help thinking about what Charlotte had asked.

"I found your sister's questions fascinating," she admitted. "Though what the ability to carry fire a great distance has to do with the strength of stitches on silk and the tightness of woven reeds for a basket and propulsion...oh!"

She stopped on the pavement and stared at him as realization hit. "Really, Worth? Ballooning? That's so...so frivolous!"

Heat rushed up him, followed by an icy cold, as if he'd jumped head first into the Thames on a summer's day. He'd done everything he could to keep his course of study a secret, from his peers in the Royal Institution, from his friends, even from his team members. Charlotte was the only one who knew, and she would not have confided in Lydia. And that meant, despite all his precautions, Lydia had divined the truth.

And found it less than satisfactory.

He took her elbow. "I must insist that you keep the matter to yourself. And I assure you these studies are not in the least frivolous."

"If I chose to study ballooning, people would consider it frivolous," she said, but she fell into step beside him.

"That is because they fail to see its promise," he told her, releasing her elbow. "Right now, transportation is confined to sailing ships and horse-drawn vehicles."

"And Mr. Trevithick's Catch Me Who Can," Lydia put in.

"Steam locomotives like the one Trevithick invented will have their place," Worth allowed. "But imagine harnessing the very air to propel you. You could cross mountains, oceans, the icy wastes at the poles, places a steam engine would be impractical. You could transport goods to where they were urgently needed, carry patients to the physician most knowledgeable about their complaint. Families separated by distance could be reunited. Geographic boundaries would become meaningless."

"You imagine it on an industrial scale, then," she said. Was that a note of awe he heard creeping into her voice?

"Industrial and international," he admitted.

"Oh, Worth."

They had reached the foot of the townhouse steps, and Lydia turned to him with all the wide-eyed wonder he'd once found so compelling.

"My apologies," she said. "That doesn't sound the least bit frivolous. It sounds quite admirable. I'm so glad you invited me to participate."

He should not be so warmed by her approval. "I must caution you again, however, not to speak about our work in public."

Her admiring look faded. "But why? It's highly commendable."

"And highly speculative. Hot air has proven problematic, but the last attempt at combining various gasses cost Monsieur de Rozier his life when he tried to unite hydrogen and hot air.

"But that was nearly thirty years ago, before I was born," she protested. "Surely we have advanced since then."

"Not nearly far enough," he insisted. "Charles reached ten thousand feet, but no one else has matched him. Few flights have lasted longer than an hour or two. No one has sent up weight beyond a couple hundred pounds. If we are to make this more than an adventurer's hobby, we must do better."

Lydia nodded. "I see. So what is your goal?"

He drew a breath. This was all written in his journals, but saying it aloud to anyone but Charlotte was a gamble, risking his reputation, his honor. If he was wrong, he forfeited any claim to advancing knowledge. His forebears would be ashamed had they known.

"I intend to build a balloon capable of carrying more than three hundred pounds across mountains," he said, "sustaining a height of ten thousand feet for at least twenty-four hours as the balloon travels. To do so, the fabric must withstand greater pressures, the basket must be able to carry greater weight, the air used to carry the balloon must remain buoyant much longer, and we must find a way to steer the craft. It is a small achievement in the scheme of things, but a significant advance in the science."

"A great advance." She shivered as if she could not imagine it. "When will you demonstrate it at the Royal Institution?"

Worth raised his chin. "We are to present our findings to no less than the His Royal Highness the end of May. Only a few know this. I would prefer the matter to remain quiet until then. I would not want to raise expectations."

She nodded again. "Of course. Thank you for telling me. I will keep matters to myself, as you wish, but I will work all the harder knowing what we hope to achieve. Until tomorrow, Worth."

He inclined his head, and she tripped lightly up the stairs to let herself in the front door, just as a gentleman was coming out. The fellow tipped his top hat to her before stepping onto the stoop.

Worth blinked. "Julian?"

Julian Mayes, who had attended Eton with him and many of the men he still called friends, came down the steps with a ready smile and an extended hand. "Worthington. A pleasure. How go the experiments?"

For a moment, he nearly recoiled, then he realized his

friend was merely being polite. Only Lydia, it seemed, had guessed their true purpose.

"Well enough, thank you," he said, shaking his friend's hand. "And your efforts?"

"Well enough," Julian said. His smile was amused, as if he knew neither was completely at liberty to discuss what they did each day. Worth's work was secret to prevent another betrayal like the last that had jeopardized his hopes. Julian kept the secrets of his many clients. And Worth had heard the whispers that the dapper solicitor was working directly with the Crown on matters of utmost urgency.

So perhaps that meant he knew who owned this townhouse. Worth nodded toward the door. "I didn't realize you had provided your services to Miss Villers and her brother."

Julian glanced at the house as well, and his smile warmed. "I see Villers on occasion, but he is not a client. I was here visiting a friend." He seemed to recall himself and turned to Worth once more. "This is the home of Miss Thorn. Miss Villers is staying with her for the nonce."

Miss Thorn, the employment agency owner? Business must be good that she could afford to reside on Clarendon Square, though not every family around her would appreciate her presence. But to take in Lydia? Had Lydia's brother given up all responsibility?

"An interesting woman, this Miss Thorn," Worth said. "What do you know about her?"

His friend's gaze went out toward the park. "A great deal. We grew up together in Surrey."

The facts added up quickly. "Then Wey must know her as well."

Julian glanced back at him. "Assuredly. She introduced him to his wife. Sir Harry and Carrolton too. Be warned."

Worth shook his head. "I'm not looking to take a wife. But it sounds as if you are."

His smile deepened. "I admire Miss Thorn more than

words can say."

Words perhaps, but the tone and the light in his eyes said Julian cared about the regal employment agency owner. Worth envied him.

They chatted a while longer about mutual friends and plans for the rest of the Season, then Julian took his leave, and Worth turned for home. His steps felt buoyant, as if the hot air he studied had inflated his chest. How odd. His secret was out and in the hands of the one person he had vowed never to trust again.

So why did he feel so good?

# CHAPTER SIX

Lydia felt a bit like a balloon herself as she headed for her work the next day. Meredith had offered the use of her maid, Enid, who would be coming over later in the afternoon with Lydia's ballgown and accessories to help her dress. But the ball was the last thing on her mind.

She was doing something important, with the potential to improve the future for thousands of people, something that could change the world for the better. It was positively...

"Uplifting," she said aloud as she rapped on the door.

Bateman opened the door just as she was giggling. Lydia quickly schooled her face, but his stern mouth twitched as if he was trying not to smile. He stepped aside and let her in.

Charlotte appropriated her straight away. She wore a heavy dun-colored canvas overcoat on top of her day dress and handed Lydia one like it to don.

"Miss Pankhurst is busy replicating her perfected stitch on yards of scarlet silk," Charlotte reported. "I have a platform set up in the garden. I want to test containers."

A tremor went through her, and she thought her pleasure must be shining from her eyes. "How exciting!"

Charlotte led her down the corridor and through the rear door out into a small garden surrounded by high stone walls. Unlike the house, it remained separate from the adjacent garden, from which came clanks and thumps and male voices raised in discussion.

Charlotte must have noticed Lydia's puzzled glance, for she waved in that direction. "Pay no attention to them. Worth is testing the strength of Miss Janssen's basket. Beast will be assisting when he finishes his other duties. This is where we'll be working."

In the center of the garden, where the graveled paths led to a flagstone square that had once likely held a statue or sundial, someone had erected a bronze brazier and surrounded it with various transportation options, including a copper pail and what looked suspiciously like a medieval shield covered in studded leather. A pile of wood and a canister of whale oil stood not far away, as if waiting to see if they would be needed.

"Worth tells me you surmised the purpose of our research," Charlotte said as they paused before the brazier. Already coals glowed red, the heat pulsing against Lydia like a caged tiger yearning to be free.

"Yes," Lydia admitted. "But I promised not to breathe a word of it."

"Good," Charlotte said. "We have four tasks, then: to advance the construction of the basket that carries the weight, the envelope of the balloon itself, the method of heating the air, and the propulsion of the balloon. I can only hope Worth is making progress on the last."

Lydia put a hand on her arm. "He doesn't even share his results with you?"

"No." Charlotte looked just the slightest saddened by the fact. "He has been...disappointed in his previous collaborators. He prefers to work alone now. But never fear, our task is just as important."

She nodded toward the brazier. "You must see our difficulty. Currently, the air used to fill the envelope is heated before lifting, so the balloon can only stay aloft until the air inside cools. If longer-range, higher-altitude flights are to be achieved, we must find a way to keep the air hot, or at least have the capability of reheating it as needed. And that means we must have a way to transport the flame and the fuel with the basket."

"Of course." Lydia circled the brazier, mind busy. "What have you tried?"

"Nothing," Charlotte admitted. "Everything I considered proved impractical on closer examination. But your idea of using leather inspired me." She smiled at Lydia. "Shall we?"

They spent the next little while using tongs to transfer portions of the heated coal to the various containers. Charlotte's journal lay nearby. She kept going to it and noting time and changes with a pencil. To Lydia's dismay, the leather shield deformed quickly, and the copper pail swiftly became nearly as hot as the coals themselves.

"Not ideal for a woven basket," Charlotte said, wiping sweat from her forehead with the back of her gloved hand.

Lydia eyed the remaining coals. "Why not simply use the brazier itself?"

"Too large," Charlotte said. "And how would we suspend it so that the heat entered the envelope rather than spread to the winds?"

"Make it smaller then," Lydia countered, "and lift it on a pedestal."

Charlotte cocked her head, studying the brazier as well. "Wouldn't that design just direct the heat into too small a space?"

"Not if we add feet and insulate them. Felted wool, perhaps? We could raise the base of the brazier on flame-retardant wood like cork so that the heat was diverted directly into the mouth of the envelope. Air flowing beneath the brazier might keep it cool."

Charlotte cupped her chin, eyes narrowed. "Would too much cooling cause the heat to dissipate?"

"Not if the fire was sufficiently hot to begin with," Lydia reasoned.

Charlotte's russet brows rose. "Just how hot would that

have to be?"

"Hotter than what we have now, I should think."

"Could we devise some sort of additive to make it burn hotter?" Charlotte mused.

Lydia glanced to the other fuel waiting nearby. "What about whale oil?" She took up the container, opened the spout and sprinkled some over the glowing coals.

Flames roared skyward.

On the other side of the stone wall, Worth was watching Miss Janssen bounce up and down inside the pale wicker frame they had suspended from four stakes driven into the dirt of the yard.

"You see?" she said over the squeak of the material. "It's flexible yet firm, just as you asked."

"So it appears," Worth said. "Now, to test it for weight. Bateman, climb in with Miss Janssen."

Standing to one side, his bodyguard didn't move. Bateman's gaze was on the grey stone wall that separated them from the garden of the other house. Worth hadn't removed the barrier when he'd combined the houses. For one thing, it gave him two spaces for experimentation. For another, it kept the work nicely compartmentalized. The fact had offered some comfort. This time, no one would steal his work.

"Bateman?" he nudged.

"Is your sister working with Miss Villers in the garden?" the boxer asked.

"That was the plan," Worth said as Miss Janssen ceased bouncing and waited.

Flames shot into the sky, accompanied by cries. Of fear? Of pain?

Bateman was moving a moment before Worth. He leaped into the air, caught the top of the wall, and hauled himself up and over. Another time, Worth would have followed more slowly, knowing the big man would protect Charlotte.

But Lydia faced the same danger.

He could look for handholds in the stone, calculate their ability to hold his weight, carefully scale the surface. But fear for her drove him up and over, following Bateman.

As Worth dropped into the other garden, he could see that his bodyguard had Charlotte in his arms, well away from a brazier that was engulfed in flames, smoke clouding the garden. Coughing, he waved his hand in front of his face, gaze darting here, there. Where was Lydia? If anything happened to her...

"One side, if you please." Lydia bustled past him, pail of water in her arms. She swung it, and the bright liquid arced through the air. The fire hissed and popped as the water hit, smoke changing to steam. Worth caught her arm and drew her back from the hot clouds.

Face streaked with soot, Lydia smiled at him. "I'm not sure that was sufficient to put it out. Perhaps you could help?"

Worth stirred himself, grabbed up an oddly shaped leather platter that rested nearby, and followed her to the garden pump to fill the receptacles with water. After two trips, nothing but a soggy mass of coal remained.

"Well, that was eventful," Charlotte said, stepping away from Bateman at last.

"That was a farce," her rescuer said. "You could have been burned." He aimed his scowl at Lydia.

Very likely the greater blame lay with his sister. Charlotte knew the possible dangers of the work she was doing. Lydia was still relatively new to her role.

"I asked you to take precautions," Worth told his sister as he lowered the platter.

"And I did," Charlotte informed him. "We had it well in hand. There was no need for you to intervene." She glanced at the brazier and shook her head. "Now we won't be able to proceed for hours."

Lydia did not appear the least abashed at nearly catching herself on fire. "A shame, but there was nothing for it. We'll simply have to consult another expert."

Worth stiffened. "I believe we agreed we would not discuss the work with others, Miss Villers."

Her smile remained sunny, but her voice held just the hint of an edge. "I didn't intend to, my lord. I'd like to talk to your cook."

Worth blinked.

Bateman snorted. "Mrs. Hestrine's not likely to know much about such things."

Lydia did not take umbrage at his disparaging tone. "She might surprise you, Bateman. In this case, she might hold the key." She turned to Charlotte. "Surely she has some ideas on how well various materials conduct heat. We might have missed something."

Interesting approach, and one that might gain them some unexpected insights. Besides, if she and Charlotte spent the rest of the afternoon in the kitchen, he wouldn't have to worry about his research or them.

But there was one sure way to safeguard his sanity.

"Excellent suggestion," he said. "I'll join you. Charlotte, perhaps you could work with Miss Janssen on her testing, then help Bateman set up a new test platform for you and Miss Villers."

He thought his sister might argue. She had enough on her hands with completing her own task to jump in with his basket weaver.

But she slid a glance toward his bodyguard before nodding. "Yes, of course." She turned to Lydia. "We'll regroup afterward. I'm sure you'll have a great deal to relate."

As it turned out, not as much as Lydia had obviously hoped. Their cook, Mrs. Hestrine, directed her undercook and pot boy to keep working while she answered Lydia's questions at one side of the bustling kitchen. Worth had never spent much time in the space, but he wasn't surprised to find it bright, clean, and well organized. Charlotte would have had it no other way. For his part, so long as food arrived on a predictable schedule and was largely edible, he saw no need to interfere in his staff's domain. And on the rare occasion when interference was needed, Charlotte saw to it.

He had met his cook at the once-a-year Boxing Day festivities, when his parents and now Charlotte held a party for the staff. The older woman was heavyset, with a round face and meaty hands that looked equally capable of wielding a rolling pin or a battle axe.

"Thank you for allowing us to interrupt you, Mrs. Hestrine," Lydia said when introductions had been completed. "We had a question about the pots and pans you prefer in your kitchen."

His cook glanced at the bright copper pots hanging on the sunny yellow wall to their right. "Always preferred copper myself."

Interesting. "Why?" Worth asked, leaning forward. "I've found it altogether difficult to manage for my applications."

Mrs. Hestrine stared at him. Lydia stepped in smoothly.

"What his lordship means is that copper seems to heat too readily, unlike iron."

"But cast iron can be terribly heavy when filled for a large event," the cook protested. Then she blushed. "Not that I'm complaining about cast iron, mind you. Miss Charlotte keeps us well equipped."

"I'll be sure to let Miss Worthington know how much you appreciate that," Lydia promised her.

"Have you found a particular metal that does not conduct heat well?" Worth asked, gaze going over the various cookware. Porcelain, perhaps? Or would it not tolerate the changes in altitude and temperature?

"Conduct heat?" She glanced from Worth to Lydia and back. "I'm your cook, my lord. Not my place to conduct anything."

Worth felt a tug of impatience, but Lydia showed not the least of it. "Of course. Forgive us. What I believe his lordship meant was, have you ever cooked in a pot that simply didn't heat well?"

"Well, certainly." Mrs. Hestrine pulled up on the strap of her voluminous apron as if preparing for a fight. "You have to season the iron, you know. If you don't, the fish won't fry evenly."

Seasoning. Would some coating make the metal less vulnerable to overheating?

Lydia had brought one of Charlotte's journals and a pencil with her. Now she made a note of something. "Interesting. With what do you season it? Wouldn't salt affect the taste of the food?"

"Salt?" Mrs. Hestrine shook her head. "You season with drippings—pork fat, perhaps, or beef. You rub it into the iron. Keeps it cooking nicely."

"Fascinating," Worth said, while Lydia made another note.

Again the cook glanced between them. Then she drew herself up with a sniff that must send her pot boy scurrying for cover. "I have been working in this house since before you were born, my lord. Never have I had anyone complain about my work, much less make fun of it."

Lydia glanced up, face bunching. "Oh, Mrs. Hestrine. I wasn't making fun of you."

The cook sniffed again, as if she highly doubted that.

The floor seemed unsteady under his feet. Here was his greatest lack. He could have told Lydia the exact temperature each of the cook's vessels could tolerate, but he struggled to understand why Mrs. Hestrine had decided not the tolerate their questions.

"I'm sure Lord Worthington has nothing but respect for

your culinary skills," Lydia said with a glance his way.

Mrs. Hestrine glanced at him too, waiting.

They both expected him to set things right.

He was sweating, but he squared his shoulders. "Of course. My father praised your work, my mother praised it, and Charlotte praises it. I may have been remiss in not letting you know how much I appreciate it, but it is because of the faith I have in you that I accompanied Miss Villers to consult you."

He held his breath, hoping he'd judged the situation correctly.

The cook's nose came down, and a smile turned up her generous mouth. "Thank you, my lord. I am always at your service. Is there anything else you wanted to know?"

Worth exhaled.

Lydia asked some more questions, followed the cook around to examine various metal pots and porcelain bowls, then thanked her for her time. After Worth had reiterated his thanks, they left the kitchen together.

"I hope you have a good dinner tonight," Lydia said as they headed back for the garden. "I didn't consider the possibility that she might see our questions as interloping. It's almost as if she expected that from us."

Worth held open the door to the laboratory side of the house for her. "Perhaps she did. I wasn't exaggerating when I said I have failed to praise her work. I may even have suggested at some point that my efforts were not to be interrupted for meals."

She shook her head. "You gave her the impression your work is more important than hers. Small wonder she isn't eager to share her thoughts."

"But my work *is* more important than food," he said with a shrug.

Lydia stopped just short of the rear door to the garden, and he stopped as well.

"What an interesting theory," she said, green eyes bright

as grass in spring. "Let's test it. For the next forty-eight hours, you may work as long as you like, but you may eat nothing."

Worth chuckled. "Point taken. I was wrong."

Lydia pressed a hand to her chest. "What! The great philosopher made an error? What is the world coming to?"

"The world continues to advance," Worth said, moving forward to open the door to the garden for her. "Regardless of whether I make an error in judgement."

"That," she said, passing him for the yard, "is one of the most intelligent things you've ever said."

The words held no rancor, simply observation, but they made him pause on the back stoop, while she continued on to where Charlotte and Bateman were studying the brazier as if trying to determine the best way to resurrect the fire. Why was it Lydia's insights so easily disrupted his thinking? With seemingly little effort, she made him stop and consider.

And she was more right than she knew, for he could not tell her that it was exactly his errors in judgement that had landed him where he was. And he still had not recovered from them.

# CHAPTER SEVEN

Lydia, Worth, and Charlotte spent the rest of the afternoon debating ideas for augmenting and transporting the coal. They worked in Charlotte's study, Worth roaming about the room while his sister and Lydia perched on stools at the table. Worth and Lydia looked up recent research; Charlotte sketched promising concepts. Unfortunately, every avenue they pursued quickly proved itself useless.

"I begin to see why balloon flight remains a curiosity," Lydia said, laying down a volume of *Philosophical Transactions* and rubbing her temples, which were beginning to throb.

Worth lowered his volume from the German Academy of Sciences as well, grey eyes focused on the day outside, which had turned rainy. "There must be an answer. I refuse to believe long-distance flight impossible."

"Perhaps we should consult the other members of the Royal Society," Lydia said. "John Curtis has done outstanding work in determining the various elements that might compose gasses."

Worth snapped the book shut. "No. Out of the question."

His shoulders had tensed, his head was high, and the view of the rain no longer seemed to provide any source of calm.

"Do you have something against Mr. Curtis?" Lydia asked.

Charlotte, who had been finishing one of her sketches, stilled her quill to look at her brother expectantly.

"I have only the highest regard for those who excel at their work," Worth assured them both. "But I prefer to keep my theories private until they have been proven to my satisfaction."

Charlotte sighed, tipping her quill into its brass stand. "You realize you are an aberration, Worth. Most natural philosophers consult with others when possible. Why, researchers from different countries have corresponded for years to share their work and learn."

"Science advances on itself," Lydia agreed, "one person building on the foundation of another." She waved at the books scattered across the table before them. "Why else are we searching for precedent?"

Worth shelved the book. "Perhaps I prefer to set the precedent rather than follow it." He turned to his sister. "Forgive me, Charlotte, for taking up so much of your time. I should be working on my own task, not intruding on yours. And I know you hoped to prepare for the ball this evening."

Charlotte consulted the silver-cased watch pinned to her day dress. "It's only half past four. Perhaps another hour?"

"I would not dream of being so selfish." He bowed to his sister and Lydia. "I will have the carriage brought round at a quarter to eight. Until then." He strode out of the door before either could comment.

"Well," Charlotte said. "I certainly don't require so much time to prepare for a ball. Do you, Lydia?"

Lydia smiled, glad to hear Charlotte call her by her first name again. "I've prepared for a ball in less than a quarter hour when Beau managed a late invitation." She leaned forward. "Where else shall we look for our answers?"

Charlotte regarded her notes with a frown. "I wish I knew. Natural philosophy appears to have failed us."

Lydia studied the books remaining on the upper parts of

Charlotte's shelves. She could not agree with Worth that past inquiries were meaningless. If nothing else, they could illustrate what *not* to try. Most of Charlotte's books were scientific in nature—pontifications on nature, chemistry, physics. But she spotted a few historical tomes among the leather-bound volumes, as well as more than one recent novel.

"If natural philosophy has failed us," Lydia said, turning her gaze to Charlotte's, "perhaps history will save us. How did the Romans keep fire burning?"

Charlotte stuck out her lower lip. "Or the Greeks. I seem to recall something about an eternal flame. Polybius's history, perhaps?"

She located the thick books and took the first two volumes while Lydia began wading through the third. She wasn't sure how long she'd read about various conquests and conquerors before she heard a loud *harrumph*. She looked up to find Bateman framed in the doorway, shoulders of his sturdy brown coat nearly touching each side.

"A woman is here claiming she's supposed to help you change," he declared, voice and look heavy with suspicion.

Lydia set aside the book. "That would be Enid, Miss Thorn's maid. I thought we might need help."

Once more Charlotte consulted her watch. "Half past six? Where did the time go? Let her in, Beast, and send her to my bedchamber. Ask the other ladies to meet us there."

With a nod, he left.

As Charlotte came around the table, Lydia tipped her head in the direction the manservant had gone. "Your brother calls him Bateman, but you call him Beast. Surely that's not his first name."

A dusky rose bloomed in Charlotte's cheeks as they headed for the door. "Certainly not. I understand Beast is the name he was given when he was a pugilist. The Beast of Birmingham."

Lydia's brows rose. "Bateman was a boxer?"

As they started down the corridor, Charlotte glanced at her as if surprised she would question the matter. "Yes, a rather good one, recommended to us by Gentleman Jackson himself."

Lydia knew the name. Few among the *ton* didn't. Most of the gentlemen subscribed to his school on Bond Street, taking lessons from him twice or three times a week. A fellow did not count himself among the sporting class until he had sparred with the Gentleman.

"How did he come to work for your brother?" Lydia asked as they made for the stairs.

"Worth was looking for a bodyguard," Charlotte said.

Lydia frowned. "A bodyguard? Was his life in danger?"

"Perhaps." Charlotte stopped at the foot of the stairs and put a hand on Lydia's arm. "Please, say nothing to him or the others about the matter, Lydia. Last year, shortly after you and my brother stopped keeping company, we received several notes with vague threats. The sender seemed to think Worth could be induced to stop his inquiries. The notes only served to spur him on. But, to make sure he and I were safe, he hired a bodyguard. I understand Beast became bored with the fighting square. Worth may be tiresome at times, but he is rarely boring."

Now, that she had no need of research to confirm. Just when she thought she understood him, Worth did something inexplicable. Setting precedent indeed. Why spend hours poring over the annals of the Royal Society, then?

"I won't say a word about the matter," she promised Charlotte. But she didn't promise not to talk further with Worth about this issue of precedent.

Unfortunately, she had no time to question him for a while. They climbed to the chamber story and followed the wood-paneled corridor to Charlotte's room. Now, this was a bedchamber Lydia could appreciate. A shame Beau had never been able to manage one in the many houses he had rented over the years. Folds of blue satin fell from a gold half-crown near the ceiling to drape around the polished wood headboard of the bed. Similar draperies, held back by gold-tasseled ribbons, embraced the multipaned window overlooking the park. Even the Pier glass mirror was framed in ornamented gold. It was as if she'd wandered into a palace in the sky.

"How lovely," Lydia said with a sigh she hoped wasn't too envious.

Charlotte smiled as she went to the walnut wardrobe along one soft-blue wall. "I like it. Excuse me while I ring for my maid Tess. Between her and Enid, we should be in good hands."

Miss Pankhurst and Miss Janssen did not appear nearly so certain when they joined Lydia and Charlotte a short time later. They milled about just inside the doorway, like pigeons expected to be startled into flight. Tess, a sturdy blonde old enough to be Charlotte's mother, glanced from one woman to the other as if trying to decide whether to shoo them from the room or put them to work.

Enid, however, was a godsend. Short and curvaceous, with bright blue eyes and capable hands, the dark-haired maid bustled into the room, Lydia's gown draped over one arm and a satchel on the other. Like her mistress, she was efficient and practical, and soon had one lady changing while Tess brushed out the hair of another at the dressing table and a third tried on jewelry before the long mirror.

Charlotte was ready within a half hour, dressed in the grey she favored, this time of a matte satin with a silver embroidered net overskirt that shimmered in the light. Miss Janssen was ready a short while later, turning in front of the long mirror as if surprised how well she looked in celestial blue with a white satin ribbon tied under her ample chest.

Miss Pankhurst, however, could not seem to settle. She asked Lydia's opinion on everything from how to curl her brown hair to whether to take up the hem on her rose-colored gown. And then, she disagreed with everything Lydia suggested!

It was considerably after eight when the four of them made their way downstairs. Worth was pacing about the entry hall, lean form swathed splendidly in black from his velvet-lapeled tailcoat to his satin breeches and leather evening pumps. He stopped and stared at them, and Lydia readied herself for a scold. If dinner must not delay his work, taking time to dress for a ball must be sheer rebellion.

"Forgive us for being tardy, my lord," Miss Pankhurst sang out before he could speak. "It takes a great amount of time for some of us to make up our minds." She looked pointedly at Lydia and giggled. Miss Janssen gave a half laugh as if she felt she must but wasn't sure of the joke.

Lydia understood, feeling cold all over. It was one thing to constantly berate her work. She had to earn her place on the team and was prepared to do so. This was something more, something she had thought she'd left behind when she'd eschewed the crowded Mayfair ballrooms for the excitement of natural philosophy.

Jealousy.

Miss Pankhurst was intent on vying with her for Worth's attentions. She was clever about it, Lydia would give her that. The comment was true. The lady had been unable to make up her mind. But she'd made it seem as if it were Lydia who had delayed them. She meant to diminish Lydia in Worth's eyes.

How very sad. Lydia could have told the woman she was wasting her time. Worth no longer admired Lydia in that manner. He saw her only as a way to spur his efforts, and she was fairly certain he felt the same way about Miss Pankhurst and Miss Janssen. On such occasions, she had learned, there was only one recourse: smile and get on with more important things.

She aimed a carefree smile in his direction and caught

her breath.

He was gazing at her as if she was the fuel to his fire, the perfect stitch on his silk envelope, as if she held every answer to every research question he might want to pose. Could he still admire her after all?

Worth was vaguely aware of the others descending the stair, but his gaze had latched onto Lydia and refused to let go. Dressed in white silk with lush peaches and dusky green leaves embroidered along the dip of her neckline and the hem of her graceful skirts, she was summer personified. He wanted to rush to her side, whisper praise in her shell-shaped ear, hear her promise she would be his forevermore. Why did these feelings persist? They were as demanding as a new hypothesis, yet he didn't dare test them. Why did she still have the power to captivate him, even when he knew what lay beneath the fair façade?

A quick mind.

A warm heart.

A woman capable of breaking his.

He shoved those thoughts aside as Bateman came out from behind the stairs, arms loaded with cloaks.

"Take what's yours," he ordered straightening out both arms.

Miss Pankhurst and Miss Janssen glanced at each other, clearly perplexed.

Charlotte stepped forward. "Allow me. Worth, this long one must be yours."

He took the crimson-lined black velvet cloak from her and slung it about his shoulders as she doled out smaller, simpler versions that must belong to Miss Janssen and Miss Pankhurst.

"Two left," she declared. "Worth, if you'll help Miss Villers, I'm sure Beast can assist me."

Worth accepted the spring green wool lined with lavender satin and held it up. Lydia turned dutifully, and he draped it about her shoulders. His knuckles brushed her neck. Even though he wore his evening gloves, he was certain her skin was warm. How soft it had once felt to his touch.

As if she remembered the days when he'd held her close, she pulled the cloak more tightly about her and stepped out of reach. But both she and Charlotte were blushing as they left the house for the coach.

In the cramped space, his awareness of Lydia only grew. Built to seat four comfortably, the padded leather seats of the carriage made five a pinch. Charlotte maneuvered it so that Worth sat between her and Lydia, his thigh pressed against Lydia's, while Miss Janssen and Miss Pankhurst sat across from them. In the light from the carriage lamps outside, both the ladies seemed to be watching his every move.

What did they think? That he would turn, take Lydia in his arms, and profess his undying devotion?

Ridiculous idea. He couldn't even shift without bumping into her or Charlotte.

"You will remember me to Lord Stanhope, Miss Villers," Miss Janssen said as the coach rolled through Mayfair for the Baminger ball. "Miss Worthington read his recent paper on the development of lenses to us. Inspiring."

"Of course," Lydia promised. "And I'd be happy to introduce you as well, Miss Pankhurst."

Miss Pankhurst sniffed. "No need. I came tonight only as a favor to dear Miss Worthington. You don't find me posturing to catch a gentleman's eye."

Miss Janssen dropped her gaze and rubbed her fingers against each other in her lap as if she would have preferred to be back at her weaving. He could not easily turn his head to see how Lydia reacted to the statement. Once her entire world had been about posturing to catch a gentleman's eye. Her brother had introduced her to Worth and most of his friends, including Carrolton and Sir Harry.

"Pity," Lydia said cheerfully to Miss Pankhurst. "I imagine more than one will be looking your way."

Miss Pankhurst blinked. Very likely she was unaccustomed to hearing herself praised after spending years, Charlotte had told him, as her family's poor relation, shuttled from one relative's home to another. Then her brows drew down as if she suspected she'd just been insulted. He could have told her Lydia ever used flattery, never irony, to win her conquests.

Charlotte evidently did not take Lydia's statement amiss.

"You will have to be on your guard tonight, Worth," she said. "Or you just might lose an assistant."

Despite the warmth of the tight-packed coach, Lydia shivered beside him. It was all he could do to keep from putting his arm about her and anchoring her to his side. He knew it wasn't just for warmth. Of the members of his team, her loss once more would cut the deepest, despite all his attempts to reason otherwise. But he could not bring himself to vie for her again.

Which meant any gentleman was free to approach Lydia and offer himself instead. It was her right to marry, to be happy. Surely he could be happy for her.

He had a feeling Lady Baminger's ball was going to be the longest of his life.

# CHAPTER EIGHT

It was a tremendous crush. Lady Baminger's ball always was, even if her guest list was far more varied than that of most hostesses. The cavernous space of the rented hall boasted high ceilings painted with scenes from Olympus, marble pillars crowned with gold, and velvet couches along the plastered walls. London's finest rubbed elbows with those of the creative class. The lady was involved in any number of charitable pursuits and had been known to sponsor scientific, artistic, musical, and literary endeavors. Those she had funded came from gratitude. Those of her own class came from curiosity. Others came hoping to benefit from her largess.

Lydia's brother Beau usually belonged to the last group.

He must have been watching for Lydia, for he showed up at her side the moment she and the other ladies finished the receiving line at one end of the ballroom, leaving Worth to greet their hostess and her husband. Even with Beau's sleek black hair and aquiline nose, her brother did not pull off the black eveningwear nearly as well as Worth did, a flickering candle to Worth's bright flame.

"I see Lady Baminger continues to favor the young and beautiful," he said, gaze sweeping over her companions as he sketched a bow.

Charlotte eyed him, brows raised. Miss Janssen blushed. Miss Pankhurst tsked. "You will not turn our heads with such flattery, sir," she declared. "We recognize a wolf in sheep's clothing when we see one."

Either she knew of Lydia's brother or had correctly determined his scheme. Beau put a hand over his paisley waistcoat, about where his heart would be. "Madam, you wound me."

"Come now, Mr. Villers," Charlotte said. "You must admit you have a certain reputation."

Beau's mouth dipped down, as if the fact saddened him. "Surely you've heard I've reformed."

"Have you?" Miss Janssen looked positively disappointed.

"My brother is engaged to be married," Lydia explained. "To Lady Lilith."

"Sister to the Earl of Carrolton," he confirmed, chin up as he preened.

"And when is the happy day?" Charlotte asked. "I don't recall seeing an invitation."

"Some difficulty with the printer, I understand," he said with a wave of his gloved hand. "I expect them shortly. Lady Lilith is at Carrolton Park at the moment. Miss Worthington, might I persuade you to take the floor with me in my beloved's absence?"

Though Charlotte and Lady Lilith were friends, Worth's sister snapped open her ivory fan. "Perhaps another time, Mr. Villers." She looked to Miss Janssen, who stepped forward eagerly.

"I will have to make do with my sister, then," Beau said, ignoring the other woman and offering Lydia his arm.

Lydia rapped it with her finger. "I'm not wasting a dance on my own brother. Besides, the musicians haven't even stationed themselves in the alcove above the supper room yet. I can take my time determining my first partner. Come along, Miss Janssen. Let's find better sport."

Miss Pankhurst giggled, at Beau's expense or Lydia's, Lydia wasn't sure. But Miss Janssen scurried to accompany her, and they set off around the edge of the floor, leaving

Charlotte, Miss Pankhurst, and Beau behind.

"I heard your brother is a great scoundrel," her companion said.

"My brother is a mediocre scoundrel at best," Lydia told her. "But I do believe associating with Lady Lilith has made him a better person."

"And he approves of you working?" Miss Janssen asked as they detoured around a group of young ladies on their first Season. Oh, how lovely not to have to endure the posturing, to smile when she wanted to shout.

"Not in the slightest," Lydia said. "Beau finds work, of any sort, abhorrent. But my parents didn't leave me an inheritance, expecting him to take care of me. At least I'm sparing him the expense. Oh, look, there's Lord Stanhope."

Tall and impossibly lean, with a nose as sharp as his mind, the earl was a familiar sight in London when Parliament was in session. His hair had deserted his head, leaving a greying wing on either side of his long face, but his smile was always welcoming. He was standing by one of the pillars, in discussion with another man Lydia didn't recognize. His companion was short and slight and also balding. Unlike Lord Stanhope, he was apparently unwilling to accept the fact, for he had taken pains to hide the skin by combing his blond hair across the spot. He was older than Worth and more flamboyantly dressed in a vivid blue coat, silver-shot waistcoat, and white satin breeches.

Miss Janssen followed Lydia's gaze, then blanched. "Oh, Miss Villers, we shouldn't."

"We most certainly should. He will not bite, I promise you." Lydia took Miss Janssen's arm. The lady resisted, but Lydia managed to tow her over to the pair.

Lord Stanhope glanced her way as they approached, then smiled. "Miss Villers. What a pleasure. Come to renew our argument about the uses of electricity?"

The suggestion was nearly enough to make her forget her purpose, but the tug on her arm grew more insistent.

NEVER VIE FOR A VISCOUNT

"Nothing would suit me more," she assured him, "except perhaps to introduce you to a dear friend of mine, Miss Janssen. She is also keenly interested in scientific pursuits and was most desirous of making your acquaintance."

Lord Stanhope inclined his head to the weaver. "Miss Janssen. I believe I heard your name in connection with Lord Worthington's work."

"My lord," Miss Janssen said with a bob of a curtsey. Her voice came out breathless and fast. "Such a pleasure it is to meet you. I must not keep you to myself. Come, Miss Villers."

She transferred her grip to Lydia's arm so fervently she forced Lydia back a step to two. Lord Stanhope frowned, but his companion closed the gap, smile pleasant.

"No need to hurry off. I'd love to hear more about what course you're pursuing."

Miss Janssen let out a squeak, released Lydia's arm, picked up her celestial blue skirts, and fled.

"Extraordinary female," Lord Stanhope said. "I don't usually frighten them away."

"Ah, but you have been known to reach some frightening conclusions," his friend reminded him with a laugh.

Lord Stanhope smiled as if recognizing the reference to his sympathy for the French Revolution. "Forgive my manners, Miss Villers. May I present Mr. Curtis. He's interested in scientific pursuits as well."

Lydia offered his friend her hand. "I know the name. Your work on the chemical reactions of hydrogen was fascinating."

His eyes lit. They were a faded blue, as clear as the apothecary jars Gussie favored. "A lady who reads *Philosophical Transactions*," he said. "How refreshing."

"And one who puts action to interest," Lord Stanhope assured him. "Miss Villers was instrumental in helping Augusta Orwell develop the salve that's all the rage."

The light in Mr. Curtis's clear eyes dimmed only the

slightest. "Stillroom crafts can be quite efficacious."

"Did I hear you are also working with Lord Worthington now, Miss Villers?" Lord Stanhope asked.

Lydia dimpled. "I am. It's delightful work, engaging all my attention."

"Ah, then the gentlemen of London must be in mourning," the earl teased her.

Mr. Curtis perked up. "What are you studying that could possibly require all your attention, Miss Villers?"

Behind them came the sound of a violin. The orchestra was tuning up. That meant the first set would begin shortly. This was her cue to slip away. She really couldn't tell Mr. Curtis everything he wanted to know. She'd promised Worth. And she certainly didn't want to say anything that might imply the work was secret. That would only invite more questions.

She glanced around for a partner to rescue her and sweep her onto the dance floor, only to find Worth bearing down on her, color high and face set. Now what had she done?

She turned to Lord Stanhope. "I'm certain I must owe you a dance, my lord," she said, seizing his arm. "Shall we?"

Intent on rescuing Lydia from the company of a scoundrel, Worth pulled up short as Lord Stanhope led her out onto the floor. Or was Lydia leading him? It was difficult to tell by the bemused expression on the earl's lean face. His wife, seated on one of the velvet sofas along the wall, whispered something to her friends behind her painted fan, and they all shook their heads.

He might not understand motivations, but he thought he knew the reason for their reaction. His face warmed on Lydia's behalf. She might once have been hunting a title, but she would never dally with a married man. That much he could say with one hundred percent certainty.

The alliance would only alienate her from the Society she could otherwise have ruled. Very likely, she had chosen Stanhope because he could gratify her desire to talk about scientific advancements. Worth smiled just thinking about the exchange.

A movement caught his attention. Near the marble pillar, John Curtis inclined his head in greeting.

Worth turned his back on the fellow.

The cut direct. No doubt someone would notice and comment, but it was no more than Curtis deserved.

Charlotte must have seen him as well, for she hurried to Worth's side, Miss Pankhurst puffing in her wake.

"Worth?" she asked, brows knit in obvious concern.

"I'm fine, Charlotte," he said, though even he heard the tension in his voice.

Charlotte put her nose in the air. "I am shocked Lady Baminger would allow toads at her ball," she said with a look in Curtis's direction. "I'd think they'd make a mess of the flooring."

Worth shook his head, a chuckle rising even as his shoulders came down. "You always know what to say, Charlotte."

"That's because I know you," his sister said.

Miss Pankhurst glanced between them, lips more pinched than usual. "I fear I don't understand. A toad? Mr. Curtis? Has Lord Worthington taken him in dislike?"

He was not about to discuss the details with her, particularly in the middle of a crowded ballroom where anyone might overhear.

"That is a tale for another time," he told her. "Miss Pankhurst, when this set ends, might you honor me with a dance?"

She fluttered her lashes, cheeks turning pink. "But of course, my lord."

He did his duty for the next while, partnering Miss Pankhurst as well as Miss Janssen. Indeed, he was pleased to see his sister and her team in much demand, their smiles engaging, their movements graceful. He lost sight of Charlotte only when he escorted Lady Stanhope out onto the floor.

"I understand I have you to thank for the young lady who has stolen my husband's attention," she said when the pattern of the dance forced them to stand out for a time.

Worth glanced to where Lydia was dancing down the center of the line of couples, arm-in-arm with Lady Baminger's oldest son. She hadn't sat out once, her bubbly laughter and bouncing curls evident in each set.

"Lord Stanhope was simply indulging a young lady's interest in natural philosophy," he assured her.

"Natural philosophy," she said, accepting his arm as they returned to the line. "Is that what they call it now?"

The dance prevented him from responding until he led her back to her seat. As he bowed over her hand, he met her gaze. "Miss Villers is a valued member of my staff, Lady Stanhope. I would not like to see her reputation diminished because of a mistaken belief in her interests."

She inclined her head. "No more than I would, my lord."

Satisfied he'd made his point, he went to find his next partner. He was near the sofa where several of the dowagers had congregated when a gentleman moved to block his way.

"And what's this about you imposing on my sister?" Beau Villers demanded.

Fans stilled, necks craned, eyes brightened. Worth took Villers's elbow and steered him out of earshot.

"To be precise," he told the fellow, "my sister is imposing on her. If you are concerned, I advise you to take up the matter with your sister and not link our names in the middle of a ballroom." He released his hold and started around the fellow, but Villers dodged to cut him off.

"Lydia and I have spoken," he assured Worth. "But she doesn't seem to understand her role in your household.

Surely you aren't allowing her to assist in your work."

Worth studied him. Villers was as sleek as a panther, from his ebony hair to his polished evening pumps. Poised on his feet, he even gave the appearance of being ready to pounce.

"Your sister has experience and a number of excellent insights," Worth said. "Why shouldn't I include her in my work?"

Beau shook his head slowly, as if amazed Worth had to ask. "Her enthusiasm sometimes puts her in untenable positions. As her devoted brother, I would be remiss if I did not ensure her safety."

Worth raised his brows. "Safety? What do you imagine she's doing?"

"It's well known you dabble in chemicals, my lord. Certain combinations can be dangerous."

He wasn't sure which was more insulting—the assumption that he would "dabble" in anything, that he might not realize the dangers in his work, or that he would in any way subject Lydia to them.

"I no longer pursue chemistry as my subject," he told Villers. "Your sister is safe with me."

The fellow's smile was sly. "I am very glad to hear that, my lord. I would not like to have to demand compensation for the ruin of her health. Or her reputation."

Worth's jaw tightened. "A gentleman should not demand compensation but satisfaction when a lady has been harmed."

Villers laughed. "Oh, I would never challenge you to a duel, my lord. If you harmed Lydia, I know your honor would demand that you do the right thing and marry her. You once considered marriage, I believe."

Had come within hours of proposing, but he wasn't going to admit that either.

"Congratulations on your own nuptials," he said instead.

"I am the most fortunate of mortals," Villers answered

quickly, as if the line was well rehearsed. "Now, about my sister…"

"Yes, what about me?" Lydia asked, appearing at Worth's elbow. "You two look entirely too glum. This is a ball, you know. You should be dancing."

# CHAPTER NINE

Really, but Beau could be tiresome. For three years, she'd followed his advice scrupulously—dance with this fellow, flirt with that one. If she'd questioned him, he'd trot out his excuse for constantly pushing her forward.

"I promised Mother and Father I would see you well wed."

She shared that goal, though it had become apparent she and her brother defined *well wed* differently. To her, it meant marrying a gentleman with compatible ideals, a common purpose, two hearts and minds beating as one. To Beau, it meant only a gentleman of wealth and prestige. He had not been born to the peerage, but, through her, he might marry into it.

A year ago, she'd thought she'd found a way to satisfy them both in Worth. Since then, she'd learned there might be a better goal for her. She was not about to allow Beau to push her forward again.

"Go on," she told him, shooing him with her hands. "Lady Lilith may not be in attendance, but any number of dowagers would enjoy your company. Go!"

Blinking, Beau went.

"So that's how one handles your brother," Worth said. "I would not have thought to dangle a dowager."

"Beau is very good about furthering his cause," Lydia said, watching her brother bow to an elderly duchess who had been sitting a little farther along the wall. "He simply forgets I am no longer his cause." She turned to Worth. "I hope he wasn't bothering you."

His look was more amused than annoyed. "He said nothing that need concern you, but thank you for asking. I was looking for you earlier."

She glanced around him but could not catch sight of Charlotte, Miss Janssen, or Miss Pankhurst. "Oh? Did your sister have need of me?"

"No. I do."

Lydia stiffened, gaze slowly moving back to him. His smile brushed her softly, like tender fingers. But he could not mean that statement as it sounded. Viscount Worthington needed no one, especially her.

As if he noted her surprise, he bowed and explained himself. "I have danced with everyone else on the team. I didn't want to leave you out. Would you consider partnering with me?"

Her heart leaped up and lodged itself in her throat. Perhaps that was why her voice came out so high. "Certainly."

Another set was preparing to start. He offered her his arm and led her out.

Earlier, she'd focused most of her attention on her partners, only tangentially aware of Worth down the set. Now he filled her senses. She'd forgotten how well he danced, or perhaps she had not allowed herself to remember. It wasn't just his athletic grace. Many gentlemen possessed that. No, Worth danced as he did everything else, with an intensity, a fire. While others minced through the steps, he claimed the floor. When he took her hands and turned her, she thought all eyes must watch him. That smile, that power. She wanted only to be closer to the blaze, for all she knew it could burn her.

She was breathless by the time the set ended, and she knew it wasn't from the exertion of the dance. Worth didn't look as winded, but his hands disappeared behind his back as they left the set, and his gaze dipped to the complicated pattern of the floor. "Lydia, I…"

"My lord Worthington." Miss Pankhurst hurried up to them, gloved fingers fluttering before her rose-colored gown and tightly curled ringlets trembling. "Your sister would like to leave."

Worth immediately turned to accompany her across the room, Lydia at his side. "Is she unwell?" he asked with a frown.

Miss Pankhurst didn't answer. Instead, she led them to a quiet corner, where Miss Janssen sat beside Charlotte on one of the sofas. Worth's sister was once more plying her ivory fan, this time before her face.

"The room is crowded," Miss Janssen was lamenting. "Best you should rest."

"I have brought your brother, Miss Worthington," Miss Pankhurst said as if Charlotte wouldn't notice them standing in front of her. "Is there anything else I can procure? Lemonade, perhaps? A slice of cake?"

"No, nothing," Charlotte assured her. Her sculpted cheeks were stained pink, and sweat beaded her brow below her swept-back auburn hair. "Worth, could we go home?"

"Certainly," he said. "I'll ask for the carriage to be brought around now. Are you comfortable waiting here?"

She nodded, and he strode off.

Lydia sat beside the woman she was beginning to consider a friend. "Is there anything I can do?"

Charlotte's smile was a ghost of its usual self. "I'll be fine, Lydia. Please don't worry."

"How can we not worry?" Miss Janssen asked, fingers rubbing each other in her lap again. "That horrid Mr. Curtis. He is to blame. I saw him talking with you. How he encroaches. If I had known he would be here, I would have told you we should not come."

"He does seem to have an odd effect on you all," Miss

Pankhurst said, eyes bright as she glanced from one lady to the other. "It seemed to me Lord Worthington gave him the cut direct earlier, and then you seem to have been overcome after speaking with him, Miss Worthington."

Charlotte met the woman's blue-eyed gaze, her own grey eyes implacable. "It is crowded and close in here, just as Miss Janssen noted. I merely need fresh air."

"Oh, of course," Miss Pankhurst hurried to assure her. "Do you not find it odd, though, that…"

"No," Charlotte snapped. "I do not." She closed her eyes, and Miss Janssen began flapping her fingers at her as if trying to push the air in Charlotte's direction. Miss Pankhurst said no more.

An idea burst upon Lydia. "A fan!" she cried.

Charlotte opened her eyes, fingers clutching the ivory. "I have one. Did you need it?"

"No, but we do," Lydia insisted. "A bellows. A blacksmith uses it to increase the heat of his fire. Why couldn't we?"

Charlotte straightened. "Of course! Just the thing! Oh, Lydia, you're brilliant!"

Lydia's cheeks were probably as pink as Charlotte's. "No, but I like to think I'm observant."

"As am I," Miss Pankhurst said. "And Mr. Curtis appears to be headed in this direction."

Immediately Charlotte pulled in on herself, as if trying to sink into the velvet upholstery behind her. Miss Janssen waxed white. Miss Pankhurst looked entirely too interested in their reactions.

"Allow me," Lydia said. She rose, shook out her silk skirts, and went to meet the man.

Mr. Curtis inclined his head in greeting as they drew closer. "Miss Villers. What an accomplished dancer you are. Might I request you partner me?"

What was it about this man that so discomfited Worth and his sister? Lydia looked him up and down but saw only a fellow approaching middle age who dressed perhaps too much like a dandy to be taken seriously as a natural philosopher. He associated with Lord Stanhope, so at least that gentleman approved of him. Lady Baminger had invited him to her ball, but Lydia didn't know whether he belonged in the creative camp, was a sponsor, or, like her brother, had come with his hand out. She did, however, know what to do when a gentleman offered to dance with her.

She smiled with just the right amount of regret. "Alas, Mr. Curtis, but I shall be leaving as soon as the Worthington coach can be brought to the door. Miss Worthington is feeling unwell."

He frowned in Charlotte's direction, and Lydia shifted just enough to block his view of her friend.

"I'm very sorry to hear that," he said. "Did she mention the reason for her discomfort?"

Lydia was fairly sure she was looking at the reason, but she still didn't understand why the man held such power over the usually unflappable Charlotte.

Lydia waved her hand before her face. "Well, it is rather crowded."

He angled his head as if trying to see around her, and his hair slipped, revealing more of his balding pate. "Perhaps I should sit with her while she waits."

"She has her assistants at her side," Lydia assured him. "Sometimes a lady merely wants the company of another lady. As a gentleman, I'm sure you understand."

He could not argue and still maintain the façade of a gentleman. He offered her a bow, and she returned to Charlotte's side.

"What did he say to you?" Charlotte hissed, face now devoid of all color.

"Nothing of import," Lydia told her. "He wanted a dance, but I explained that we were leaving. He seems harmless enough."

"Yes," Charlotte murmured, fan moving more from habit

than need now, Lydia thought. "So he seems."

Worth didn't like Charlotte's look, first red, now white, and so very stilted in her movements, as if something pained her. His sister was rarely sick, rarely indisposed. She moved through life with a placid grace that admitted no interruptions.

It had been that way since their parents had died—first their father from pneumonia, and then their mother a year later. The physician had been perplexed as to what had caused her death, but Worth had always suspected a broken heart. Just because no one had documented the malady yet didn't mean it couldn't exist.

Still, Charlotte had been his rock, his stalwart companion, through it all, despite the fact that she was younger. The thought of losing her too was untenable.

"Could it have been something you ate?" he pressed as they headed for home. In deference to his sister, he had insisted that she sit beside him on the forward-facing bench. Lydia had squeezed in between Miss Pankhurst and Miss Janssen opposite them. In truth, that was probably for the best. Dancing with her had brought back too many memories. He had to remind himself their purpose for associating now had nothing to do with courting.

"No, Worth," Charlotte answered him. "Stop fussing. I'll be fine now that we're out of that crush." She drew in a breath and sat taller, adjusting her cloak around her as if determined to regain her usual composure. "Now, what about tomorrow? Does everyone have an assignment?"

"I will work with the cabinet maker to secure a floor to the basket," Miss Janssen supplied. "Light, but strong."

"I am making rapid progress in stitching the silk, now that certain impediments have been removed," Miss Pankhurst said with a glance at Lydia.

Impediments like Miss Pankhurst's unwillingness to try anything new? As far as Worth could see, that had been more of an impediment than Lydia. Her efforts had only been a boon to their work.

"Shall I help you with your heat experiments?" Lydia asked Charlotte, look and voice eager.

"Absolutely," Charlotte said, turning to him. "Worth, Lydia had an inspired idea. Instead of augmenting the coal, why not use a bellows?"

He nodded, the idea taking shape in his mind. "Like a smith. Excellent thought."

"Perhaps you could work with Lydia tomorrow morning on the approach," his sister ventured.

"Oh, how disappointing," Miss Pankhurst put in. "I could make so much more progress with another pair of hands."

Hands she had just complained of, if he had understood her correctly. He thought Charlotte would complain as well, demand that she needed Lydia more, but his sister merely smiled.

"I'd be happy to sew with you, Miss Pankhurst. Worth and Lydia can work in the garden until I'm needed. A day or two helping you catch up would be well worth the effort."

"How…kind," Miss Pankhurst said. "But I wouldn't want to put you out. Miss Villers has some talent for the work. All that embroidering for a trousseau, I expect." She giggled.

Lydia didn't so much as twitch at the mention of her lost opportunities. "Very likely. But I defer to Charlotte's excellent plan. How may I help you explore this new approach, my lord?"

A dozen answers leaped forward like horses freed to run. They'd have to review his propulsion work to see how the devices he had in mind might be affected by the addition of another. He and Lydia could visit a smithy, her presence a light in the dark space. Their fingers might touch as she handed him the bellows. The warmth of the fire would glow in her cheeks.

He was mad. Utterly mad.

"Let's start by hearing more about your idea, Miss Villers," he said.

Her smile brightened the coach.

It brightened his laboratory the next day as well. Both Miss Pankhurst and Charlotte had appointments that morning, but Lydia arrived right on time. He had planned to work in the rear yard. Unfortunately, a steady rain had begun falling, and he needed to calculate the dimensions and other requirements of the apparatus in any regard. Leaving the door open to the stairs so the others could hear them, thus protecting Lydia's reputation, he set about summing up their progress.

"Hot air rises, this we know," he said as he paced past the center table, where Lydia sat on a bench, muslin skirts brushing the plank floor. "The problem is keeping it hot without destroying the container, basket, or envelope."

Lydia nodded, pale curls bouncing. "Charlotte said as much. That's why she's trying to determine how to transport fire."

"Exactly. I originally thought to come at the matter from another direction. Might there be another type of air that rises without heat?"

She rubbed at a stain on the table with one finger, as if she longed to touch the instruments just beyond. "Another type of air? Like the noxious air in coal mines?"

"Or what Volta discovered over the marshes in Italy, yes."

She wrinkled her nose as if she could smell the fetid odor from here. "But those appear to sink, if I understand correctly."

"They stay close to their origin. Something else might rise. I considered hydrogen, which the French have been using with some success, but ruled it out because of its known flammability."

"Oxygen?" she suggested.

Worth shook his head. "Too difficult to produce in pure form, particularly for industrial purposes."

She pouted. "How unfortunate. But you see what I mean about precedent, Worth. You're building on what others have learned."

He was. He knew that. It wasn't the building but the taking that incensed him. How was he to make a mark on the world if no one knew his contribution? Was he to be the least famous Viscount Worthington?

"In this case, precedent has failed," he told her. "Davy may discover another gas any moment, but we must demonstrate at the end of the month. Heated air will have to do. An equally important question is how to steer the balloon."

She shivered, and he realized the moment came from anticipation, not cold. "If I understand correctly, balloons move at the mercy of the winds."

"At the moment, they do," he acknowledged. "A balloonist's sole recourse is to rise or fall into favorable wind, and we have no way to veer right or left. Yet Napoleon is certain his balloons can cross the Channel from France, in direct opposition to the prevailing winds."

"How?" she demanded.

He picked up his propeller model from the table and gave the cedar paddles a spin. "Through propulsion."

She watched the angled paddles turn. "You would affix something like this to the basket?"

"To all four sides," he said. "With cranks so they would be turned by hand."

Lydia frowned. "Foot pedals too, I would imagine. Otherwise the balloonist's arms would weaken over the time you have envisioned."

Foot pedals. Why hadn't he thought of that?

"Foot pedals would be so much more practical if we add the bellows," he mused aloud.

She dimpled.

Simply having her there, listening to his theories and supplying facts that proved or disproved them spurred him to consider alternatives he'd ignored before. Together, they determined how big the bellows would need to be to effectively increase the heat of the fire and debated ways to outfit the balloon with the additional device. When his sister rang the bell for tea, he almost resented the break.

Lydia didn't show such concern. She paced him down the corridor, already talking about their next steps. He'd always admired her energy. How invigorating to pair it with his work. Both his loves, in one package.

He reined in his thoughts. He did not love Lydia Villers. He could not allow it. Today natural philosophy enthralled her. Last year, it had been flirting. Who knew what it might be tomorrow? His mind leaped as agilely, but within a central sphere. He still could not trust Lydia's motivations.

His sister had returned earlier and was going through the mail as he and Lydia joined the others in Charlotte's study. The tea cart rattled through the door as Bateman trundled it into the room. When Charlotte glanced up at him with a smile, he folded his arms over his chest.

"Don't look at me," he said. "I'm not pouring."

Miss Pankhurst tsked. "Certainly not. That is a lady's function. Would you like me to pour, Miss Worthington?"

Charlotte waved a letter. "Yes, please do."

Miss Pankhurst lifted the teapot in the violet pattern his mother had favored and proceeded to hand out the cups as she filled them. Miss Janssen joined her on the sofa, while Lydia plunked herself down on a chair near Charlotte's table. She took up the *Times*, scanning quickly through the newspaper as if searching for something. Was she seeking key Society news the paper occasionally covered? Or looking for items of a scientific nature? His mind was so busy he had to force himself to take a seat by the window.

"Miss Worthington and I had a very productive morning,"

Miss Pankhurst announced as she offered Miss Janssen the plate with little slices of lemon cake, his favorite. "But I believe we could do with your help, Miss Villers, if Lord Worthington can get on without you."

"I'll do whatever is needed," Lydia said, but her voice lacked its usual enthusiasm, and she looked down at her tea as if resigned to her lot.

If he were half as intelligent as Charlotte liked to claim, he'd let Lydia go work with Miss Pankhurst. One more opportunity to advance the envelope task. One less distraction for him. He could visit the smithy alone, request a prototype to their specifications. He could work with Charlotte to test it.

But the idea had originated with Lydia. As with the thread and water experiment, she had every right to see it through.

"I begin to believe I cannot get by without Miss Villers at my side," Worth said.

Lydia's head came up. She beamed at him, and the world was a better place.

Miss Janssen's hand trembled as she set the plate back on the tea cart without passing it to the others.

"Oh, no," Charlotte said.

Lydia blinked, and Worth glanced his sister's way. She held a thick vellum note. The window seat seemed to be sinking as all color drained from his sister's face once more.

"Charlotte?" he asked. "What is it?"

"Someone has died?" Miss Janssen asked, fingers anchored on her cup.

Charlotte managed a breath, the bodice of her grey gown rising and falling with the effort. "It's one of those notes, Worth. I thought we were beyond them."

She held out the paper with a trembling hand. All eyes were on him as Worth rose to take it.

"I know what you're doing," Worth read aloud. "You will never succeed. Stop now, before someone dies."

# CHAPTER TEN

M iss Janssen gasped and clutched her generous chest. Miss Pankhurst begged for an explanation. Charlotte was as white as she'd been last night at the ball.

"Well, that's silly," Lydia said.

Worth blinked as he raised his head from the note.

"Silly?" Miss Pankhurst cried. "Someone is threatening our lives!"

Lydia wrinkled her nose, rising to go study the note in Worth's hands. Good paper—as thick as a formal invitation. Someone with money or employed by a wealthy household, perhaps? She didn't recognize the dainty hand, so at least it wasn't one of her brother's poor attempts at managing her life. Someone with some education, however. Those vowels were precisely inscribed, and everything was spelled properly.

"Not much of a threat," Lydia said, straightening. "It's all rather vague, if you ask me."

"Someone trying to frighten us," Worth agreed, folding the note in half.

"And succeeding," Charlotte said. "You must show Bateman, Worth."

"I will," he promised, sliding the note into his coat pocket. "Rest assured, ladies, that you are all safe in this house. We have important work to do, and this cowardly missive won't stop us."

NEVER VIE FOR A VISCOUNT        101

Miss Janssen nodded. "Glad I am for Mr. Bateman."

"Indeed," Miss Pankhurst put in. "Though perhaps Miss Villers shouldn't be the only one to be escorted home in the evenings."

Worth cast Lydia a glance so quick she could not be sure of his thoughts. "Charlotte, make the arrangements."

Charlotte nodded. "Of course. I'm sorry I mentioned the matter to you all. It just caught me by surprise."

Worth as well, Lydia thought, though he seemed to have recovered.

"Anything else of import in the mail?" he asked as if Charlotte and he had been discussing nothing more interesting than what ball to attend.

Charlotte roused herself. "Yes, actually. We received an invitation to Lady Lilith's wedding to Lydia's brother, a week from today."

A week's time? Why had her brother been so evasive last night? Trust Beau not to remember the date of his own wedding.

"How lovely," Lydia declared.

No one else looked amused. She understood. That threatening note had upset them all. Besides, her brother had annoyed any number of people over the years. Not everyone would be forgiving as he set out to redeem himself.

"Yes, lovely," Charlotte said. "We'll all go, of course." She shot Worth a look as if daring him to disagree.

Worth nodded thoughtfully. "If you have no other news to impart, Charlotte, I propose that Miss Villers and I visit the smithy this afternoon about the bellows."

Miss Janssen's face puckered. "You would leave us alone?"

Did she truly think danger stalked the corridors? Lydia could not put any faith in such a flimsy threat.

"Hardly alone," Charlotte said. "Beast will be here to protect us. I'd like to see the fellow who could take him on and win."

"So would I," Miss Janssen said dreamily.

"Still, a change in plan may be warranted," Charlotte continued. "The heat and basket tasks are moving along nicely. Miss Pankhurst is gaining ground. I propose the four of us who sew competently combine on her task and complete the sewing of the silk."

Worth frowned. Did he want to spend more time together? She did.

Dangerous thought. Perhaps Charlotte was right.

"I'm happy to help," Lydia said.

"Very well," Worth said. "Good afternoon, ladies. I'll report what I learn from the smith." He strode from the room. Lydia refused to allow her enthusiasm to go with him.

A short while later, the three women gathered around Miss Pankhurst as she demonstrated the stitches that had survived the most tests.

"With no need for wetting," she reminded them all.

"Well, I didn't know we were creating a balloon then," Lydia pointed out.

Miss Janssen's eyes widened. "A balloon?"

Charlotte set down her portion of the fabric. "Yes, a balloon. A very particular balloon, capable of long-distance flight. Miss Villers, I must caution you again about sharing such information."

Lydia's face heated. "I'm sorry. I thought the others must have been told by now."

"I knew," Miss Pankhurst said, calmly taking a stitch. "I surmised the matter some time ago but deemed it unwise to speak out. Lord Worthington has taken pains to keep the matter quiet."

"Yes," Charlotte said. "He has. Our goal is a demonstration to His Royal Highness at the end of this month. We have much to do to be ready. Sew, ladies."

They sewed. That afternoon and most of the next day, until Lydia's fingers threatened to cramp from clasping the needle and her neck ached where she'd bent her head over the scarlet fabric. How did seamstresses manage it day after day? She would never demand a new gown quickly again.

Worth poked his head in from time to time to inquire on their progress and report his. Always his gaze strayed to Lydia. Did he wish for her company? Did he find his mind worked better in tandem? She felt as if any intelligent thoughts she'd had were marching down the thread and away from her brain with each stitch, like ants on their way to a picnic.

Bateman was equally as attentive, escorting anyone who left the house after dark and dividing his time between Worth and Charlotte during the day. Miss Janssen seemed to have accepted Worth's word that the threatening note had been a sham intended to rattle them, though Miss Pankhurst still insisted on an escort even though she left in broad daylight. Worth had consented to walk her home or send her in the carriage. Bateman had not been amused.

Miss Janssen walked out with Lydia the second evening. She'd donned a wide-fronted bonnet that formed a cone around her broad cheeks. She turned with Lydia to the left even though Lydia was certain her boardinghouse lay in the opposite direction.

"I wanted to talk to you, Miss Villers," she said, clumping along beside her. "I have done you a great disservice."

Lydia glanced at her. The lady's head was down, her gloved fingers plucking at the fabric of her sensible wool dress where it draped below her spencer.

"I don't see how you could have done me a disservice," Lydia said. "You have always been kind to me."

"*Nein.*" She sighed. "Sorry. I find when I grow weary the German comes out too easily."

"You're from Hanover," Lydia guessed.

"*Jah.* Born and raised in the capital itself. My parents came over when I was a girl. We have always served the nobility." Her voice rang with pride.

"How did you end up working with Miss Worthington, then?" Lydia asked as they moved past the trees in the center of the square.

"After my father died, my mother was laundress to the Worthingtons and others in the area. She made her own baskets. I learned from her. I took over the laundry three years ago, but already I was tired of it. The work is long, hot, and wet."

Lydia hid a shudder. "I would imagine."

"Miss Worthington came to me about a year ago and asked me to weave a special basket. It must be done in secret, in her home. She said I would be like her companion. It was a great elevation."

Indeed it was. Like Miss Janssen's mother, most laundresses died in the trade. "So you've been working on that basket for a year."

She made a face. "His lordship kept changing his mind. That didn't trouble me so much. Sitting and weaving is much better than working with lye."

"I admire your patience," Lydia told the older woman.

Miss Janssen kicked at a stone on the pavement. "But I was not so patient. Working with Miss Worthington gave me ideas. She treats us so well, like we are family. I began to dream of being a family in truth. I thought if I worked hard, showed promise, Lord Worthington might notice me."

She knew the feeling. "I take it he didn't."

"*Nein!*" She sighed again. "I am a servant, someone to complete a task. But a fierce heart beats in my breast." She thumped her chest as if to prove it. "And when he showed interest in another, I acted to protect what I hoped would be mine."

Another? Was Worth courting again? Her own heart beat fiercely at the thought.

"Lord Worthington expressed interest in a lady?" she asked as they neared Meredith's house.

Miss Janssen nodded. "You."

Lydia started, then forced a laugh. "A momentary folly, I assure you. Lord Worthington decided that we would not suit."

"I decided." Miss Janssen stopped on the pavement, fingers now bunched in her skirts. "I was jealous, shameful though that is. I knew he would not listen to me. So I gossiped with Miss Pankhurst. She loves it so."

"I've noticed," Lydia murmured, dread gathering. "And what did you share?"

"I had heard stories from the maid about your brother. Everyone in the great houses knew of his ambitions."

Beau would be so proud to hear that his name had been bandied, even with poor report, in high circles. Her dread only grew. "And Miss Pankhurst went to Lord Worthington."

Miss Janssen rubbed her fingers together, until she nearly tore the gloves from her hands. "I heard them speak. The way she talked, you had ambitions too. She is very good at such nuances. She said you wanted to marry above yourself. To marry for money. She made it seem as if you could never have loved Lord Worthington himself."

"I see." Indeed, she thought she saw a great deal. She had cared deeply for Worth, had dreamed that at last she had found a way to make Beau happy while marrying for love. She had made no secret of her admiration. Lacking family and fortune and being no great beauty, all she had had to offer was her love and devotion. To hear she cared only for his title, that her sweet attentions stemmed only from calculation, would have seemed to Worth the ultimate betrayal.

"I am very sorry," Miss Janssen said, entire body trembling now. "You have been so kind to me, so clever with the work. I was wrong to try to part you and his lordship. You are good together."

"Sometimes." Her mind was whirling once more,

offering picture after picture of what might have been. Then another thought intruded, shaking her with its truth.

She regarded the older woman, whose face was puckering. "Thank you for telling me, Miss Janssen. I truly cared for Lord Worthington, and I thought he cared for me. Yet why would he so readily believe that story? He ought to have known me, believed in me. Then again, few do."

Tears were gathering. She despised them. They made her feel wet and miserable, and they accomplished nothing. She'd long ago learned to turn aside criticism with a smile, find opportunity in any cloud. At the moment, she struggled.

"He knows better now," Miss Janssen insisted. "I see how he looks at you when he thinks no one notices. He still cares for you."

Hope leaped up. She had to contain it. For the first time, people were taking her seriously. How could she jeopardize that for the chance that Worth's feelings would prove reliable this time?

"Perhaps," she told Miss Janssen. "But I fear Lord Worthington has far more on his mind then me, and always will."

He could not get Lydia off his mind. Neither the work to create and test the bellows nor the note threatening death to one of the team fully claimed his attention. Where Lydia had been the distraction, now his work proved the most intrusive. He even troubled to focus when he, Charlotte, and Bateman attended church services that Sunday.

"Mind what you're doing," Bateman ordered during one of their sparring matches. The boxer hadn't been as convinced as Lydia that the note was a sham.

"Different hand than the original set," he had insisted, studying the note. "Seems you have more than one enemy."

Or two working together. The thought brought no comfort. The need to protect Charlotte and the other members of his team had never been more important. So why did his brain fixate on Lydia?

He simply could not sit in his laboratory, listening to the cheerful voices down the corridor as she sat sewing with the others. He found himself prowling along the edge of the square, energy uncaged. Perhaps that was why he nearly bumped into Julian coming out of Miss Thorn's again. His friend took one look at him and whisked him off to an inn in the City, bespeaking a private room.

"I take it your experiments are going badly," Julian said after they had settled themselves into comfortable overstuffed chairs near a glowing fire, cups of tea in their hands.

"It's not the experiments that trouble me," Worth admitted. "Do you plan on attending the wedding between Beau Villers and Lady Lilith?"

If Julian wondered at the shift in topic, he didn't comment. Instead, he leaned back. "I haven't been invited."

Worth raised his brows. "I thought everyone in London had been invited. Lady Lilith doesn't do things by half."

His friend's mouth quirked. "We had a disagreement recently. She didn't care for my stance on the issue. And remember, I'm simply a solicitor."

Worth shook his head. "A solicitor who has the ear of the highest levels of government and is welcome in the most noble houses. I certainly wouldn't want to alienate you."

Julian laughed. "Should I take it you'll be missing out as well?"

Worth sighed. "No. We'll all attend."

Julian toasted him with the cup. "I predict it only a matter of time before I'm not invited to your wedding too. Miss Thorn and her cat Fortune have a way of seeing to her clients' future."

He and Lydia, matched by a cat? He remembered how Fortune had regarded him when they'd first met, as if she could see his inmost thoughts. Still, he couldn't shake the feeling that he was moving in the wrong direction.

"I'm not ready for marriage," he told his friend.

Julian eyed him. "Why? You're established in your field. You have a suitable income to support a wife. Some might consider you kind on the eyes, if one can stomach all that red in your hair."

Now Worth laughed. "Said the flame to the blaze."

Julian patted his red-gold mane. "Exactly." He sobered. "So why hide away as if you had nothing to offer a lady?"

Worth shifted, the chair feeling suddenly hard. "You of all people should know my record when it comes to judging a person's character."

"You're talking about Shubert," the solicitor surmised. "That could have happened to anyone. You were still a boy."

"Sixteen," Worth corrected him. "And my father's heir. When he died, I shouldn't have simply trusted those who had been left in charge to care for me, my mother, and Charlotte. Shubert had been the family solicitor for years, and he embezzled thousands before you caught him at it."

"But you had the idea to hire me to review your accounts," Julian reminded him.

Worth cocked a smile. "Well, you needed the job."

Julian shook his head with a wry chuckle. "You have a good heart, Worthington."

"A soft heart," Worth replied. "I can offer more evidence of it. One of my first acts on graduating from Eton and returning to London as the viscount was to replace our aging butler. The fellow had earned his retirement. The man I chose was tall and imposing, with impeccable references. He so browbeat the rest of the staff that I had to sack him within a fortnight."

"You aren't the first to have trouble with your staff,"

Julian pointed out. "If everyone had a perfect household, my Miss Thorn wouldn't be able to place her ladies so quickly."

He suspected Miss Thorn placed her ladies not so much from need as from savvy negotiating. "Very well," he allowed. "But you can't deny Curtis was a disaster."

Julian finished his coffee. "No argument here. You were lucky to escape with your dignity intact."

"And little else," Worth agreed. Even as he thought back on it, his shame rose anew. How could he have been so blind?

He'd met John Curtis at a Royal Institution lecture, two idealists determined to revolutionize the nation. Curtis seemed to understand Worth's theories, encouraged him to dream big. For once, someone had understood him. To have the attentions of the older man, already an icon of the prestigious Royal Society when Worth had only just been put up for membership, had told Worth he was on the verge of greatness. He could finally feel his portrait deserved a spot with his forebears' in the family picture gallery. Curtis, whose protégé had recently passed away, appeared eager to help another young gentleman. Within a week, Worth and Curtis were meeting daily to compare notes. Within a month, they shared laboratory space. Worth hadn't worked at home, then, but in a warehouse along the wharves.

Everything had been going splendidly, his work progressing faster than he had hoped. Then Curtis had published a paper in *Philosophical Transactions*, claiming the innovations as his own.

Worth had stormed to his flat, demanded an explanation.

"What's the fuss, old chap?" Curtis had asked. "We both worked on those experiments. You would have eventually published the results. I merely helped highlight the work sooner. And the Royal Institution is interested. We're no longer confined to the musty halls of the Royal Society.

The Royal Institution makes all these theories practical. That's where the money is, the chance for advancement. Do you think glory so easily attained and held?"

"Money and favor," Worth had raged. "That wasn't my aim."

Curtis had made a face. "Then what does it matter who takes the credit? Science will be served. You've accomplished your goal."

Not in the slightest. "If names don't matter," Worth had returned, "then you won't mind if I write to the editor and request a correction in the next issue."

Things had turned uglier from there.

"You parted with Curtis more than a year ago," Julian reminded him now. "You said your experiments were going well. Why dwell on the matter?"

"Because Curtis wasn't the last to disappoint me," Worth said. "I'd thought I'd learned my lesson. I purchased the adjoining townhouse and brought my work home, where I could control it. I refused to accept Curtis's card when he called. I even took a different direction in my studies. No more far-flung theories. No more relying on others. I decided to pursue something practical, useful. I wouldn't publish, I'd demonstrate, so it was clear to my colleagues, to the world, that the work was mine and my team's. I congratulated myself on my victory. And then I met Lydia Villers for the first time."

Julian grimaced. "You did seem top over toes. I take it you decided otherwise."

Worth nodded. "She provided ample evidence that I still don't understand those around me."

"Strange, then, that you allowed her in your home," Julian mused, watching him.

Worth barked a laugh. "Even stranger? All my life my intellect has led. I find it retreating now, for my heart demands that I take another chance, on her."

Once more Julian raised his cup in toast. "May we both find success in our pursuits, of the mind and of the heart."

# CHAPTER ELEVEN

L ydia had to endure a third day of sewing, after church services, before all the panels of the scarlet fabric had been fastened together. At that point, anyone might have guessed they were manufacturing a balloon. The silk spread across the hardwood floor and rippled with every movement of the air through the room.

"So beautiful, it is," Miss Janssen said, watching it.

"It's the durability, not the beauty, that matters," Charlotte said, sticking her needle into a pincushion for the last time. "And that only Worth can tell us."

A little thrill went through Lydia, like a candle brightening the night. She snuffed it out. Sewing beside Miss Pankhurst had been all the more difficult now that Lydia knew the role the woman had played in forcing her and Worth apart. Small wonder the little companion had been so eager to jab at her, thinking she understood Lydia's character. Lydia would prove her wrong. She wasn't here for Worth. She was here for herself. Worth wasn't coming to see her, was no longer interested in her as a potential partner in life. He was coming to inspect their work. Any anticipation she felt should be aimed in that direction.

They all gathered in Miss Pankhurst's room the following morning. As if to commemorate the occasion, Miss Janssen had pinned an ivory cameo broach on her broad chest and swept up her hair in a more elaborate braid around her face. Even Miss Pankhurst was looking her best in a lavender round gown that drew attention to the blue of her eyes. Lydia in one of her muslin dresses felt as pretty as a butterfly among flowers.

If Worth noticed the changes in their attire, he gave no indication. He walked up one side of the envelope where it was spread across the room, around the top, and down the other side, gaze latched onto the scarlet fabric.

"And you are satisfied the panels will hold when expanded?" he asked Miss Pankhurst, who was scurrying along beside him, hands fluttering in front of her gown.

"Quite satisfied, my lord," she assured him. "I tested each stitch myself."

That seemed an overstatement. The woman generally left the house at the end of the day before Lydia. She had arrived at about the same time as Lydia and had sat beside her sewing. When had she tested any stitch but her own?

"Well done," Worth pronounced, and the little woman preened.

Worth turned to Charlotte. "We'll have to confirm it, of course. I'll have Bateman set up the rear garden for the task. Would you care to oversee his efforts?"

"Yes, thank you." Charlotte gathered up her skirts and swept to the door.

"And what would you have us do, my lord?" Miss Pankhurst warbled.

He eyed her a moment as if considering the matter. Instead of answering her directly, he turned to the weaver. "Miss Janssen, we had discussed finding a way to pad certain parts of the basket to better support the propulsion devices. Please consult with Miss Pankhurst about which fabrics might be more efficacious."

Miss Pankhurst smiled like a cat among the canaries. "Delighted to offer my expertise, Miss Janssen."

The older woman nodded, but her shoulders slumped. It seemed she still was not entirely above attempting to catch her employer's eye.

"I'd be happy to help too," Lydia put in.

Miss Janssen managed a smile. "*Danke*."

"I'm afraid that won't be possible," Worth said. "Miss Villers, I need you with me."

Her heart leaped up. It was the prospect of the science, of course. She'd been sewing for so many days that she would likely have brightened to be back turning her skin blue as she tested Gussie's preparations. At least, that was what she told herself as she followed Worth from the room.

"I appreciate your flexibility," he said as they descended to his workroom in the old kitchen. "I realize other natural philosophers focus on a specific discipline. This effort requires us to think more broadly."

"I like that," Lydia said, stepping down into the room. "When I worked with Gussie, we experimented with plants, animal products, and minerals, but we were focused on one goal, perfecting skin lotion. You must perfect the geometry of the basket, the tensile strength of the fabric, and the heat of the fire. You must master the very air!"

"Yes, that's it exactly." They shared a smile before he hastily looked away.

Lydia took pity on him. "So, how are things coming?" she asked, advancing on the table.

"Not as well as I'd like," he said. "The bellows did well in testing. The bronze brazier appears to be a suitable container. But I find it difficult to concentrate."

Lydia nodded. "I have the same trouble. We are so close! The idea of sending the balloon soaring is intoxicating."

"It's not that." He paused beside her, bare inches between them. "Lydia, I seem to have made a grave error."

She leaned over to look at the notebook open on the table. She could see the numbers they'd discussed—height, length, width, and weight of the bellows. "The calculations appear to be in order."

Worth reached around her and closed the journal. "The

calculations aren't the problem." His gaze brushed hers, soft as a caress.

Lydia held herself still. "I'm not sure what you're trying to say."

He blew out a breath. "I'm trying to say that I still care."

She couldn't believe him. "You can't. You don't trust me. I'm not sure you even like me."

"I like you quite well indeed."

The tone warmed her more than the words. Yet how could she accept them? "I have always liked you," she admitted cautiously. "But I fear that wasn't enough then and isn't now."

Slowly he raised his hand, and she closed her eyes, willing his fingers to touch her cheek, to help her remember how it felt to be admired, if only for a moment.

"My lord?"

Lydia's eyes popped open. Worth was frowning toward the open door, where Miss Pankhurst stood framed. Her face was reddening, as if she'd run a great distance, but she gamely held up two squares of material. "I thought perhaps felt to cushion the devices, but I feared it would be too heavy. Would you perform the calculation for me, so I know the tolerances I must not exceed?"

"Yes, of course," he said, turning for his notebook.

"We could use Miss Villers's help as well," Miss Pankhurst ventured as he scribbled. "Many hands make light work."

"Miss Villers is essential to my task," he said, but he tore a sheet from the journal and offered it to the other lady. "This should provide you a range, Miss Pankhurst. If the combined weight of the fabric remains within these margins, we can accommodate it with the envelope we currently have."

She accepted it from him. Their fingers brushed, and she tittered. Worth didn't appear to notice, but Miss Pankhurst shot Lydia a look of triumph.

So she was still vying for the viscount's attentions. Did

Lydia truly wish to fight her? Worth may have been distracted from his purpose. She refused to be.

"I'm not sure how much help I can be, my lord," she told him. "It would be wiser if I assisted Miss Pankhurst."

She wasn't sure who looked more surprised by the statement as she moved toward the door: Worth, Miss Pankhurst, or herself.

Four days later, Meredith tucked a pearl-headed hairpin into her coiffure and turned from side to side to examine the effect. She still couldn't quite conceive that Lady Lilith had invited her to the wedding. If a well-respected solicitor like Julian didn't warrant inclusion, the owner of an employment agency, however polished and polite, should be excluded as well. Very likely her invitation had come through Lydia's urgings.

*Scritch, scritch, scritch.*

"Miss Fortune wants out," her maid Enid said, laying a painted-silk fan and white silk gloves on the dressing table in front of Meredith. "Again."

Meredith swiveled on the bench and eyed her pet. Fortune arched her back and straightened her front legs as if she hadn't just rasped her claws against the wood of the paneled door.

"I don't know what's gotten into her," Meredith said. She rubbed her nails over the edge of the walnut dressing table, and Fortune's ears pricked to the sound. Her pet eyed her a moment over one shoulder, then faced the door again, tail twitching.

"She likes Miss Villers better than us," Enid said with a sniff.

Not likely. Fortune had been her closest friend since the dark days when Meredith had been accused of murdering her previous employer. Alone in London, with no family or friends to come to her aid, Meredith had huddled in a tiny room at the back of a boardinghouse that was just this side of respectable. One day, coming home from the bakery on the corner in the pouring rain, she'd heard a mew. Fortune had appeared at her side, accompanied her home, and shared the meager loaf of soggy bread with her. The cat had never left her side since.

True, Fortune had shown a marked preference for Lydia's company the last few days, but then, Lydia had been unaccountably blue, and Fortune tended to gravitate toward those in need. On one occasion, when Meredith had passed the girl's room, she was certain she'd heard crying. But Lydia's face had been as sunny as usual when the girl had answered Meredith's knock. The answers to Meredith's questions, however, had been less than satisfactory.

*Yes, work was coming along well.*

*Yes, her brother was in fine health, as far as she knew.*

*No, she needed nothing, thank you so much for asking.*

Strange how so pretty a smile could look so wooden.

"It's as if she's in mourning," Meredith had confided to Julian when he'd called yesterday.

Julian had stretched long legs to the fire where they once again took tea in the withdrawing room. "Worth seemed equally troubled the last time we spoke. He seemed fixed on the past."

Meredith raised a brow. "The past? Whose past?"

"His and Miss Villers's." Julian held out his cup, and she refilled it with the lavender-scented brew. "He was very much smitten with her last Season, but it didn't last. I'm not sure why you chose to match them again."

Fortune jumped up onto her lap, and Meredith slid her hand down the silky fur. "It was Fortune's idea."

Julian cocked a smile. "Somehow, I thought it was."

"You're humoring me," Meredith accused, and Fortune regarded him, somber-eyed.

Julian set down his cup and raised his hands in surrender.

"Far be it from me to question your cat. Her record speaks for itself. Three clients and three marriages. Rather impressive."

Meredith lifted her chin. "Three clients, three successful matches in occupation. And I see no reason Lydia cannot be number four."

"You might if you knew Worth," Julian said, lowering his hands. "I cannot betray client confidence, but, suffice it to say, the fellow has reason to doubt his judgement."

"Good," Meredith said. "His judgement was in error last year. I want him to question it."

Julian laughed. "Believe me, you have succeeded."

He would give her no more than that, but Cowls had already related that Lord Worthington appeared to be in as dark a mood as Lydia. How was Meredith supposed to take encouragement from that?

She rose now, shaking off her concerns. "Very well, Fortune. If you will not come to me, I will come to you."

"Your gown, miss," Enid protested, reaching out as if to protect the satin she'd recently ironed.

"Is a lovely grey chosen to compliment Fortune's coat," Meredith assured her. She moved to the door and picked up her pet. Normally, Fortune cuddled and purred, the perfect tonic for any ailment. Now she squirmed to be free.

"What is it?" Meredith murmured, struggling to keep hold of her.

Fortune twisted so her eyes met Meredith's for a moment, then focused on the closed door.

With a sigh of resignation, Meredith tucked her closer and opened the door.

Lydia was standing in the corridor, shifting from foot to foot as if uncertain whether to go forward or retreat into her room. Her gown was as pink as tulips in the spring, with a white-net overskirt spangled with beads that picked up the light. Once more, Fortune squirmed.

"I begin to see your concern," Meredith murmured. She raised her head and marched up to her houseguest. "Ready to go so soon?"

Lydia blinked her great green eyes as if surprised to find Meredith at her side. Then her gaze dropped to Fortune in Meredith's arms, and her smile blossomed.

"And how is my sweet kitty snookums?" she crooned, reaching out to caress the cat's head.

Meredith had never particularly appreciated the sugary tone or the words that accompanied it, but if Fortune could tolerate it, so could she. Now her pet turned her head to allow Lydia to rub behind one delicate ear.

"You're spoiling her," Meredith realized.

Lydia drew back her hand, even as Fortune regarded Meredith accusingly.

"I'm sorry," the girl muttered.

"I didn't mean you," Meredith said. "Really, Fortune, you are becoming a bother. Is Lydia not allowed some peace?"

Fortune put her nose in the air as if she had no idea what Meredith was talking about.

Lydia's smile returned, soft and fond. "She is a dear friend, and so are you. I'm sorry I haven't been better company lately."

"No need to apologize," Meredith said. "I would, however, appreciate a confidence. What's troubling you, Lydia?"

Lydia sighed, the breath so strong it ruffled Fortune's fur. "It's odd, really. I've always been accused to trying to rise beyond my reach. It's rather unnerving to find the accusation true."

Meredith set Fortune down at last, and the cat began rubbing around Lydia's ankles. "Do you mean by attempting to better yourself? There's no crime in that. If we have no ambition toward anything, we cease to grow."

"True," Lydia allowed, gaze on the cat. "But lately, I wonder whether natural philosophy is enough."

Meredith frowned. "Should we look for another position, then?"

"No, no," she hurried to assure her with a ghost of her usual smile. "The work is so interesting. Usually. I've learned a great deal already, and there's always more to know."

"But?" Meredith encouraged.

Lydia sighed again. "Nothing. It's likely a momentary aberration. It was last time, for him." She started to bend, then hesitated. "May I?"

Meredith nodded, and Lydia scooped Fortune into her arms, where the cat snuggled against the rose-colored velvet of the girl's bodice. Very likely there'd be a pattern of grey hairs against the fabric when she was done, but perhaps that was all to the good. A touch of Fortune would remind Lydia that she was loved, and that might be the greatest gift of all.

# CHAPTER TWELVE

Why had he agreed to come? Worth tugged at his cravat as he and Charlotte sat in the church, Miss Pankhurst and Miss Janssen beside them. St. George's Hanover Square was crowded, each paneled box pew filled from side to side. He wouldn't have been surprised to find the galleries above teeming as well. Certainly hushed voices echoed against the vaulted ceiling. It seemed not everyone disliked Beau Villers as much as Worth did. Or perhaps they were curious as to whether the scoundrel would follow through on his promise.

Villers wouldn't have had much choice. Lady Lilith's brother brooked no opposition as he led the bride down the center aisle. Worth had known Gregory, Earl of Carrolton, since they had been at Eton together. He was easily the largest, strongest fellow Worth had ever met. One of the nicest too. Even now his chest was high, his smile bright as he escorted Lilith. And only Gregory could have made his sister look petite.

An Amazon of a woman, the raven-haired Lady Lilith's head was an inch or two higher than her groom's as the two stood and recited their vows at the canopied altar.

"For better for worse, for richer for poorer…"

Worth couldn't help glancing to the other side of the aisle. A row ahead of them, her face in profile to him, Lydia sat, mouth trembling as if she were reciting the words as well. Once he'd been certain she could not have spoken them truthfully, that wealth and position were all that mattered to her. He knew many women, and men, felt the same. Arranged marriages had once been the norm, and even today couples on the *ton* were as likely to marry for advantage as for love.

But he remembered his mother and father together, the tender care, the devoted looks. They had held hands when walking through Hyde Park, decades after they'd wed. They'd shared a bedchamber, not from financial necessity but from a desire to be close to each other. That was the kind of marriage he wanted. That was the kind of marriage he'd envisioned with Lydia.

He'd nearly confessed as much the other day in his laboratory, might have kissed her if not for Miss Pankhurst's timely intervention. He had decided to listen to his heart again when it came to Lydia, and she'd been the one to run from any opportunity to renew their courtship.

Why? Surely she could see he was weakening. He'd confessed as much. Had she truly given herself over to the pursuit of knowledge? Or had he been right, and she had never harbored feelings for him and no longer needed to pretend that she did?

The service ended, and all rose as the bride and groom walked down the aisle side by side. He had never seen Lady Lilith look so happy, face radiant, dark eyes sparkling. Her groom looked more stunned than happy, as if he couldn't believe the matter resolved. As the sister of the groom, Lydia filed past in their wake.

"She's so lovely," Charlotte said as they joined the procession out of the church to the carriages waiting to take the guests to the wedding breakfast.

"Lady Lilith is striking," Worth agreed, escorting his sister and their two assistants to the carriage. Bateman was leaning up against the lacquered wood with his arms crossed as if he was annoyed the ceremony had taken so long.

Charlotte looked at Worth from the corners of her eyes. "I was speaking of Miss Villers."

"Everyone seems lovely in their finest," Miss Pankhurst put in as Bateman handed her into the carriage. "That is the wonder of a wedding. I daresay we'll all return to our senses soon."

Very likely.

Until then, Worth accompanied Charlotte and the others to the breakfast and joined many of their family and friends in toasting the bride and groom. Carrolton had spared no expense for his sister's wedding, renting a large hall with alabaster columns that had been festooned with swags of white roses intertwined with pink lilies. Other plants clustered here and there in elegant jasperware vases. The food was equally fine, with lobster cakes in a rich cream sauce, delicate slices of ham, and a massive wedding cake with so many furbelows decorating the yellow icing he wondered whether the thing was meant to be displayed rather than eaten.

"Many considered her a spinster, you know," Miss Pankhurst told no one in particular as they exited the hall for the antechamber following the sumptuous feast.

"All the more reason to celebrate that she has found love," Miss Janssen insisted.

Lady Lilith wasn't the only one who had met her match. As the guests milled about in congenial company, Worth had time to chat with his old friend Sir Harry Orwell, who had recently married his sweetheart, Patience Ramsey. The pretty blonde had served as companion to Carrolton's mother before taking a turn as assistant to Harry's aunt Augusta. Lydia had replaced Patience in that role for a time. Even Carrolton had married, to an intriguing red-haired Frenchwoman with an air of mystery about her.

"Why, I do believe it's an epidemic," Charlotte teased as Carrolton and his countess turned to greet other guests.

"Not a statistically viable one," Worth said. "Men our age with titles are generally expected to marry and carry on the line."

Miss Janssen heaved a mighty sigh. Miss Pankhurst looked at him expectantly. Charlotte merely raised her brows.

Worth laughed. "I realize I'm a statistical aberration. I have no plans to marry soon."

Miss Janssen slumped, and Miss Pankhurst's bright light dimmed. Odd. Worth was about to ask what concerned them when Charlotte nodded toward the door of the hall. "Oh, look. Here comes Lydia."

Worth turned slowly. Lydia was indeed headed in their direction, pink skirts sweeping across the floor. Her eyes were bright, her head high, and something inside him ordered him to run and meet her. He kept his feet from moving with difficulty.

"Lydia," Charlotte greeted her as she drew near. "You must be so happy for your brother."

"I am," Lydia assured her. "But I begin to find myself discontent."

Charlotte glanced between them as if waiting for Lydia or Worth to confess they longed for their own wedding. Worth clamped his mouth shut.

Miss Pankhurst tsked. "Weddings can make any spinster discontent with her life."

Miss Janssen sighed again.

"Oh, I'm not discontent with my life," Lydia said, smiling around at them all as if to prove it. "I'm discontent at remaining. And so I have a question for you, my lord."

All gazes swept his way. Hers was wide and encouraging, and he stood manfully before it, ready for whatever she might ask. "Yes, Miss Villers?"

Her smiled brightened. "When can we get back to work?"

They all stared at her. Truly, was it so much to ask? She'd done her best to avoid working directly with Worth the last few days before the wedding, but that didn't mean she'd changed her mind about the work itself. Things had been rather invigorating, especially since Miss Pankhurst had taken several afternoons off as if certain she'd earned them. Lydia and Miss Janssen had watched as Bateman and several men he had recruited stood around the envelope in the walled garden and tugged it in every conceivable direction. They were as strong as he was; that was apparent by the muscles rippling under their coats. But no matter how they tugged, the envelope remained intact.

It was a significant achievement, yet so much remained to be done, and time was growing short.

"An excellent question," Worth said now. "I hope to see you all at the house first thing in the morning following church services."

Lydia could hardly wait. Nice, orderly natural philosophy. Devices that didn't look at you as if you might hold the key to their future. Heating calculations that didn't ask whether you were still enamored of them. The work might at times be messy, but it was seldom emotionally taxing. That's what she needed right now.

She was smiling as she rapped at the door the next morning. Bateman answered and directed her to the garden. As if the others had been as eager to begin work again, Miss Pankhurst and Miss Janssen were there ahead of her, along with Charlotte and Worth. Miss Janssen's basket sat on the gravel, ropes running from each side to stakes in the ground. Spilling over one side and trailing off on what remained of the shrubbery was Miss Pankhurst's silk envelope. It had been threaded through a rope lattice, the ends of which were lashed to the basket. Lydia wiggled with excitement.

Worth had been adjusting the brazier seated on the center pillar but turned as she came up to the others.

"Good," he said. "You're all here. As you have probably surmised, our steps thus far have gone toward creating an advanced balloon."

"Yes," Miss Pankhurst said. "So Miss Villers told us."

Worth's gaze swung to hers, and she raised her chin against the challenge in it.

"If I recall," Charlotte put in, "you said you'd known for some time, Miss Pankhurst."

Her smile was smug. "Yes, well, it wasn't terribly difficult to determine for anyone with a logical mind."

Worth looked a bit shaken by the news, but he quickly rallied. "Nevertheless, we are now at a critical juncture. Today, we begin bringing each of our accomplishments together to see if we can make a whole."

"A hole?" Miss Janssen asked. "Why would a balloon need a hole?"

"To allow the air to enter, of course," Miss Pankhurst said with a shake of her head.

"I believe Lord Worthington means that we are assembling the various pieces of the balloon," Lydia offered.

"Yes, precisely." Worth strode around the basket, pointing. "We'll build the fire here, in the brazier and on the pillar Charlotte and Miss Villers designed. This arrangement will allow us to test the bellows Miss Villers suggested to manage the fire's temperature. The heated air will fill the envelope that Miss Pankhurst and Miss Villers stitched with your help."

Lydia stared at him. Her name, associated with nearly every task? She truly had contributed. Did he know what it meant to her to hear him acknowledge that?

"We will fill the envelope," he continued as if he hadn't noticed the smile that was growing on her face, "then allow the balloon to rise on a tether. Every step must be timed for comparison with future efforts. I've asked Mr. Bateman to enlist the aid of some of his colleagues, the ones who helped us test the envelope last week."

As if he had been waiting for the introduction, the former pugilist moved out of the house with three others, each more muscular than the last. Miss Janssen goggled.

Charlotte stepped forward. "You heard the plan, ladies. Miss Pankhurst, Miss Janssen, I will issue you each a watch. Please time the filling of the envelope and keep an eye out for any difficulties as the fabric stretches. Miss Villers and I will monitor the fire itself. Lord Worthington will man the bellows. Once the balloon ascends, we will take shifts in teams of two to watch it until it sinks to the ground again."

"Every hour of every day," Worth added, "noting changes in temperature, wind velocity, and wind direction."

"Precipitation as well, I would think," Lydia mused. "Brilliant."

Was that pink creeping into his cheeks? "Yes, we must note any environmental differences that might account for changes in the balloon."

"Any questions?" Charlotte asked.

"Who will partner Lord Worthington on his shifts?" Miss Pankhurst asked. Miss Janssen raised her head.

Worth's gaze veered to Lydia, and her own cheeks warmed.

"I will," Bateman said with a frown in Worth's direction.

"Of course," Worth said, but she thought she heard disappointment.

The plan set, they began working. Charlotte had Bateman and his friends build the fire in the footed brazier Lydia had suggested, the contraption mounted on the pressed cork pillar. Lydia kept notes as to how much coal had to be added and how often to keep the fire hot. Worth estimated the amount of heated air filling the balloon. From time to time, he pumped the bellows, making the coals glow redder. Lydia noted that too.

But no matter how busy she kept herself, Worth dominated her attention. He moved about the inside of the balloon, watchful as a new father over his babe. Long-fingered, capable hands tugged on the ropes to confirm strength, ran along the wicker to test its integrity. The light shining in his eyes mirrored the excitement building inside her.

The envelope expanded, the scarlet widening as breath filled it. When the crown lifted off the bushes to edge skyward, Worth shot her a grin. She felt it to her toes. Everything they had worked for was coming true.

By dinner, however, the envelope was only half full by Lydia's estimation.

"If only we could fill faster," she told Worth as he finished pumping the bellows. "When the outside air cools with the night, the envelope will lose heat. There's too much surface area to do otherwise."

"Agreed," he said, mopping his brow with a handkerchief. Bateman and his friends had long since stripped down to their shirts and trousers as they ferried more coal to the site. By the lift of her nose, Miss Pankhurst found this scandalous. By the look in her eyes, Miss Janssen found it fascinating.

Now Worth turned to Charlotte. "Can we build the fire hotter to compensate for the night air?"

"That brazier was designed for a certain heat," Charlotte answered as Bateman brought more coal from the bin. "I don't know what would happen if we surpassed it. We could catch fire to the basket and the envelope."

"But the night air will cool the brazier as well," Lydia countered. "It will be a difficult balance, but it might work."

Charlotte and Worth agreed, and the work continued. Lydia wasn't aware that Miss Pankhurst and Miss Janssen had left until Charlotte handed her a watch.

"You and I will take the first shift," she told Lydia. "Worth and Beast can take our places at midnight. Miss Pankhurst and Miss Janssen will return around dawn."

Lydia wrapped her fingers around the silver-cased watch and nodded. She had seen the work this far. She had no intention of leaving now.

Worth climbed out of the basket to stalk around the circumference of the envelope, estimating height, width. Based on their progress so far, they had at least six hours left to expand the silk to its full size. Last he had read, the French hydrogen balloons often took the better part of two days to fill. They could stay aloft for only six hours. His team had succeeded in shortening the filling time, even compensating for the cooler air tonight, with a safer design. Had they managed to extend the time aloft?

"Careful, if you please," Charlotte was instructing one of the pugilists. "We must know exactly how much fuel we're using. You can't just dump it into the brazier."

His usually polite sister was beginning to sound testy. It had been a long day. The hair in Charlotte's bun was coming free—curls teased her ears. And her practical canvas overcoat was speckled with ash.

Lydia, however, looked as if she'd newly woken and dressed. How she'd kept her overcoat that clean he had no idea. Her pale curls still bounced as she moved around the balloon, gaze on the envelope and watch in her hand. She was so focused, in fact, that she nearly walked right into him.

"Ahem," Worth said.

She glanced at him, clearly startled, then smiled. "Oh, sorry, Worth. I didn't see you there." She transferred her gaze to the envelope once more. "Isn't it marvelous?"

He refused to be jealous of a balloon. "I'm glad everything is going so well. I'll be even happier once we beat the ascension record."

She slid the watch into one pocket of her overcoat and pulled the journal and pencil out of the other to note something. "How likely are we to achieve that with this balloon, do you think?"

"I give us one chance in ten," Worth said. "But it's a start."

Her smile rewarded him, but suddenly faded. "Why it is doing that?"

Worth glanced up. The envelope was tilting, sagging toward the bushes from which it had recently risen as if wishing to sleep for the night. He ran to Bateman and Charlotte where they stood by the coal bin.

"What happened?" he demanded.

Charlotte was nearly as red as the envelope. "I don't know!"

Bateman pointed toward the brazier. "Who added peat?"

Worth saw it too. The thick mat of plant material was already smoking as it smothered the heat. In a moment, it would ignite and blaze up, catching the silk on fire as well.

"It was with the coal," one of the pugilists said. "I figured it wouldn't hurt."

"Take it out," Worth ordered. "Now. Dump the whole thing if you must."

Charlotte caught his arm. "Worth, look!"

The balloon wouldn't wait for the heat to be rebuilt. It was continuing its fall, the heavy silk cascading down, straight toward Lydia.

# CHAPTER THIRTEEN

It was the most graceful thing. The scarlet balloon bent toward her, for all the world as if it was bowing. Lydia reached up a hand to touch the silk and pulled back her fingers in surprise.

A moment before Worth leaped on her and dragged her off to one side.

She blinked to find herself clasped in his embrace. His eyes above hers were wide and wild; his breath came fast.

"Worth?" she asked.

He gathered himself and disengaged. "I was concerned the envelope might fall on you."

Lydia glanced past him to where the silk puddled around the basket. If all that weight had landed on her…

"I might have been smothered," she realized aloud. She grasped his hand and held on tight. "Oh, Worth! You saved my life!"

"Not necessarily," he assured her. "I'd give you a fifty percent chance of survival."

"I wouldn't." She shuddered. "The silk was warm, Worth, as if I had sat too close to the hearth. I didn't expect that."

He frowned at the balloon. "Neither did I."

Charlotte rushed up to them. "Are you both all right?"

Worth merely nodded, but he removed his hand from Lydia's.

"Fine," Lydia told her. "Thanks to your brother." She

reached into her pocket for the watch, a little surprised to find her fingers trembling. She drew out the silver case carefully. "I estimate this mishap occurred at a quarter past nine. Do you concur, Charlotte?"

Charlotte shook her head. "You amaze me. Once that envelope started slipping, all other thoughts flew from my head. I suppose I should have been tracking how long it took to fall. I'm sorry, Worth."

He was studying the balloon, which flopped about as if trying to rise again. "No need for concern, Charlotte. We hardly expected that. But I concur with your estimate, Lydia. Now we must see what this mishap, as you called it, cost us."

He was so cool, as if he hadn't just exhibited the most daring act of heroism. She wanted to throw her arms around him, tell him how grateful she was. He wouldn't allow it. He couldn't believe it. He might even discharge her for it.

She did it anyway.

"Thank you, Worth," she said, arms about his waist and head to his chest. For one mad moment, she thought she heard his heat rate speeding. Then she released him, and he stepped back out of reach, where he'd been for the last year.

Charlotte had obviously gathered her dignity, for her chin was once more high.

"Things are not hopeless," she declared. "We've removed the peat and are rebuilding the fire. I sent the fellow who added the contaminant home. But what I want to know is why that peat was even in with the coal. I was quite specific in my requirements."

Lydia glanced to where the coal pile had dwindled to a few scattered lumps. They had all been so focused on timing the inflation that only Bateman and his colleagues had attended much to the fuel. Yet peat, while plentiful in parts of the country, was uncommon in London. How had a thick mat of it landed in the coal bin?

"Perhaps Mr. Bateman can tell us," Lydia said.

Charlotte cocked her head as if trying to see around the mess that was their balloon. "Where is Beast?"

"Gone to fetch more coal, very likely," Worth said. His hands were clasped behind his back, his gaze off in the middle distance, as if he no longer saw the garden, his balloon, or them. "Are you and Miss Villers still prepared to keep watch until midnight, as you planned, Charlotte?"

Charlotte eyed Lydia, who nodded. "We are," she told her brother.

"Good. I have some notes I must record." With a nod that passed for a bow, he strode for the house.

"You frightened him," Charlotte said, watching the door close behind her brother.

"It was rather frightening to see the balloon fall," Lydia agreed. "I couldn't think to move."

"I'm not sure the balloon incident is entirely to blame," Charlotte said, turning for the envelope. It had risen to the top of the basket and sat rather like a mushroom just above the brazier. Only the position of the bellows had prevented the silk from sagging into the coals and catching fire.

"Has my brother broached the topic of your previous courtship?" Charlotte asked.

Lydia's skin felt hotter than the silk of the balloon. "Not directly."

"Pity," Charlotte said. "My impression is that much explanation is needed, on both sides."

"Very likely," Lydia said. "But it wouldn't change anything. He decided I wasn't the sort of woman he wanted in a wife. I don't particularly need to hear all the many ways he thought I was deficient."

"Lydia." Charlotte put a hand on her arm. "You are in no way deficient."

"Of course I am." When Charlotte looked as if she might argue, Lydia hurried on. "I'm not stupid, Charlotte. I know my assets and my debits. I am pretty, but I am not beautiful. I can sing, but no one would ask me to lead a musicale. I am clever, and I remember much of what I read, but I'm not highly intelligent like Worth and some of the other natural philosophers. He must have had high expectations of his bride. I did not meet them."

"He's not perfect either," Charlotte informed her. "He's dictatorial and capricious, and he frequently takes those around him for granted."

"I know," Lydia said. "But I don't mind his imperfections."

"You should," Charlotte insisted. "If he asks so much from you, you should not be expected to settle for less."

"No one should ask for perfection," Lydia said. "But I have found it happens far too often in the marriage mart. That's why girls purchase hair to thicken their own, use cosmetics to whiten their skin, wear chest enhancers to provide what Nature failed to supply."

Charlotte glanced down at her bodice. "Chest enhancers?"

Lydia shrugged. "Men pad their calves and shoulders too."

Charlotte shook herself. "Some men, perhaps. I still say fah to the notion. People should be what God intended them to be."

"Amen to that." Bateman moved out from behind the balloon. When had he returned? Had he heard everything? Her skin heated all over again.

"We just delivered the next batch of coal," he told Charlotte. "Care to inspect it before we start shoveling it in?"

"Yes, of course, Beast," Charlotte said. "Lydia, would you note the time and amount?"

"Of course." Lydia pulled out her notebook and pencil. She felt heavy, and not just because of the long day. For a moment, holding Worth, her dream of marriage for love hadn't seemed so far away. Her conversation with Charlotte had only served to remind her that that dream would never come true, at least as far as Worth was concerned.

Coward! Worth paced back and forth before the rear door, as far as the narrow corridor would allow. He'd claimed the need for documentation when all records of this experiment were out in the garden. The only thing that required documentation was his sanity.

Lydia had wrapped her arms around him, and all conscious thought had vanished.

He could reason out the sequence now. Fear for her safety had driven him to respond before the balloon fell. Thanksgiving for his action had prompted her to react. He should not read more into it than that. Even if her body pressed against his had awoken feelings he had thought dead and buried.

Feelings of joy. Feelings of delight. A desire to protect and cherish her all the days of her life. He'd wanted to hold her, kiss those lips and feel them warm against his.

A daring experiment. He gave it a less than ten percent chance of success.

And what was success? Love, marriage, a future together? Why did he persist in thinking such things were possible? She didn't care about him, only about the work they were doing together.

So, here he was, hiding in the house, while the balloon they'd worked so hard to build expanded slowly skyward.

Worth squared his shoulders and opened the door.

Charlotte smiled as he rejoined them. Lydia was consulting the watch, and he shoved off the disappointment that she didn't smile as well.

"How goes it?" he asked.

"We have about reached the circumference and height we had before the mishap occurred," Charlotte reported, gaze on the fire before her. "That means we're only off by thirty minutes. Correct, Lydia?"

"Thirty-six," she answered, frowning at the watch. "Though I wish we had a more precise way of keeping time."

"A shame we haven't one of Halston's chronometers," Charlotte said. "He can register time on a scale of seconds."

"Lord Halston has made a study of time and watches," Worth explained to Lydia. "He claims the Swiss far superior to the English in designing accurate time pieces."

"Yes, I know," Lydia said, studying the watch as if she would find a way to improve it right then and there. "I read his last paper in *Philosophical Transactions*. Oh!"

Worth tensed, but her frown was gone when she glanced up, and her eyes sparkled in the firelight.

"I just remembered," she declared. "Lord Halston will be lecturing on the measurement of time the day after tomorrow. I saw the notice in *The Times*. We should go."

Quite possibly. He had avoided many of the Royal Institution lectures since the debacle with John Curtis. He didn't want to hear the fellow's research praised, nor was he ready to share his own results just yet. But the watches they used barely tracked to the quarter hour accurately, and he would have preferred minutes or even seconds. If Lord Halston had a better approach, he'd like to hear it.

"I'll go," he said. "No need for you and Charlotte to subject yourselves."

Her face fell, and the night felt colder, though he was certain the temperature couldn't have dropped so quickly. "But I'd like to attend."

Worth cocked his head. "Really?"

She raised her chin to allow her gaze to meet his, the soft green surprisingly hard. "Really."

Charlotte made a face. "A few can be exciting, Lydia, but most are dull as ditchwater. These fellows tend to prose on and on about their accomplishments."

He'd never found them all that dull. Lydia seemed to

agree with him.

"I assure you," she insisted, "it would be no imposition to attend. I love to hear what other natural philosophers are studying."

"Why?" Charlotte demanded.

Worth frowned at his sister. Why would Charlotte question her? Did she have reason to doubt Lydia just as Worth was beginning to believe in her?

Lydia didn't take umbrage. Indeed, she seemed to expect more opposition to her request. "Because," she said, "when one part of science advances an inch, others may build on the idea to advance feet, miles. Take our work, for example. Being able to measure time more accurately could show us which parts of the process require additional study. Why focus on the fire when it's the expansion of the fabric that holds us back?"

"Precisely," Worth agreed. "Or is it the very act of shoving coal that slows the process?"

Lydia wiggled her lips. "It might at that." She brightened. "Perhaps we need an automaton, something that regulates the amount, size, and timing of fuel addition. That would have prevented the incident with the peat."

"Yes, excellent idea," Worth said, pacing back and forth in front of them as the idea settled in. "We can start on that tomorrow. I seem to recall a fellow who creates automatons for the king. Make a note of that, Charlotte."

"Delighted," Charlotte drawled. "As soon as you agree to attend the lecture with Lydia."

Worth stopped. Lydia beamed. Glancing between the two of them, he felt his own smile forming. Why not?

He bowed to Lydia. "Miss Villers, would you do me the honor of attending the lecture at the Royal Institution this week?"

She curtsied. "I would be delighted, my lord."

"Excellent." He straightened and regarded his slowly rising balloon. They were behind schedule and now had a new task to add to the scope of work.

So why did he feel insufferably pleased with himself?

Julian strolled through London's famous gentleman's club, White's, attuned to every sound. He kept his smile pleasant, his look vague. No one would have guessed he was listening. But listening, he had found, was far more advantageous to his career than speaking.

In truth, he hadn't been sure what sphere to pursue when his parents had sent him to Eton. The son of some of the most respectable gentry in his part of Surrey, he'd grown used to associating with the titled and wealthy. One of his best friends then was now the Duke of Wey. Friends Harry Orwell and Carrolton had also ascended to their titles.

And here was Julian, still untitled. Unless he found some miraculous way to distinguish himself, he always would be.

Thus, he listened—for problems he might solve, for needs he might meet. Even for secrets that could be shared with the right person for the right reason.

"Penny for your thoughts, my boy."

Julian drew up at the sight of the older gentleman standing in his path. Lord Hastings might look like a jolly good fellow with his brown hair and walrus mustache, his tailored coat and spotless trousers. But he led an aristocratic team of intelligence agents, listeners like Julian. Julian had assisted him from time to time, including with the recent case of the French agent sent to capture Yvette de Maupassant, now Countess of Carrolton. But he had never officially joined Lord Hastings's cadre.

"I fear my thoughts tonight aren't worth your copper, my lord," he allowed.

Hastings wasn't deterred. He took Julian's arm. Anyone looking would be warmed by the fatherly gesture. Julian felt the steel in those fingers.

"Now, you let me be the judge of that," he joked. "Come along, my boy." He led Julian to the back of the room, where two cozy armchairs braced a small table and glowing lamp.

Julian sat across from him on the soft leather. "How might I be of service, my lord?"

Hastings leaned back, the side wings of the chair framing his lined face. "Always to the point. I like that about you, Mayes. Have you spoken with your friend Worthington lately?"

Was the old codger having him followed? Julian hadn't noticed any of Hastings's men dogging his steps, but that meant nothing. One never knew exactly how many men he had. And nothing said they couldn't have set some street urchin on his tail.

"Yes, as a matter of fact," Julian told him.

"And how goes his work?"

Was that what interested the spymaster? What had Worth gotten himself into?

"He reports his work is going well," Julian acknowledged.

"Excellent. His Highness will be attending a demonstration shortly. I've arranged for you to accompany him."

Interesting. "And what profit to you is Worthington's work?"

Hastings smiled. "I find natural philosophy fascinating. And I'd like your assessment as to how these advancements might be useful in our work."

Julian nodded. "Happy to oblige."

Hastings leaned forward. "You're well-known for being obliging. Watch that it continues to benefit you."

The room felt colder. "Have I offered offense, my lord?"

"You?" Hastings laughed. "I've heard nothing but praise for you, my lad, and in high circles. That's why I'm offering you this opportunity to impress the prince."

It was an excellent opportunity. Once drawn to His

Royal Highness' attention, Julian might find additional opportunities to shine. The prince had to approve the nomination for honors, after all. It wasn't unknown for his friends to advance.

"Thank you," Julian said, inclining his head.

"See that you use the opportunity wisely," Hastings said. "A fellow is known for the company he keeps, male, female, or feline."

Julian stilled. "I don't take your meaning," he said, though he feared he understood it all too well.

As always, those brown eyes missed nothing. "I think you do," Hastings said. "A certain cat-toting beauty has come to the attention of the wrong people. Can't have a poor relation profiting from the death of a family member. Where would we be?"

"I assure you the lady is innocent," Julian said, hands tightening on the arms of the chair.

"Of murder? Nothing was proven. But you cannot deny her fortune came from her mistress' death. That sort of scandal stays with a person."

Before Julian could respond, Hastings rose. "I look forward to hearing your thoughts on this demonstration. Until then."

Julian rose and bowed, watching as England's spymaster continued his stroll through White's. Listening, just like Julian.

For once, he could not like what he'd heard. It seemed Meredith was becoming as well known as Hastings.

Julian had worked most of his life to reach his current position in Society. He had curried favor with some of the wealthiest, most powerful men in the Empire. He had earned respect from most. He was so close to the recognition he craved he could almost see it, like a shining city on a hill.

But never once had he considered he might have to choose between his dreams and the woman he loved.

# CHAPTER FOURTEEN

L ydia almost didn't get her wish to attend the lecture. The afternoon before, the Prime Minister was assassinated in the lobby of Parliament, throwing London into turmoil. Rumors of conspiracy raced through the aristocracy like wildfire. Worth sent everyone home, while Gentleman Jackson requested Bateman's aid in subduing the mobs gathering. Though Clarendon Square was far from the trouble, Lydia and Meredith stayed away from the windows, and Fortune divided her time between them, offering cuddles.

By Tuesday, however, calm had been restored, and the murderer, a disturbed man named Bellingham, had been imprisoned to await trial. The group that gathered at the Royal Institution lecture appeared determined to put a good face on matters. In fact, Lydia could hardly sit still as she and Worth waited for the lecture to start.

The Royal Institution had a splendid lecture hall, with tiered padded seats in a semicircle around an expansive desk and more seating in galleries above. She was glad to be wearing her darkest gown, a spruce green wool with a high collar. She wasn't the only lady in the room, but she was the most seriously dressed. She wanted no misunderstandings as to her purpose here.

She wanted to learn anything that might help Worth improve his balloon.

It had taken seven hours for the envelope to inflate after the peat incident, two more than Worth had wanted. But the balloon had stayed aloft for eighteen hours, nearly reaching his goal.

"Next we try it with weight," he'd said after congratulating the team.

Since then, they'd been refurbishing the various components for reuse. Charlotte had gone over the coal order with Bateman to remove any possibility of peat reappearing. Miss Janssen had noticed a deterioration of the reeds closest to the brazier and set about reweaving them and coating them to prevent further trouble. Miss Pankhurst rechecked every stitch in the envelope and reinforced a few. Of course, she ascribed them to Lydia.

Lydia couldn't care. She had been too busy working with Worth to determine whether an automaton could serve as a coal feeder. They'd interviewed the collier who supplied the house and discovered he had a lever to tip the coal into the chute and down into the storage bin. Lydia had immediately seized on the idea of using a similar lever attached to clockwork. They'd tried the first mockup this afternoon, but keeping the coal high enough in the basket to be dispensed had posed a problem for balance, and the dispenser had quickly overwhelmed the brazier, burying it in coal.

"Timing again," Lydia had said, and Worth had agreed.

Now they sat among so many of the scientists whose work she had read about and admired. How interesting to see whether they looked as she had imagined. Somehow, she'd thought Sir Humphry Davy older, but the newly married chemist was surprisingly boyish, with curly brown hair and bright eyes, as if he was as delighted as she was to be in such company. Sir Joseph Banks, on the other hand, was a craggy fellow with grey hair and jowls like a bulldog. She hadn't realized he was confined to a wheeled chair now. A special place had been made for him near the front.

She had convinced Worth to introduce her to him.

Sir Joseph had nodded his heavy head. "A pleasure to meet you, Miss Villers. You are exactly what we need, charming young ladies taking an interest in natural philosophy."

"A great interest," Lydia had assured him. "I read your *Circumstances Relative to Merino Sheep*. I promise you, I will never look at wool the same way again."

He blinked. "Well, certainly. That is…who are you again?"

Lord Battersby had been less complimentary when he'd stopped by their seats to greet Worth.

"What do you mean by bringing Miss Villers to a lecture?" the earl had demanded. "You'll merely bore the chit. See? She's already looking about for better game."

Worth's arm had tensed against hers. Lydia had met the earl's gaze. "I certainly am. I came tonight hoping to discuss scientific advances. If you prefer social commentary, I'd be happy to direct you to Lady Jersey's set." She'd batted her lashes for effect.

The earl had leaned closer, a decided curl to his lips. "Scientific advances, eh? What would you know about any scientific endeavor?"

She had been ready to answer him, but Worth had stood to face the fellow, his height far exceeding the earl's.

"Miss Villers assisted Augusta Orwell in inventing the salve that cured your daughter's skin affliction, my lord," he had told the earl. "Charlotte said you praised it the last time she saw you. You might want to thank Miss Villers rather than making an assumption. We both know the effect an assumption can have on the scientific process."

"Yes, well." He had taken a step back. "Excellent work, Miss Villers. Dolly made her first appearance in Society after weeks hiding at home. I'm sure she'd be delighted to thank you in person. Feel free to call any time."

"Thank you, my lord," Lydia had said. "And I do hope you'll be willing to show me what you're currently working on in identifying new elements."

He had glanced from her to Worth and back again. "I look forward to it."

So did she. Opportunity seemed to be crowding on all sides. She couldn't wait to hear the lecture.

But even as she sat up taller to gain a better view of the lectionary, she became aware of Worth moving beside her. He shifted back and forth on the seat as if considering jumping up and running away. If he adjusted his cravat one more time the thing would probably fall right off his neck.

"What's the matter?" Lydia whispered, mindful of the people in front, behind, and on either side on the sharply sloped theatre.

His smile was tight. "Nothing of import to our work. Forgive me. Let's just enjoy the lecture."

She intended to and was not disappointed. Lord Halston had a pedantic way of speaking, as Charlotte had predicted, but his comparisons between the marine chronometers and the standard watch set her mind to humming.

"We must ask him to recommend a manufacturer," she told Worth as the lecture ended and everyone prepared to leave.

Worth nodded, gaze on the group surrounding the lecturer. "If you'd stay here a moment, I'll see if I can beat my way to his side."

Lydia waited, thoughts churning. To be able to stabilize the watch against movement, as chronometers did at sea—how perfect for balloon flight! Worth wouldn't have to depend on those on the ground. He could time various aspects within the balloon itself.

Assuming, of course, he chose to fly the balloon. She frowned. He had said weight. Surely that meant a person at some point. Someone needed to pilot the balloon, turning his propellers, working the bellows. That tingle shot through her—oh, to have such an opportunity!

"Did you enjoy the lecture, Miss Villers?"

Lydia turned to find John Curtis beside her. He was dressed more conservatively tonight, in a navy coat and tan breeches, as if he sought to impress as well. His hair had been combed over the bald spot on his head. The blond tresses gleamed with pomade. His smile was equally shiny.

"Yes, thank you," she said. "And you?"

"Oh, of course. Having a movement-hardened watch would be very useful in my chemical experiments."

"Lord Worthington's too," she assured him.

His brows rose. "Worth is back working in chemistry? I thought he was determined to perfect ballooning."

She blinked, then realized that Worth must have told him. The pair had worked together once. True, there was some antipathy between them now, but surely Worth would have sought his mentor's advice.

"You know?" She beamed at him. "Oh, how delightful. I've so wanted to discuss our progress with another natural philosopher, but Lord Worthington has been determined to hold things close."

"Understandably," he said with a commiserating smile. "His work carries such promise. Industry will no doubt latch onto any advances he makes, and I understand the military is keenly interested in using balloons for observation purposes. I'd be delighted to help in any way I can. Perhaps we could meet at Gunter's tomorrow afternoon and discuss the matter further."

In the past, the treat of eating at the famed confectioner's would have thrilled her no end. Now, all she could think about was the amount of work ahead of them if they were to be ready for the demonstration to the prince.

As if he saw her indecision, he leaned forward. "And I could share some recent studies of my own on heat conductivity."

Oh! That could be just the thing to speed their work.

"I'll ask Lord Worthington," she promised.

He leaned back. "Alas, Lord Worthington seems to have

taken me in dislike. He has chosen to make our work a rivalry, I fear. I would love to mend the rift. Perhaps you could help."

Perhaps she could. She knew a great deal about navigating Society, when to placate, how to play the fool. And if Mr. Curtis and Worth reconciled, they'd have another scientific mind to help advance the work.

"Very well, Mr. Curtis," she said. "I am due for a half day. I will meet you at Gunter's tomorrow. Shall we say eleven?"

Worth finished his discussion with Lord Halston and turned to retrace his steps to Lydia's side. Her smile was bright, as if she couldn't wait for what lay ahead. She'd been nothing but a delight all night.

Even if some of his fellow philosophers had not thought as much.

Lord Nampton had been the worst. "What a pretty little ladybird," he'd murmured to Worth as the two of them had waited to speak to the lecturer. "Must be the patient sort to sit through one of Halston's lectures."

"More patient than I am," Worth had assured him, "particularly when I hear a lady slandered. I will have your apology, sir."

Nampton had stared at him, porcine face glistening in the lamplight. "My apology? To a tart?"

Worth gritted his teeth. "Your apology to the *lady*, sirrah, or the name of your second."

The marquess had drawn back. "My apology then. But for pity's sake, man. That's Beauford Villers's sister. Why would you threaten a duel over the likes of her?"

"I suggest," Worth said, hands bunching at his sides, "that you consider the answer to the question yourself, while you examine your behavior. Good night, sirrah." He'd turned his back on the fellow.

Just remembering fueled his steps now. Did every gentleman on the *ton* look at her and see nothing but the fluff of a dandelion, blown on the wind of her brother's avarice? Was this the sort of thing she'd endured the last few years? Small wonder she found solace in science.

*And were you any better?*

The answer shamed him. He had mistaken others so often that to hear he had mistaken her had been all too easy to believe. He'd been quick to disassociate from her a year ago, and just as quickly thought the worse of her when she'd reappeared in his life.

But Lydia wasn't that woman. He'd seen a bright light and mistaken it for artifice. The light was there, a warm glow that encouraged everyone who saw it. She had been nothing but helpful since she'd joined his team, spurring him to new ideas, new approaches. Because of her, they had a chance to achieve his dreams.

"How do you abide my arrogance?" he asked as he came up to her.

She blinked, rapidly, as if her thoughts moved in time with her golden lashes. "The same way I abide other people's arrogance. With a smile."

Worth shook his head. "You continue to astound me. I treated you abominably last year, yet you willingly return and offer your help."

"Well," she said, taking his arm, "I will accept that as another apology. Now, what did Lord Halston say?"

He led her through the thinning crowds toward the door. "He recommends Thomas Earnshaw, the fellow who's been making chronometers for the Navy."

"But a chromometer of that size would surely disrupt your weight calculations," she said as they collected their wraps. She flung hers about her shoulders before Worth could offer his help.

"Quite possibly," he acknowledged. "I understand,

however, that Earnshaw has a pocket version."

"Oh! We must go see him." She swished her skirts aside as they descended the stairs to the pavement. Bateman, who had been waiting near the door, peeled himself away from the building to join them.

Out of the night, something hurtled toward him. Worth recoiled, but Bateman pushed him aside, separating him from Lydia. He heard his man grunt.

"Bateman!" Lydia caught his arm as the boxer swayed.

Worth moved in against his other side. "What was that?"

Bateman shook them both off, glaring into the shadows. Red trickled down his temple.

"You're bleeding!" Lydia cried.

He wiped away the blood with the back of his hand. "Wouldn't be the first time. Get in the carriage, both of you."

Worth hurried Lydia down to the next carriage, where his coachman sat waiting. Petersham must not have noticed anything, for he held the horses steady with a ready smile as Bateman opened the door and hustled them in. Then the boxer darted back into the shadow of the building.

Lydia clutched Worth's arm. "What's he doing?"

Worth shook his head before his man jumped in beside them.

Petersham started the carriage forward as Bateman wiped at his face again. As if she thought he wasn't doing a good enough job, Lydia took a handkerchief from her reticule and offered it to him. Her hand was shaking.

"What hit you, Bateman?" she asked.

"Brick," the boxer said, accepting her gift. The fine lawn turned pink as he held it to his forehead. "Someone threw it at his lordship."

Worth reared back. "At me? Nonsense. Why would anyone want to brain me?"

"Same reason they threatened to kill you," Bateman said.

"Or had you forgotten why you hired me?"

Lydia gasped. "Oh, Worth! That note!"

Worth put his hand over hers but addressed his bodyguard. "You think this has something to do with those threats?"

"Don't you?" He set down the bloodied handkerchief. "I know you keep your head in your work, but you have to think of your ladies. The last note warned of harm to them too. That brick could as easily have hit Miss Villers as you."

The very thought chilled him.

Lydia sighed. "It couldn't have been meant for me. I doubt I'm important enough to warrant such treatment right now. If I was vying for Lord Worthington's attentions, perhaps. But I've made no secret of the fact that I'm only in his company to learn more about natural philosophy."

Hearing it said aloud was still lowering.

"That's not what people expect," Bateman argued.

"Then perhaps they should reconsider their expectations," she said sweetly. "I believe I have given sufficient evidence of my true purpose."

She certainly had, at least to him. He could not conceive that another woman was so jealous that they'd attack her, in public no less. And how would anyone have known she would be at the Royal Institution's lecture, of all places? No, the brick had to have been meant for him.

But why? And by whose hand?

"Perhaps the stories were true," Bateman said. "There's more than one madman in London set on hurting those in power."

"This has nothing to do with Perceval's assassination," Worth insisted, as Lydia's eyes widened. "Bellingham made no secret of his dissatisfaction with government in general. Our threatening letter writer appears to be aggrieved with me specifically."

"So, who did you set off?" Bateman demanded.

One name came to mind. John Curtis had been at the

lecture, for all Worth had tried to ignore him. Was his former mentor so angry over their falling out that he'd aim a brick at Worth's head?

# CHAPTER FIFTEEN

What a night! Lydia was still shaking when she walked into Meredith's townhouse. Why would anyone want to hurt Worth? She could imagine a few young ladies who'd go so far to remove her as a rival, and her brother had enough enemies that someone might have wanted to take their vengeance on him by hurting her. But the direction from which the brick had come made it seem far more likely that Worth was the target.

"You could probably have caught the culprit," she said to Fortune, who had come to the door to greet her. She bent and swept the cat up into her arms. Amazing how a few cuddles against that silky fur made breathing easier.

"Everything all right?"

Lydia raised her head to find Meredith standing on the landing, head cocked as if she could see inside Lydia. Her elderly butler ambled forward.

"May I take your wrap, Miss Villers?"

Lydia turned so he could remove it from her shoulders, juggling Fortune in the process. "Thank you, Mr. Cowls." She carried the cat up the stairs to join her mistress.

"I doubt Lord Halston's lecture could have you in such a state," Meredith said, stepping aside so Lydia could follow her into the withdrawing room.

"It was fascinating," Lydia allowed. "And I met some interesting people. But you didn't have to wait up."

Meredith eyed her pet, who was purring, the rumble tickling Lydia's chest. "Someone refused to settle until she knew you were home."

"Sweet little kittykins." Lydia lowered her head and rubbed her nose against Fortune's. Fortune sneezed.

Lydia smiled. "Very well. I know when I have overstepped." She bent and released the cat, who traipsed over and began winding around Meredith's skirts, ruffling the lavender silk.

Meredith's look softened, then she glanced up at Lydia. "You haven't answered my question. You looked troubled when you came in. What happened?"

Lydia sighed, going to sit on the sofa. Meredith joined her.

"There was an incident after the lecture," Lydia confessed. "Someone threw a brick at us."

"Us?" Meredith's dark brows arched.

"Lord Worthington and me."

"One brick doesn't seem a sensible weapon against two people," Meredith said with a shake of her head.

"And there lies the question," Lydia said. "Was it meant for him, or me?"

Fortune jumped up onto the sofa and eyed each of them as if trying to determine which lap held the most promise. She must have decided on Lydia, for she made herself comfortable on the spruce gown.

"And there was no one else about?" Meredith questioned.

Lydia shook her head. "Only Mr. Bateman. He pushed Worth aside and took the brunt of it, poor man. The wound wasn't serious, just bloody."

Meredith shuddered. "Well, I suppose we should be thankful it wasn't any worse. Still, why would anyone assault Lord Worthington? He hasn't done anything notable, unless you count this balloon he's building."

Lydia threw up her hands, startling Fortune, who glared as if deeply offended, jumped down, and stalked off behind the sofa.

"How does everyone know what we're doing?" Lydia demanded. "Worth makes it seem a dark secret."

"I was informed by Mr. Cowls," Meredith said, "and I am no longer surprised by what he can ferret out. Nor do I question how he acquires his knowledge. One should not look a gift horse in the mouth. So, Lord Worthington wishes the matter kept quiet. Why? Does he fear failure?"

"He estimates failure whenever asked," Lydia admitted. Something tickled her skirts—Fortune, sneaking up on her mistress. "But I truly believe he thinks we will succeed in the end."

"Interesting," Meredith said, leaning back. "Could this assault this evening have been from a rival, attempting to prevent him from that end?"

A rival. John Curtis had commented along those lines, but he had implied the impetus for the rivalry lay on Worth's side. Lydia could certainly imagine that. Worth had taken a dislike of her on no more evidence than a story from a colleague. Perhaps someone had said something bad about Mr. Curtis. She certainly couldn't see the slight fellow heaving a brick at Worth's head.

Then again, it was difficult to imagine anyone she knew doing such a dastardly deed, except, perhaps, her brother. Beau was off on his honeymoon to the Lakes District and likely had no reason to accost Worth regardless. Blackmail was more his style. She might have blamed him for the vague note someone had sent to the Worthington establishment, but that hand hadn't belonged to him. And he would never have convinced his thoroughly-proper bride to help him.

"I can't think of anyone who would want to brain Worth," Lydia said.

Meredith cocked her head. "Except you, perhaps."

Lydia laughed. "Well, maybe once. But I need Worth now. He's providing me with the opportunity to advance."

Meredith trailed her fingers along the edge of the sofa.

Fortune popped out from behind Lydia's skirts to watch, ears twitching as if she listened for the slightest sound. "And is that the only reason you're interested in Lord Worthington?"

"Of course," Lydia said.

Either she said it too readily or too flippantly, for Meredith's brows arched once more. Why did that look demand she confide?

"Very well," Lydia said. "I still admire him. But he treats me like any other member of the team, with no more than professional courtesy, if that at times."

Meredith's fingers stilled. So did Fortune. "Nothing more?"

His apologies came to mind. He did seem to regret the way they'd parted. He'd said he liked her, that he still cared. And once in a while, she thought she saw something like admiration shining from his grey eyes. Miss Janssen had noticed it as well.

"In truth, I'm not sure," Lydia admitted. "Perhaps I merely want to see more. Is it foolish to hope?"

Meredith drew back her hand, and Fortune jumped up and into her lap as if in search of her fingers. "It depends on the hope. What is it you want, Lydia?"

*To hear him say he admires me.*

*To hear him say he loves me. To feel his arms around me, his lips against mine. To know I am cherished, just for myself.*

Her eyes felt warm. She blinked back tears. "For most of my life, what I wanted and what was possible were two different things."

"And now?" Meredith challenged.

Lydia spread her hands. "Now, working with Worth, it seems as if anything might be possible."

Meredith smiled. "Excellent. That is exactly what I want my clients to feel. I believe I should begin looking for my next opportunity."

The sofa seemed to sink beneath her. "Will I need to

leave?"

Meredith waved a hand even as Fortune climbed off her lap and sidled over to Lydia as if giving her another chance to share her lap.

"Not at all," Meredith said. "Most of my clients are placed into living situations, and I have another room I can outfit if need be. You are welcome to stay as long as you like."

Lydia drew in a breath. "Thank you."

"Allow me, however, to make a prediction," Meredith said. "Very shortly, you will have a new place to live, one that you can call home for the rest of your life."

If only she could believe.

Worth woke early the next morning. The sun was shining. The air smelled new. Odd thought. He knew the origin of air, its movement and properties. Nothing had re-created it anew. Yet he couldn't help the feeling that the very breath inside him was different, better, than it had been only yesterday. He defied his valet to throw on his clothes, knotted his cravat, and ran down the stairs.

Charlotte was generally up before him, had breakfasted and planned her day before he arrived. She hadn't even started her first cup of tea when he peered into her study.

"I'll be in the garden," he said.

"And good morning to you too," she said, rising to follow him down the short corridor. "What's the hurry? Did you learn something last night?"

*Yes, that I still have feelings for Lydia Villers, and someone hates me enough to attempt to kill me.*

He shook his head. "Nothing that can help us immediately. Halston's thoughts on time pieces were very helpful. I'll send a note this morning to the watchmaker he recommended about a new chronometer. With any luck, it will arrive before the demonstration."

Charlotte hurried to keep up with him as he reached the rear door. "You are in a good mood."

*Because I'm in love.*

"Just eager to start the day," he told her. "We have a great deal of work to do."

"I fear we will be short-handed," Charlotte said as they stepped into the garden. The scarlet silk had been taken inside for safekeeping, but the basket and brazier stood waiting, dew setting them to sparkling. From the garden next door, he heard birds singing, the merry sound making him smile.

"Oh?" Worth asked, eyeing the coal feeder and remembering how hard Lydia had worked to make her idea a reality. "Has Miss Pankhurst requested time off again?"

"No, Lydia has."

He froze, cold slipping over him. "Has something happened to Lydia?"

His concern must have leaked out, for Charlotte regarded him oddly.

"Not to my knowledge. She sent round a note early. She has an appointment this morning but hopes to join us afterward."

Relief and disappointment vied for his attention. "Good. We'll need all the help we can get."

Bateman came out of the house just then. "Why didn't anyone call me?" he demanded. "You shouldn't be out here alone."

Charlotte laughed. "Really, Beast. I doubt anyone would accost us in our own garden."

"I don't." He came abreast of them and scowled at Worth. A jagged red line marred his forehead under his thatch of brown hair.

Charlotte must have seen it as well, for she sobered. "What happened to your head?"

"You didn't tell her?" Bateman asked Worth. When Worth

shrugged, his bodyguard turned to Charlotte. "Someone tried to smash your brother's head in last night."

His sister turned white as she glanced between them. "What!"

"He makes it sound worse than it was," Worth assured her. "Someone threw a brick as we were leaving the lecture. It could have been aimed at anyone."

He thought that might assuage at least some of his sister's concerns, but she turned on Bateman. "And I suppose you stepped between it and Worth?"

Now Bateman shrugged. "That's my job."

Charlotte glared at Worth. "He could have been killed."

"I wager my head's harder than his," Bateman said.

"That is immaterial," Charlotte scolded. "Honestly, how can you two stand here so casually? Someone might have died!"

Worth caught her hands. "No one was seriously hurt, Charlotte. Bateman likely had a headache last night, but he's here and ready to work this morning. That's what's important."

She pulled out of his grip. "You and I will never agree on what's important." She turned and marched back to the house.

"You worried her," Bateman said watching her.

Perhaps. But Worth had the unsettling feeling that it was the boxer's injury that had most concerned his sister.

"I appear to have worried you too," he told his bodyguard.

Bateman's jaw was tighter than usual as his gaze swept back to Worth's at last. "I don't like it. We don't know who did it, whether it will happen again."

Worth nodded. "Point well taken. Let's apply some logic. It was dark. Most of the others had gone. Likely the few who remained never noticed the culprit."

Bateman crossed his arms over his chest. "That's true enough. I tried looking but couldn't see anything or anyone that might be associated. Petersham claims he saw nothing until we arrived to get in the coach."

"So either the fellow had been waiting in hiding for more than an hour during the lecture, or it was someone who had left the lecture before us."

Bateman dropped his arms. "One of your fellow philosophers? They don't seem the type to get their hands dirty. But it could have been one of their servants. Or a thug they hired. Some will do anything for money."

From what Gentleman Jackson had said about Bateman before Worth had hired him, the boxer had cause to know. Thousands of pounds changed hands at any boxing match, none of it strictly legal. That was one of the reasons the magistrates tried to ban such sporting events from the city proper.

"Then we're back where we started," Worth said, "the culprit's identity and motivation unknown. What do you advise?"

Bateman glanced around the garden. "You should be safe enough in here. Nothing can get over that wall without being noticed. But we'll be more careful when you leave the house."

"Agreed," Worth said, turning for the basket. "However, I don't plan to leave the house in the near future."

Aware of a distinct disappointment that Lydia wasn't there beside him, he threw himself into the work. The others arrived shortly afterward. While Miss Pankhurst made her final inspection of the envelope and Miss Janssen reinforced the padding on the basket, he and Charlotte worked on the coal feeder. The device continued to fight him, delivering too much coal one time and too little another.

"There's nothing for it," Charlotte said, wiping sweat from her brow. "The only way we can deliver the right amount of coal to the fire is if someone introduces it by hand, alternating with the bellows."

"Meaning someone must remain awake at all times,"

Worth said. He cleaned the coal residue from his hands with a rag. "Combined with the propellers, we'll need a two-man crew."

"Or a two-woman crew," Charlotte amended.

He tossed the rag aside. "Either way, we've increased the weight."

"You'll want a higher weight rating eventually anyway," Charlotte pointed out. "To transport goods, people. And you know if this demonstration goes well, His Highness will insist on a ride."

"His ministers will prevent that," Worth predicted. "We can't risk England's ruler in a balloon."

Charlotte put her hands on her hips. "Since when have any of his ministers been able to stop Prinny from doing as he likes?"

Miss Pankhurst sidled closer. "Pardon me, my lord, Miss Worthington. The stitches appear to be satisfactory, except for a small set on the very crown. I could complete the work faster if I could have Miss Villers's help. When do you expect her back from Gunter's?"

Charlotte frowned. "Gunter's? Why would she be out eating ice cream?"

Miss Pankhurst tittered, the sound more irritating than usual. "I'm sure I couldn't say. Perhaps her interest in natural philosophy is waning. She is such a busy little bee."

Worth felt as if the woman had landed a punch more surely than Bateman. "I believe she is expected this afternoon," he said, voice coming out hard.

"Ah." Miss Pankhurst pouted. "Pity. Well, if she returns, perhaps she'll be willing to help."

She wandered back to the envelope, humming to herself.

"Did you know about this?" Worth asked his sister.

"No," Charlotte, ever the unflappable, said. "But Lydia hasn't had time away since her brother's wedding, and we did promise a half-day off every week in our work agreement."

"Then why not ask for time off?" Worth pressed. "Why claim an appointment?"

"Perhaps she had an appointment," Charlotte countered, "and stopped by Gunter's afterward, though how Miss Pankhurst would know is beyond me."

"We need her here," Worth said, legs taking him past the brazier and back again. "This coal feeder was her idea. And you heard Miss Pankhurst. Only Lydia's stitches will do."

"Until Miss Pankhurst rips them out again," Charlotte said. "And I cannot like your tone, Worth. Lydia is our employee, our colleague. She isn't your slave."

He recoiled, stung. "I'd never consider any person a slave."

Charlotte's grey gaze, so like his own, was implacable. "And yet, you continue to expect us all to be at your beck and call—Lydia, Miss Pankhurst, Miss Janssen, Beast. Me."

Worth raked his hand back through his hair. "You hold high a mirror, and I cannot like the image I see. Forgive me, Charlotte. It was never my intention to take advantage of any of you. Perhaps you could draw up a schedule, ensure every member of the team and our staff has time off each week. With pay. I will endeavor to be a more understanding employer."

"Generous," Charlotte said. "I'll arrange the schedule and bring it to you for approval. Thank you, Worth. I think everyone will work better with a little time to themselves, even you."

She was likely right. But, with the insights into his character that Charlotte and Lydia had given him recently, the last thing he wanted was more time alone with his thoughts.

# CHAPTER SIXTEEN

Lydia sat on a park bench in Berkeley Square, across from Gunter's, swinging one foot under her muslin skirts. The white-fronted confectioner's with its wide glass windows was crowded. The fashionable entered and left every few minutes, and waiters ran ices and candies out to carriages waiting under the trees of the square.

"You are kindness itself to meet me like this," John Curtis said for the third time since she had arrived and they had taken a seat in the park at the center of the square. "But if you could just explain a bit more about what Lord Worthington hopes to accomplish, I might be able to offer advice."

Before answering, Lydia swallowed another spoonful of the tart pineapple ice Mr. Curtis had purchased for her. "I fear I've shared as much as I feel comfortable. Let's discuss your work. Advances in chemistry, I believe?"

He glanced around at the other wrought iron benches nearby, which were mostly empty at the moment, then lay a hand on her arm and gazed deep into her eyes. "My dear Miss Villers, Lydia, if I may, I sense we are kindred spirits. There is much I long to say to you, to share with you, if only I could be sure of your heart."

Lydia pulled away. Once she had had to put up with unfounded declarations of adoration, usually followed by an offer of a *carte blanche*. No more.

"My heart has nothing to do with the matter," she told him cheerfully, pausing to finish the last of the ice. "You invited me to talk about our mutual interest in natural philosophy. So far, I'm the only one talking."

He leaned back. "And you're remarkably close-lipped."

"Am I? I don't mean to be." She set aside the little crystal cup with a sigh of regret. "I explained to you that Lord Worthington would prefer to keep some matters to himself. You were going to tell me more about heat conductance."

He waved a gloved hand. "A matter far above your understanding, my dear."

And that was quite enough of that. "Pity," Lydia said, rising and forcing him to his feet as well. "Thank you for the treat, Mr. Curtis. I fear I will be too busy in the coming weeks for another."

"Busy?" He seized on the word. "Busy how? What is Worth planning?"

He was so interested. She knew desperation when she saw it.

"You will have to ask him," she said, turning to go.

He grabbed her shoulder. "Wait! You've told me nothing."

Lydia eyed the fingers digging into her rose-colored pelisse, and he released her.

"Neither have you," she pointed out. "Please don't approach me again, Mr. Curtis. I so dislike giving people the cut direct. Good bye."

She walked past him for the street. He did not call out to stop her.

A few establishments beyond Gunter's, she let out a sigh. Did it have to be this way? Why did pale blond curls, big green eyes, and a friendly demeanor equate to a lack of intellect and a disinterest in anything of substance? Her brother had certainly worked hard to make sure no one guessed she might have a brain in her head. She'd grown used to wearing gowns cut too daringly for propriety, uttering giggles at a man's attentions when she wanted to gag. She'd twisted out of unseemly embraces, stomped on an instep or two, and endured too many pecks on the cheek. Mr. Curtis seemed to think that her only role in life. She refused to return to it, even if that meant walking across Mayfair for a couple miles.

It was nearly two in the afternoon when she reached the Worthington townhouses. Bateman answered her knock.

"'Bout time you showed up," he greeted her.

"How sweet that I was missed," Lydia said, moving into the entry hall.

He shut the door behind her. "Any trouble?"

Lydia glanced at him. His face seemed tighter than usual, the planes sharply defined by nose and brow. The angry red mark from the brick stood out against his pallor.

"Why, Mr. Bateman, were you worried about me?" Lydia asked.

He snorted. "Of course, I was worried. We still don't know whether last night was on account of his lordship or you." He lowered his head to meet her gaze on a level. "You all right?"

Lydia smiled at him. "You know, I feel quite fine at the moment. Thank you, Bateman."

With a nod, he straightened. "I'll make sure someone walks you home tonight."

Worth perhaps? Well, that would be silly, if Bateman was as worried about him. "Thank you," she said again. "Where is everyone?"

"Garden," he said with a tip of his head in that direction. "We'll start filling the envelope again shortly."

The words galvanized her. She hurried back.

The automaton had been removed, she saw as she entered the garden, but the coal was high in the bin, and Bateman went to man the shovel. Charlotte was watching the fire in the brazier. Miss Pankhurst and Miss Janssen were smoothing out the envelope as it lay across the space, preparing it to be filled. Worth was peering into the basket.

"Sorry I'm late," Lydia said to Charlotte. "How can I help?"

Charlotte smiled at her. "Welcome back. Worth was worried."

The idea was even more warming than Bateman's concern. What need did she have for grasping fellows like Mr. Curtis when she had friends who cared?

As if to prove it, Worth closed the distance to her side. Perspiration stood out along the edges of his hair, darkening the auburn to walnut and spiking the wave. His look was sorrowful, grey eyes dipping at the corners.

"You must forgive me, Miss Villers," he said, voice deeper than usual. "Charlotte tells me I'm driving you too hard."

Lydia glanced between them. "Not at all! I love working here."

His smile turned up, as if she'd lifted a weight from his shoulders. "I'm delighted to hear that. How was Gunter's?"

"Crowded, but that's no surprise with the warm weather." When he merely regarded her, brows up, she paused. "How did you know I was at Gunter's?"

"That is immaterial," Charlotte interrupted. "You could have been at Gunter's or Almack's or the moon, for that matter. The point is that every member of this team has more than earned time off. I will be setting up a schedule to formalize that later. For now, would you look over Miss Pankhurst's stitches? She has been fussing with them all morning."

Though the sewing task was her least favorite part of their work, Lydia nodded and went to the envelope. She could feel Worth watching her.

"Ah, the prodigal returns," Miss Pankhurst said with a giggle at her own wit. Miss Janssen shook her head good-naturedly.

"Forgive me for leaving you short-handed," Lydia said, pacing along the scarlet fabric. "But I see I wasn't needed. You've done a fine job."

Miss Pankhurst drew herself up. "That is for Miss Worthington or his lordship to say."

"Oh, Miss Worthington asked me to look," Lydia said. She turned to find Miss Pankhurst's color high and lips pressed together.

Miss Janssen lay a hand on her colleague's shoulder. "Miss Worthington must trust you if she saw no reason to inspect the work herself," she reminded the other woman.

Miss Pankhurst pulled away from her. "We'll just see about that." She moved off toward Charlotte.

Lydia sighed. "I didn't mean to offend her."

"She can be difficult," Miss Janssen allowed. "She is what is called a poor relation—a lady with no inheritance of her own, no husband to support her. She was sent from one part of the family to another and wanted by none of them, I hear. I think she likes the freedom to come and go as she pleases."

"I can understand that," Lydia murmured.

Miss Janssen nudged her with her shoulder, nearly oversetting Lydia. "His lordship didn't like that you were gone. He missed you." Her smiled broadened her already broad face.

Lydia glanced to where he was tightening the ropes that held the basket secure. "I thought I had found someone to advise us on heat conductance. The gentleman in question only wanted to flirt."

Miss Janssen nudged her again. "Ha! That must happen a lot."

"Not if I can help it," Lydia assured her. "Excuse me. I should report to Miss Worthington."

Miss Janssen nodded and went back to smoothing the fabric, and Lydia hurried around to the other side of the envelope.

She expected to find Miss Pankhurst with Charlotte. Surely the other woman wouldn't lose such an opportunity to complain about Lydia. But Charlotte was alone, gaze on the fire building in the coals.

"Everything ready?" she asked.

"The envelope appears ready," Lydia told her. "Have you seen Miss Pankhurst?"

"I believe she went into the house a few minutes ago," Charlotte said. "Did she need more supplies or some such?"

"Not that I know of," Lydia said. "I think she took umbrage that I was to inspect her work."

"She's certainly inspected yours often enough," Charlotte countered. "We are none of us above having our work reviewed. That's the nature of a scientific endeavor."

"Perhaps someone should explain that to Worth," Lydia said.

Charlotte sighed. "I know it must seem odd to you, Lydia, but Worth has his reasons for keeping things so close. I'll explain when I'm able. For now, I must ask for your help again."

Lydia perked up. "Whatever you need."

Charlotte stepped to one side and pointed to the long lever of the automaton sticking up on the other side of the coal bin. "Worth and I were unable to completely automate the filling process. The shuttle fills appropriately, but the timing is off. For now, Beast will fill the brazier. Someone must climb into the basket and work the bellows on my command."

Lydia stood taller. "I'll do it."

Charlotte grinned. "I was hoping you'd say that. Put on your work coat so you won't char your dress, and let's start."

Her skin tingled as she drew on the canvas coat. She would get to try her own invention. Beau would be aghast. How lovely that Worth and Charlotte only encouraged her.

But entering the basket was easier said than done. The wicker reached above her waist. She couldn't exactly sling a leg over, especially with her narrow muslin skirts. And Worth had affixed his four propellers to the sides, making it even more difficult to find an easy way into the container. She was considering her options when Worth returned to her.

"Allow me," he said. Bending, he slipped one arm under her knees and the other around her back.

And all at once she was up in his arms, his face inches from her own, his chest against hers. As the coals began to glow, the light was reflected in his eyes. She thought her heart was reflected as well.

"If you would put her in the basket," Charlotte suggested, tone amused.

He blinked, as if he'd needed the reminder of their purpose as much as Lydia had. Gently, carefully, he angled her feet over the rim and allowed her to slide down into the basket around one of the polished cedar propellers.

Lydia righted herself, trying to catch her breath. He gripped the wicker with both hands as if he intended to vault in after her. But he merely asked. "Are you all right?"

"Fine," Lydia assured him. Too easy to bask in his regard. She had to remember they had work to do. Turning, she took up her place beside the bellows.

Up close, the brazier's warmth penetrated her coat. The wooden handles, covered and yoked in leather, stuck out at one side of the bellows. She gripped them and waited for Charlotte's order.

"We are ready to begin filling," Charlotte announced.

Worth rubbed his hands together. "Excellent. Miss Janssen, Miss Pankhurst, if I could have your help."

"Miss Pankhurst is indisposed," Miss Janssen said, but she stepped forward, rolling up the sleeves on her beefy arms.

With her help, Worth positioned the neck of the envelope above the fire, the throat wide like the mouth of a hungry child. The envelope twitched, writhed, took a deep breath of the hot air.

"Miss Janssen, will you note times?" Worth asked as they stepped back.

The heavy-set woman went for the journal and pencil.

"More coal," Charlotte ordered, and Bateman shoveled up an armload. Gritty coal tumbled down into the fire, black dust drifting upward with the heat. Red began licking around the new fuel.

"Added approximately a bushel of coal to start the process," he told the weaver, and Miss Janssen wrote on the thick parchment pages.

"Bellows," Charlotte commanded. "Five pumps, if you please. Note that, Miss Janssen."

Lydia pressed on the handles, bringing the sides together. Air whooshed out. With each pump, the coals glowed redder, and sparks floated upward to wink out as the air entered the envelope.

The pattern continued, like a country dance—coal, bellows, wait. Coal, bellows, wait. How long they worked, Lydia wasn't sure. The afternoon turned to evening. Cook sent out cheese, fruit, and crusty bread with butter at some point. Lydia took little when Charlotte offered it—too much coal dust around her. Miss Janssen gave a loud yawn but quickly smothered it with one hand before making another notation in the journal.

The envelope widened, hovered off the ground, the bushes. Rose until it became a mushroom over the basket. Lydia had to duck to keep from hitting it with her head. Miss Pankhurst must have returned, for Lydia could barely make out her and Worth moving around the sides, checking ropes, watching the expansion.

"Bellows!"

Lydia pumped.

She pumped until her arms ached and her eyes burned from the coal dust. She pumped until the great scarlet envelope towered overhead. She pumped until the floor of the basket tilted and she lost her balance as the balloon lifted off the ground.

She blinked, gazing up at the mountain of red above her.

They'd done it.

Worth must have agreed, for she heard his voice. "She's up. Note the time, Miss Janssen."

"Half past seven, my lord."

A shame the new chronometer hadn't arrived, or they'd know to the second. Still, at half past seven, they'd beaten their previous record for inflation.

The floor under her tilted higher, and Lydia slid to fetch up against the center pillar. A coal tumbled down to lay on the thin wood floor. Without thinking, she seized it and flung it out of the basket. Then she clutched her smoldering glove to her chest as pain shot up her arm from her hand.

Her colleagues must have noticed the change in the balloon, for they reacted more strongly.

"What caused that?" Worth demanded.

"That rope," Miss Pankhurst cried. "It snapped. Miss Villers threw a coal at it."

That made no sense. She'd thrown the coal because of the tilt. And her glove was merely blackened. A single coal, carelessly tossed, couldn't have burned through a rope so quickly. She struggled to rise, and the basket reared on the opposite corner.

"There goes another one!" Bateman shouted.

"Get Lydia out of there," Worth ordered.

Lydia scrambled to find purchase even as Bateman's face appeared over one side of the basket.

"Really, Miss Villers." Miss Pankhurst sounded sufficiently alarmed. "Leave the ropes alone."

With a twang that sent the twine whipping past her, the balloon broke free and leaped skyward.

On the other side of the basket, Worth felt as if someone had rained coals on his head. No time to determine how the balloon had come loose.

"Do you have her?" he shouted to Bateman.

"No!"

Nothing for it. With a leap, he snagged his fingers into the rising wicker. The container tipped, and Lydia cried out. So did Charlotte as she disappeared below him. Worth pulled himself hand over hand up and over the rim to slip down inside.

Lydia was sprawled on the floor, canvas coat bunched about her, face puckered.

"The weight's wrong," she said. "We didn't account for two."

Despite himself, Worth started laughing. "*That's* your concern?"

Once more the basket tilted, and she slid across to collide with him. Worth righted her.

"Stay low," he said, then he eased himself up and looked down.

The basket was level with the roof now. They'd never be able to scramble out in time to reach it. Worse, he could see two sets of fingers gripping the last row of the wicker. The brown pant legs swinging below told him who had tried to stop the balloon.

"Let go, Bateman!" he shouted. "You'll hit the roof otherwise."

"Won't let you get away," Bateman shouted back.

"Beast!" Charlotte's voice below was anguished. "Please! Don't leave me!"

The fingers disappeared, the balloon swung, then slowly straightened.

Lydia managed to regain her feet. "Is he all right?"

Worth craned his neck, trying to see the ground, which was slowly fading. "I don't know.

He pulled himself to the center of the balloon, the heat from the brazier pulsing at his face. He had to think, to reason. Their lives depended on it.

Lydia was peering over the side, as if she hoped to find means of escape. "We're past the chimneypots," she reported, pressing one palm to the canvas of her coat.

Forty feet or more so quickly? They'd be in the hundreds shortly. The remaining coal in the fire would continue to heat the air for perhaps a half hour, based on previous experience. With the night air, the balloon would cool, at which point they would start to descend. The prevailing winds should be from the west, pushing them to the east. How far? Beyond London? Into Essex?

Or out over the unforgiving waters of the North Sea?

# CHAPTER SEVENTEEN

"What do we do?" Lydia asked.

For the first time since Worth had known her, her voice was small and quiet. Her eyes, on the other hand, had never looked larger, a vivid green against her face as her skin turned rosy in the light of the coals. For her sake, he would keep his probabilities to himself.

"Now we ride it out," he said. "The others will surely follow us as they can. Eventually, the temperature in the envelope will fall."

"And so will we," she murmured.

"It should be a gradual descent," he told her. "If we land on a field or park, we should be fine. A city could pose a problem."

"So would the North Sea."

He should have known she'd surmise the danger as well. She shivered as if she felt the chilly waters closing around her even now.

"You intended this balloon for long distance travel," she said when he didn't reply immediately. "Could we reach Belgium or France?"

The thought was unnerving. He resorted to levity. "That eager to meet Napoleon?"

"Better Napoleon than the bottom of the ocean," she countered.

"Ah, the trials of balloon flight. I suppose we should

have considered that before climbing aboard."

She raised her chin. "Well, I hardly expected to leave the ground. And I must protest Miss Pankhurst's assumption. I had nothing to do with the ropes breaking."

Interesting assumption indeed. Miss Pankhurst's assertion that a coal had burned through one of the ropes was clearly wrong. It would have taken a sustained touch of the burning coal, not a mere brush. Still, Lydia had been at the advantage. Inside the basket, she could have reached all four ropes faster than the others scurrying around the diameter. And no one could watch all the ropes at once. The evidence could point in her direction.

But he refused to believe it. Lydia wouldn't jeopardize the balloon, not when she'd worked so hard to bring their vision into reality.

So how had the ropes come free? Everyone on his team and his staff had proven their loyalty. Could there have been someone else in the garden? Bateman had been so sure he could control the space, that Worth would be safe there. They hadn't considered Lydia's safety.

"I believe you," he said. "We'll look into the matter when we return."

She rubbed her temple. "Good. Truly, it's been a beastly day. First that ridiculous meeting with John Curtis and then walking back to the house and now this."

Worth stilled, stomach dropping as if the balloon had suddenly jerked higher. "Curtis? Why would you meet with John Curtis?"

She waved a hand, setting the basket to swaying again. She clutched the rim. "Sorry."

"Never mind the balloon," Worth said, barely keeping his feet. "What about Curtis?"

She answered readily enough. "He sought me out at the lecture, while you were talking with Lord Halston. He invited me to meet him."

"At Gunter's," he realized. Though he knew they were in

the air, he felt as if a snake slithered up his pant leg.

"Yes," Lydia said. "He claimed he wanted to help with the balloon, but he wasn't much use if you ask me."

Curtis understood what they were working on? "How did he know about the balloon?"

She met his gaze with a frown. "I assumed you had told him."

"No," he said. "I share nothing with John Curtis."

"Or anyone else, apparently," she said with a sigh. Immediately she stiffened. "What's wrong with me? I feel light-headed."

Worth glanced over the rim. Far to the west, a line of gold proclaimed the last moments of the sun. Everything below was in darkness, the sky around them growing black. He consulted his pocket watch, angling the mother-of-pearl face to reflect the red of the coals.

"We will have risen several hundred feet," he told her. "I doubt the altitude has affected us yet, but it will."

She sank to the floor of the basket with a thump that mounded her canvas coat around her. "I don't feel well."

Worth crouched beside her. Her face looked pale in the dim light, and her breaths were coming too fast. Hyperventilating, perhaps?

"Take a deep breath and let it out slowly," he advised, watching her.

She obeyed, her breath brushing his chin.

"Three more times," he urged.

Once more she obeyed.

"Better?" he asked.

She nodded. "Yes, thank you. But now I'm having trouble seeing."

Worth stood. "That's not the altitude. Night is falling."

"The temperatures will fall too." She swallowed a giggle. "Funny how many ways we've found to mention falling."

"That's the spirit." He offered her a hand and helped her climb to her feet. "The moon rose earlier today and is in the gibbous phase, so we should be able to spot it as soon as these clouds part." He nodded toward the east. "Right about there."

She squinted toward the milky section through the clouds. Enough light trickled out that he began to identify larger objects below as his eyes grew accustomed.

"So we'll be able to see when we fall," she said.

"So we'll be able to see how to steer," he replied.

Her brows went up. "Your propellers! Worth, this would be the perfect time to test them."

Once again, she turned calamity into opportunity. How could he fail to appreciate a woman like that?

"First we have to determine where we are," Worth told her. The clouds grudgingly parted then, and one rounded side of the fattening moon appeared, glowing like a pearl at a forty-five-degree angle above the balloon. Worth leaned over the rim, scanning what he could see of the ground for landmarks. The light gleamed off the silvery bend of the Thames. Tiny pricks of light, some clustered close together, spoke of inns, businesses that catered to the night.

"There," he said, pointing. "Where the Thames curves. That could be the Isle of Dogs."

She pressed against him. "Yes! It must be."

She was so close a curl tugged on the breeze brushed his chin and lavender teased his nose. He wanted to breathe it in, breathe her in.

He had to think!

"The River Lea joins it near the apex past the island," he said. "That spot is about an hour's ride outside London. We've covered that distance in less than a half hour, so we're moving at roughly twice the pace of a trotting horse, say ten miles an hour."

Lydia glanced up. "But we're still rising."

"And will be for another quarter hour, if my calculations are correct."

"I have read," she said, dropping her gaze to the brazier,

"that the winds aloft can travel faster and in different directions than those at ground level."

He'd read the same paper. "True."

"It's only forty miles from London to the North Sea," she pointed out. "At this rate, we should reach it before midnight or sooner."

Worth eyed the envelope above them. So much work had gone into it. All those tiny stitches. Just working with the fabric manufacturer to produce wider panels had proven challenging.

But he would never accomplish anything more important than protecting Lydia.

"There's nothing for it," he said. "We have to let in more cold air, force the balloon down sooner."

"How?" she asked. "We could throw out the last of the coal, but that wouldn't cool the air currently in the envelope. And there's no opening except the mouth."

"We'll have to make one," he said. "We'll have to puncture the balloon and pray."

Lydia clutched Worth's arm. He was prepared to sacrifice everything he'd tried to achieve?

"No!" she protested. "All your hard work, all Miss Pankhurst's meticulous stitches. There must be another way."

He frowned up at the envelope as if trying to find one. "Could we turn the mouth, I wonder?"

"Yes," Lydia encouraged him. "Perhaps use the bellows to fan colder air inside?"

He seemed to be considering it, face tight and mouth working. His gaze snapped down to hers.

"A quarter hour," he said. "If we haven't begun to descend by then, we'll have to take more drastic measures."

"Agreed," she said.

They set to work.

Lydia pried off pieces of Miss Janssen's insulation to cover her and Worth's hands, and together they seized the brazier. Heat built as they tugged it out of place, then tipped the coals over the edge of the basket.

"We'll have to reset it," he said. "It's too hot to risk against the wicker, and I'd hate to drop it onto someone's roof. At least the coals should have cooled before they reach the ground."

Her hand stung all the more, but she managed to help him replace the now-empty brazier.

The neck of the envelope had been left open to allow the heated air to enter. Worth took hold of the fabric now, twisted it toward the breeze to make a funnel. Once more, Lydia took hold of the bellows. With each pump, her arms ached, her burnt skin protested. Without the coals to warm the space, the air grew colder. She still broke out in a sweat.

She must have made a noise over the creak and whoosh of the bellows, for Worth nudged her foot with his. "Are you all right?"

Lydia gritted her teeth a moment, then squared her shoulders. "Fine," she made herself say in her sunniest voice.

He must have accepted that, for his shadow outline moved toward the rim.

"Still rising," he reported. He resumed his spot at the mouth, arms tensed to hold it where she could reach it.

Lydia worked the bellows faster, until her arms began to cramp. By the way his coat bunched, his lean legs braced, Worth was straining to hold the fabric open and wide. Perhaps she should have agreed to his first suggestion. But to destroy the envelope?

"What happens if we must damage the fabric?" Lydia asked. "Will we have time to repair things before the demonstration to His Highness?"

"We must," he said, and she could have built a castle on

the determination in his voice.

Just then clouds gathered, sending the moon into hiding, and darkness wrapped around them. She could barely make out Worth's shape next to her. He groaned, and the balloon swerved as he must have lowered his arms.

"Are we still rising?" Lydia asked, dropping her arms as well.

"I can't tell," he admitted. "I failed to factor in the clouds. Without the moon or the coals, I can't track the hour or determine a safe place to land. Forgive me, Lydia. I seemed to have failed you multiple times this evening." She heard the rustle of cloth then a thump as he sat on the floor of the balloon, setting it to swaying once more.

She slid down to sit beside him. The basket tilted with all their weight on one side, but she couldn't care.

"You didn't fail me, Worth," she said. "You don't have it in you to fail."

He snorted. "I fail to meet my own expectations on a far-too-regular basis."

"You aren't the only one," Lydia told him. "I am the sister of one of Society's most noted scoundrels. I was counseled never to let a gentleman know I had intelligence lest I be branded a dreaded bluestocking. Society expected very little of me. Certainly no one expected me to marry someone like you."

"So why did you try?"

The words were curious, as if their courtship had happened to someone else, long ago. She couldn't quite make herself think that way. Still, she had to answer him.

"I tried because Beau said I should. And because I hoped, I dreamed, that you might show interest."

"A viscount is not the loftiest of titles," he argued. "Why not set your sights on a marquess? A duke?"

"Oh, Beau threw me at several. But I couldn't love them."

His body shifted, as if her words made him uncomfortable. "Was love part of the equation?"

"Not for Beau," Lydia confessed. "But I kept hoping. Surely, somewhere among the *ton* was a man who would not only satisfy my brother's longing to see me marry into the aristocracy but gladden my heart as well. It didn't take long before I realized the odds were against me. You would probably have given me a ten percent chance of success. So, imagine my delight when the man I most admired showed every indication that he admired me too."

He was quiet, and she wanted to swallow her words. Perhaps it was the cover of darkness, perhaps the fact they did not know what was coming, but sharing her thoughts was too easy tonight.

"Who was he?" he asked at last. "This man you loved."

Lydia blinked. "Why, Worth, it was you. It's always been you. But I realize I wasn't the woman you wanted for your wife. I'm just glad you were willing to let me work beside you."

He twisted on the floor, pulled her into his arms, and kissed her.

Surprise swiftly melted into more—joy, delight, wonder. She kissed him back, for all the times she'd dreamed of him, for all the time they'd lost. Tomorrow he would likely come to his senses. This moment, this closeness, might be all she had.

He drew back, finger tracing the curve of her jaw, her cheek. "I wish I'd understood that a year ago."

Lydia sighed. "Would it have made a difference?"

He dropped his hand. "Perhaps not. We each had things that gave us pause. You doubted a gentleman would wish to marry you because of your brother. I doubted my ability to choose a bride."

Lydia frowned. "Why? You're intelligent and reasonable."

"Not when it comes to people. I have chosen unsuitable staff, trusted men who only meant me harm. So when it was brought to my attention that you were after a title, I thought I'd fallen prey to my own inabilities again."

Lydia lay her head against his shoulder. As if he relished the contact as well, his arm stole around her waist.

"Miss Janssen told me she'd shared my brother's nature with Miss Pankhurst," Lydia murmured. "She had hoped you would love her, you see."

"Miss Janssen?" Surprise lightened his voice. "I would never have guessed. You see how easily I misjudge motivations? A shame I didn't realize the truth, about her and you."

Lydia grimaced. "Beau was rather notorious about thrusting me at any gentleman he thought might take notice. It is all too easy for people to expect the worst of me."

His fingers groped for hers, and she flinched. Immediately he pulled back. "Lydia? Have I offended you?"

"No," she told him. "I had a slight mishap with the coal. When the first rope snapped, the brazier tilted, and I had to remove a burning coal before it damaged the flooring."

He took her hand, held it gently. "You were burned, and still you worked."

The awe in his voice made her sound a saint. "You should have seen me with Gussie. I had hives more than once trying our preparations."

"Never again," he promised. Then he sighed. "Help me, Lydia. I want to resume where we left off, if you're willing, but I have too much evidence that I trust too easily."

Was that fear? How extraordinary. She would never have thought it possible. But she would not discourage his change of heart. If he did not trust it, perhaps she should resort to what he did trust.

"You use evidence to estimate probable outcomes," she said. "It sounds as if you were unaware of certain evidence in the past, making you misjudge the results."

"Yes." He said the word so cautiously it might as well have been maybe.

"Allow me to give you more evidence. Since joining

your household, have I ever flirted to gain an advantage over you?"

"Never." Now he almost sounded disappointed.

Lydia smiled in the dark. "Have I worked unstintingly toward our success?"

"Yes." This time the word was firm in his convictions.

"Then I believe I have proven myself trustworthy."

"Indeed," he said, and the word held a world of certainty. So did his look as he gazed fixedly at her. The breeze ruffled his hair. She could imagine running her fingers through those auburn locks.

Lydia blinked. "I can see your face."

His gaze flew upward. "The moon's out. Time to save our lives."

# CHAPTER EIGHTEEN

W orth climbed to his feet and helped Lydia up beside him. What a wonder she was. The breeze brushed her curls back from her face, and her eyes lit at the sights below them. No matter how deep the conversation, how great the danger, she remained focused on what was important. At moments like this, he could only think he had been mad to ever doubt her.

"Worth, look!" she cried. "We're lower."

Indeed they were. In fact, they were dropping rather quickly. They passed a church steeple, the cross gilded by moonlight. He could make out brick chimney stacks, tiled rooftops. Beyond, a pond sparkled like a mirror. And farther yet, on what was likely the main road east, the bobbing lights of a carriage moved far too fast for the dark night.

Worth pointed. "That may well be Charlotte and the others. Quickly, now. Look for a place to put down."

She seemed to accept the implication that he could force the balloon to land where he chose. Would that he had such confidence. Too many factors played a role—the direction and velocity of the wind as they neared the ground, the terrain, the weight. Still, he had more belief in their ability to land than in what else he must do tonight.

"There!" she cried, pointing. "That field. It's broad enough and flat enough that we should be able to land safely."

And it was near nothing larger than a hedgerow with no body of water close by. Perfect.

"Come over here," Worth said, edging around the basket.

Lydia joined him, and the basket sagged to the north, tugging at the envelope secured to it. He took Lydia's hand and eased along the rim, until the greatest drag was against the wind. The balloon slowed its flight.

Now came the more dangerous part. Worth released her. "Stay here." When she looked at him askance, he bent and kissed her, quick and firm. Her eyes were wide as he pulled back.

"If anything happens, Lydia," he said, "know that I have always cared about you."

He grabbed the propeller and began cranking. The cedar paddles turned, fast, faster. His arms informed him he had overexerted himself. He ignored them.

The balloon swerved, and he lost his balance, tumbling down as the empty brazier fell with a clang.

"Worth!" she cried.

"Stay where you are," he ordered, scrambling to his feet. He grasped the next propeller, set it whirling even as the other spun to a stop. When the balloon twisted this time, he was ready for it.

He would see this landed. Lydia's life depended on it.

Lydia clung to the rim, gaze on Worth. No captain on the bridge of his ship, ordering his men to fight the storm that threatened to drown them, had ever moved so fast. He ran from propeller to propeller, tugging here, pushing there. The balloon darted like a bird in flight. She blinked and saw the top of a tree pass the basket, branches out as if to catch the bright fabric. Grasping the rim, she stared down at the ground.

They were close. The moon still held strong enough that

she could see the waving grain below. They would likely
have to compensate some farmer for his loss, but far better
to land in that green sea than the chilly waters awaiting
them farther out.

"Almost there," she called. "A little to the right."

He started laughing. "This isn't a carriage, Lydia. I can't
turn the horses to dodge through traffic."

"I think you're doing marvelously," Lydia assured him.
"To the right!"

He cranked on a propeller. Then he released his hold and
ran to her side.

"Down," he ordered, crouching and pulling her with
him. He wrapped his arms around her, bent his head over
hers, shielding her with his body. Lydia clung to him and
said a prayer.

The basket struck hard, jarring every bone in her body.
It bounced up, then came down again, the impact rattling
her teeth. The wicker cracked to one side of Worth and
broke open, reeds poking free. Worth grunted as a piece
slashed past him.

At last the basket shuddered and lay still, the envelope
sagging toward them until it blocked the light from the
moon.

"Quickly," Worth said, unfolding himself from around
her. "Before the fabric falls." He scrambled over the rim,
then reached in and helped her out. Together, they ran
away from the slumping envelope.

Worth stopped a dozen yards beyond, and Lydia turned
with him to look back. Like butter on a hot roll, the
envelope was melting over the basket, until all she could
see was scarlet, dark in the moonlight.

"Well," Worth said, dusting off his hands. "That's done."

"Can it be saved?" Lydia asked, feeling as if she'd left a
part of herself in the basket.

"We'll have to rebuild the wicker," Worth said, gaze
on the balloon as well. "Check the fabric for any strain.

Possibly reconfigure the brazier. But yes, I believe we will be able to salvage the balloon."

She felt like sagging as well. "Oh, good." She took a step away from him, and the enormity of what they'd just experienced hit her. They might have lost all opportunity to prove his work to the prince. He might have been killed. She might have been killed. She swayed on her feet.

Worth caught her, cradled her against him. "Easy. Our colleagues will be here shortly."

Lydia nodded. With his arms around her, his voice murmuring near, she could draw breath. They were alive. She sent a word of thanks heavenward.

"I realize I've put you in a difficult position," he said thoughtfully. "You and I have been alone together, for hours. Your reputation will be compromised."

Lydia snuggled against him. "Good thing I'm no longer on the marriage mart."

His arms tightened around her, as if he would keep her safe from any calamity. "I cannot be so sanguine. The *ton* is not kind to those who decide to leave it. I would not see you shunned, Lydia. This incident tonight is at least partly my fault for failing to foresee all the potential outcomes and taking steps to mitigate them."

"No one can think of everything," Lydia said, warm in his embrace. Was that his heart she heard beating against her ear? Such a firm, comforting sound.

"Nevertheless, I take responsibility," he insisted. "It would be best if we married."

Lydia's eyes popped open. "What did you say?"

"That I take responsibility for the night's problems."

She pulled away from him. It might have been the moonlight, but he seemed to have paled. He certainly did not look like a man intent on proposing to the woman he adored.

"Not that part," Lydia said. "The other part. Did you just ask me to marry you?"

He grimaced, and her heart sank faster than the balloon. "Technically, I advised you of my intention to remedy the situation. That is what a gentleman does under such circumstances."

A gentleman, not a man in love. He had said he had always cared, but not enough, it seemed. Not for her were the tender words, the yearning glances.

"I see," she said, taking a deep breath. "Thank you for your concern, but you need have none for me. Everyone assumed I'd compromise myself sooner or later. Now it's done, and I can get on with my life."

He blinked. "Are you refusing me?"

"Yes," Lydia said, though a part of her protested. "I am."

He was gaping. Really, it began to be insulting. Did he think she couldn't see what he was trying to do?

"Admit it, Worth," she said. "You don't want to marry me. I would never take advantage of the situation to force it on you."

His hands disappeared around his back. "Some would counsel you to."

"Beau? Certainly. My brother would be beyond delighted if he learned of this, which is why neither of us is going to tell him." She made her gaze as stern as possible and hoped he could see it in the dim light.

"You astound me," he said. "I endanger your life with this balloon. I kiss you not once but twice. You have every right to demand to know my intentions, to insist that I offer marriage. Yet when I do, you do nothing to seize the prize."

"A person, Lord Worthington," Lydia said, "is not a prize to be won, despite what my brother thinks."

He flinched, but Lydia's gaze went past him to where a light bounced at the edge of the field. Voices called on the breeze.

"Oh, look," she made herself say. "There's Charlotte. We're saved."

For the life of her, she couldn't understand why that fact didn't make her happier.

Lydia picked up her skirts and waded through the grain, voice raised in answer to Charlotte's frantic calls. Worth couldn't make himself follow. It was as if the balloon of his world had tilted, sending him tumbling into thin air.

Despite his misgivings, despite his concerns, despite his doubt in his own abilities, he had proposed to the most fascinating, captivating woman he'd ever met. A woman who had claimed to have once loved him.

And she'd turned him down, even knowing her reputation would be in rags and she could well be lost to all good Society.

How ironic. He now knew that Lydia could be trusted to look out for his best interests. He could trust her with his heart. She simply no longer wanted it.

He made himself trudge across the field in her wake.

"Oh, Worth." Charlotte hugged him tight as soon as he was in reach as Bateman, holding a lantern, gave him a nod of obvious relief. "Are you all right?"

"Fine," Worth told his sister. "And I believe the balloon can be salvaged."

"The balloon?" Charlotte disengaged and glared at him. "The *balloon*? Beast might have been killed trying to save you, but do you think to ask after him?"

Worth frowned as his bodyguard shifted on his feet. "Bateman came with you, evidence enough that he took no serious harm. But I am pleased to see him."

"You'll be less pleased to see that lot," Bateman said with a nod across the field to where more lanterns bobbed. "Someone's noticed us."

"I'll pay fair restitution for whatever damage I've caused," Worth told him.

Bateman nodded. "Right. Get into the carriage, and I'll make the arrangements."

Charlotte lay a hand on his arm to stop him. "What if it's dangerous?"

"I'm not afraid of a farmer," Bateman said. Then he grinned. "Especially not when I have his lordship's money to spend. Go on, now. I'll be back shortly."

Worth offered Lydia his arm, but she linked arms with Charlotte as they waded through the last portion of grain for the road beyond, where Petersham waited with the horses.

Charlotte peppered Lydia with questions as they waited for Bateman, and Lydia cheerfully answered. Not once did her gaze touch his. It was almost as if he had ceased to exist.

He shuddered at the thought, and Charlotte glanced his way where he sat across the coach from them.

"I should have thought to ask," his sister said. "Are you hurt? Cold? We have blankets and medical supplies."

"I was struck by a piece of wicker and will likely have a bruise," Worth told her. "See to Lydia's hand. She burnt it on a hot coal."

Lydia's smile remained bright as Charlotte transferred her attention to her. "A minor mishap, but a bit of cream and a bandage would not be remiss."

Charlotte pulled out a case from where it had been stored under her legs and opened it to reveal various ointments, bandages, and polished wood strips that would likely serve as splints for broken bones.

"When did you put this together?" he asked as his sister drew out a jar of cream and a long bandage strip.

"When I realized you were intent on pursuing work that could maim or burn you," Charlotte said.

"Very wise," Lydia said. She peeled back her glove with a grimace. In the glow of the carriage lamps, he could see the misshapen red patch across her palm and fingers.

Charlotte tsked as she spread ointment on the spot. "We must find a better way to handle the coals."

"Agreed," Lydia said. "I'm just glad this was the worst of our injuries."

Charlotte closed the jar and set it back among the others. Worth took up the bandage.

"Allow me."

Lydia's eyes widened as he reached across and gently took her hand. So small, so fragile, yet so capable. He wrapped the bandage carefully, then slipped the end through the folds on the back of her hand to hold the linen steady. Glancing up, his gaze met hers at last.

He might not understand people, but he knew tenderness when he saw it. As if afraid of what she had revealed, Lydia pulled back her hand and looked away.

The door opened before Worth could speak, and Bateman climbed in to sit beside him.

"You'll be getting a bill shortly," he told Worth. "But Farmer Tremont agreed to watch the balloon until we can fetch it." He thumped on the ceiling, and the carriage set off, swaying over the uneven ground.

Charlotte put away the case. "Treacherous balloon. I still don't understand how it broke free."

"It had help." Bateman's voice was grim. "I had just enough time before we pulled out the carriage to tell that the ropes didn't snap under the strain. They were cut."

Lydia cradled her hand close and made him wish he could do the same. "Who would cut the ropes?"

Bateman crossed his arms over his chest. "That's what I want to know."

"As I doubt you allowed a stranger on the premises," Worth said, "I'd say someone on the staff is out to stop us. And that person is in league with John Curtis."

"John Curtis," Charlotte cried, head snapping up.

"Of course!" Lydia cried. "How else could he have learned about the balloon?"

"Someone else knows?" Bateman glanced between them.

Worth nodded. "Curtis took Lydia aside at the Halston lecture and asked her to meet him so he could question her further."

Charlotte stiffened. "Let me guess. Ices at Gunter's."

"Yes," Lydia admitted. "How did you know?"

Charlotte drew in a breath, then sat taller. "Because he tried the same tactic with me. He approached me at the Baminger ball and begged me to meet him at Gunter's the next day so he could mend the rift between him and Worth."

"Mend the rift," Lydia echoed. "His exact words."

Worth shook his head. "The dastard. If he wanted to make things up to me, he could have approached me directly."

"Well," Charlotte said, "you did make that rather hard, Worth. You refused to see him when he called and gave him the cut direct at Lady Baminger's ball. But I'm ashamed to say I believed his heartfelt pleas. I agreed to meet, then quickly became overset thinking how you'd react if you'd discovered my plan. I'm the one who told him we were working on a balloon."

Worth stared at her. "Why? You knew what he'd done."

"I knew he published your work as his own," Charlotte said.

Lydia gasped. "What?"

"I thought perhaps it had been a mistake," Charlotte immediately protested. "He certainly acted as if he wanted to make amends. And he said certain things that made me think he had interests other than making amends."

"What interests?" Bateman asked, voice no more than a growl.

Charlotte raised her chin. "Nothing that was real or important. After a few moments in his company, it became clear his only interest was in Worth's work. I begin to think he has no ideas of his own, only what he gleans from associates. He cares for no one and nothing but achieving further glory."

She sounded so bitter. Had Curtis dared dally with her, attempted to convince her he cared about her? For the first time in his life, Worth wanted to hit someone. Lydia must have heard the same thing he did, for she put a hand on Charlotte's arm in obvious support.

He prided himself on his mental abilities, but what a fool he'd been. Charlotte had been friendly with John Curtis when the man had been working with Worth. Perhaps she'd hoped for more than a friendship. Most of the men who had once courted her had fallen away, he had assumed because Charlotte had not encouraged them to stay. Perhaps it hadn't been Charlotte but her intellectual pursuits that had deterred them. Until Lydia had returned to his life, Worth had never considered how difficult it must be for a lady of their class to indulge in natural philosophy. If Charlotte had married Curtis, she might have been able to continue her studies.

"I'm sorry, Charlotte," he murmured. "This has been a mess all around. We'll avoid Curtis, focus on our work."

Charlotte sighed. "I fear that's your response to every difficulty."

Once more Worth frowned, but Bateman bumped his shoulder. "You're forgetting something."

"What?" Worth demanded.

"Your sister may have told this Curtis fellow about your balloon, but she wasn't the one who cut the ropes."

"Certainly not," Charlotte agreed.

Bateman nodded. "That means there's someone else out to harm your work, my lord, perhaps the same person sending those notes. Until you know who, you better not bring the balloon home."

# CHAPTER NINETEEN

M eredith set aside the novel she'd been reading and went to the window. Fortune ran ahead to jump up on the sill. Pulling back the thick drape and cracking the shutters, Meredith joined her pet in gazing out into the night. Carriages, lamps a warm glow, trundled past, taking the fine ladies and gentlemen of Clarendon Square to a ball, soiree, play, or opera. Her feet twitched in her lavender-colored satin slippers. As if she felt it, Fortune glanced up at her.

"I have no wish to join them," Meredith assured her. "I had entirely enough of Society with Lady Winhaven. All the gossip, all the snide remarks. It's rather refreshing not to have to pretend I care."

Fortune's tail swished back and forth, brushing the velvet of the drape.

"Well," Meredith allowed. "I do miss the opera. Perhaps we could go sometime. That place isn't the sole possession of the *haut ton*. All we need is the price of admission."

Fortune's ears perked, and she pressed closer to the glass. Meredith saw it too. A carriage had pulled up below, the driver holding the horses steady while his passenger alighted with a swirl of a black evening cloak. From a story above, it was impossible to see who it was, but that confident walk told her who was coming to call a moment before he looked up at her window and the gaslight illuminated his dear face.

Julian.

She jerked back before he could spot her. Heartbeat speeding, she made herself close the shutters, return to the sofa, and pick up her book as if she had nothing more important to do.

Fortune had no such need to impress. At the sound of the knock, she was out the door to greet their guest. Meredith smiled a welcome as Cowls and Fortune ushered Julian into the room a few moments later. Her butler must have taken his cloak and top hat, for he looked splendid in his evening black, shirt points crisp and cravat elegantly tied.

"I didn't expect you this time of night," Meredith said as he inclined his head in greeting.

"I found my evening's engagements less than engaging." He came to join her on the sofa. "I saw your light and hoped you might be willing to receive me."

Always, but perhaps it would be best if she didn't admit that out loud. She had been enamored of Julian since she was nine and he a lordly thirteen. One Christmas when she was sixteen, she'd done all she could to catch him under the kissing bough, sure that one touch of their lips would convince him they were meant for each other. Whether it was the kiss they'd shared or the clamoring of their hearts, she had never been sure, but Julian had declared his undying devotion that day. If only she could believe him so besotted now.

"You are very welcome," she said as Fortune jumped up between them. "We had no plans for the evening."

As if to agree with her, Cowls ambled out of the room and left them alone.

Meredith frowned after him. He was getting on in years, for all she tried not to remember. But surely he wouldn't forget the need for a chaperone. Fortune, now rubbing her head against Julian's leg, hardly signified in the eyes of the *ton.*

Then again, Meredith was no longer considered a member of the *ton*, having put herself beyond the pale by opening her own business. Being accused of murder hadn't helped. And she knew she could trust Julian to behave as a gentleman.

Perhaps too much a gentleman?

He did not look the least at ease. Rather than lean against the curved back of the sofa, he sat upright, hands each gripping a knee of his black satin breeches. One foot tapped at the carpet, the silver buckle on his evening pump flashing in the firelight.

Meredith cocked her head. "What's wrong?"

His head came up, eyes on her face but in a rather vague manner, as if he wasn't seeing her at all. "Nothing. Why do you ask?"

Lies? She'd thought better of him. Her spirits slumped with her shoulders. "You've changed your mind."

He blinked. "My mind?"

"About pursuing this courtship. You've come to break things off."

Julian shook his head. "I have no intention of breaking things off. I remain your most devoted servant."

She didn't believe him. Neither did Fortune, for she pulled back to align herself with Meredith.

"So devoted, sir," Meredith said, "that you refuse to be seen publicly with me, that you feel it best to sneak into my home in the dead of night lest someone spot us together."

He grimaced, and she felt heavier still.

Meredith waved her hand, and Fortune hunkered lower. "Go, then. I suppose it was too much to hope. Between the scandal with Lady Winhaven and my audacity to ply a trade, I'm a rock weighing down your ambitions."

"That," he said, eyes lighting at last, "is nonsense."

"Is it?" Meredith challenged. "You were invited to more than one engagement this evening. I wasn't."

"You were invited to the Lady Lilith's wedding," he

countered. "I wasn't."

"Only because Lydia is my client and friend," Meredith insisted.

His mouth hinted of a smile. "If all your friends end up marrying into the aristocracy, you won't have to worry about being accepted long."

"But you do worry," Meredith said. "You have since Eton. You like the acceptance of your friends, Julian. I could threaten that."

He took her hand, held it in both of his, the touch sending a tremor through her, even as Fortune jumped down and disappeared under her skirts.

"Then perhaps I have the wrong sort of friends," Julian murmured.

How easy to slip into his smile, float in the admiration shining from his eyes. But her mother had once warned her Julian thought more for his future than hers. She hadn't believed the claim then. She feared it now.

"Julian, I would not have you regret our association," she told him. "More than anything, I want you to be happy."

"And I am convinced I can only be happy with you at my side, my dear Mary."

She pulled away from him. "I'm not Mary Rose. I'm Meredith Thorn. The girl you knew vanished ages ago. Can you love the woman she became?"

"With all my heart." He leaned forward and kissed her.

And all at once, her fears, her frustrations, melted, to be replaced by a joy and a wonder as deep as the first time he'd kissed her. Here were her dreams, her future. Here was love. Why couldn't they stay this way, always?

Something pressed against her leg, her chest, insistent, demanding. Meredith broke the kiss, and Julian leaned back. Fortune stood between them, tail slashing and ears back.

Julian rose and bowed to her pet. "I beg your pardon, Fortune. You are quite right to chastise me for my behavior.

I should go."

Disappointment pushed her to her feet. "So soon?"

If Julian heard the desperation as clearly as she did, he didn't show it. "Forgive me, Meredith. I can see I've given you the wrong impression of my feelings for you. I will rectify matters. I may not have the opportunity for tea the next few days, but rest assured I will return as soon as possible." He inclined his head and turned for the door.

Meredith took a step forward, to do what, she wasn't sure. Fortune jumped from the sofa and positioned herself directly in front of her, only to sit and begin licking one delicate paw as Julian left.

Meredith bent to pick up her pet, smoothing her hand over the silky fur. "I don't know whether to thank you or scold you."

Fortune's mouth turned up, showing her sharp, white teeth, as if she'd known exactly what she'd been doing.

If only Meredith felt the same.

The next day, Lydia stepped back from where Worth and Bateman were settling the balloon in the rear garden.

"It will be safe here, Miss Villers," Marbury promised.

The tall, imposing dark-haired butler with his hawk-like nose had managed Carrolton Park, the former home of her new sister-in-law Lilith. He had been brought to London to set up the house where Lilith and Beau would reside when they returned from their honeymoon. The three-story brick house just off Clarendon Square had a walled garden behind it and had been a gift from Lilith's brother, the Earl of Carrolton, someone Worth trusted from longstanding. It hadn't been difficult for Lydia to convince him this might be the safest place to hide the balloon until they determined who was out to destroy it.

"We know you will safeguard the balloon," she told

Marbury. "It shouldn't be long. Lord Worthington will come to remove it as soon as he can."

Once he had assured himself of his team's loyalty.

Charlotte was already at the Worthington houses assembling the others. Lydia rode back in the carriage with Worth and Bateman. Though the bodyguard kept glancing between her and Worth as if unsure what to make of them, she was glad for his company. Since Worth had proposed, and she had refused, they had not had time for private conversation. In truth, she wasn't sure what remained to be said.

He had admitted he feared that he did not choose the right people as associates. Certainly he'd been used most cruelly by John Curtis, who had claimed friendship, a desire to work together, before betraying Worth. To publish Worth's work as his own! She could imagine little more devastating to a natural philosopher. Small wonder Worth had been so leery of trusting again. He could only see the trouble with the balloon as further evidence of his inability to determine the truth about the people around him.

But when they were all gathered in Charlotte's study, Miss Pankhurst and Miss Janssen seemed just as appalled by the idea that one of them was a traitor.

"Who would attempt to damage our balloon?" Miss Janssen cried from her place on the sofa, glancing around as if seeking a suspect among the books and instruments. "So hard we all worked."

"Perhaps the balloon wasn't the intended target," Miss Pankhurst put in from where she sat beside Charlotte at the table.

Charlotte frowned at her. "Then what was?"

Miss Pankhurst's hands fluttered. "Goodness, how would I know? I have heard, however, that in such circumstances, one should look at who benefits. Certainly Miss Janssen and I had no reason to risk the balloon on a moonlit ride."

Miss Janssen nodded her broad head so vigorously both

chins disappeared.

Charlotte glanced to Lydia. "True."

Lydia felt as if she'd stepped into a stream, cold shooting from her toes to her top. "I didn't make off with the balloon. The ropes were cut."

Miss Pankhurst tsked. "You needn't dissemble, dear. We all know who cut them."

The villain! With each statement, she dropped crumbs that marked a trail leading straight to Lydia. And Worth, dear Worth, would follow the trail all too easily, not believing in his ability to do otherwise.

She glanced at him now. His brows were down, his eyes narrowed, and his mouth tight. Her heart sank.

He steepled his fingers under his chin. "Let us put aside Miss Villers for the moment. Why else would anyone seek to delay our work?"

"Jealousy," Miss Janssen said readily, with a look to Lydia. "I myself was bitter once, though I never compromised the work."

"Jealousy," Worth mused. "Of what?"

"Of whom," Charlotte corrected him. "We know Mr. Curtis was too interested in you and your work."

"Mr. Curtis?" Miss Pankhurst asked. She too turned to Lydia with a smile that was patently false. "Isn't he the man you dined with, dear, just before the balloon met with its mishap?"

Such venom. Lydia had been greeted by it many times, generally from other young ladies intent on making a match, but never when the stakes were so high. If Miss Pankhurst convinced Worth, everything Lydia had worked for would be lost.

Still, she knew only one way to counter such despicable behavior. With a sunny smile.

"Why, yes," she admitted. "I met with Mr. Curtis. He claimed to want to help with the balloon. I already explained the matter to Lord Worthington."

"Indeed," Worth said, gaze going to Miss Pankhurst over his fingers. "In a private conversation held hundreds of feet in the air and miles from London. I seem to recall you knew the meeting was at Gunter's as well. How did you learn of it, Miss Pankhurst?"

Now her lashes fluttered with her hands. "Why, Miss Villers told me."

"I most certainly did not," Lydia declared.

She dropped her hands. "Of course you did. You needn't posture. You wouldn't be the first to be taken in by his promises."

Charlotte blanched.

"So he took you in as well, did he?" Worth asked Miss Pankhurst.

Lydia started, even as Miss Pankhurst pursed her little lips.

"Why," she asked brightly, "what would a gentleman of Mr. Curtis's standing want with a mere companion like me?"

Charlotte was staring at her. "Because he assumed a companion would be as hungry as any spinster for attention. Oh, Miss Pankhurst, not you too?"

She raised her chin. "I have no idea what you're talking about."

Miss Janssen turned to Charlotte. "It can't be true. Mr. Curtis is a gentleman, even if he has shown himself to lack honor. Why would he pursue an old spinster?"

"I'm younger than you," Miss Pankhurst snapped, chin dropping. "And some gentlemen are wise enough to realize that with a certain age comes knowledge and skill."

"And the eagerness to have others recognize it," Lydia agreed.

She rounded on her. "You see! I knew you would understand. Confess now, Miss Villers, and I daresay Lord Worthington will go easy on you. That's how most men react to your blandishments, isn't it?"

Just when Lydia thought the woman hung, she threw off her noose and dropped it neatly about Lydia's neck. She couldn't swallow, couldn't breathe.

Didn't dare glance at Worth, for fear of what she would see. If he had believed the worst about her a year ago on a mere story from Miss Pankhurst, how could he do less now?

# CHAPTER TWENTY

Anger made Worth's face hot, his throat tight. Why did he continue to be plagued by the betrayal of those closest to him? Did they think him stupid, weak? Had he no reason, no character capable of seeing perfidy?

And how dare she try to point the finger at Lydia?

"Miss Pankhurst," he said. "Collect your things. We will have no further need of your services."

Both Miss Pankhurst and Miss Janssen stared at him. Lydia straightened, face lighting, but she clamped her pretty lips together as if to keep from speaking.

"I don't understand," Miss Pankhurst said, glancing at Charlotte as if for support. "I have ever given good service. Miss Worthington will vouch for my character."

"Once," Charlotte said, leaning back. "But I begin to see my brother's point. You have had several half days off recently. You knew where Miss Villers had been before she informed any of us."

"She told me!" the woman insisted.

"I can only conclude," Charlotte continued as if she hadn't spoken, "that Mr. Curtis offered you something more than we could provide. I hope it keeps you warm and fed, for I cannot in good conscience provide you with a reference."

All timidity and deference disappeared. Miss Pankhurst rose, nose up and mouth a sneer. "Why would I want a reference from you? No one in any good family would put stock in it, not after the stain of your ruin becomes common knowledge."

The woman landed punches better than Bateman. Worth felt as if he were reeling from a strike to the nose. Had he been so derelict in his duty to protect his sister?

"Charlotte," he said, "what is she talking about?"

"Nothing," Charlotte insisted, so fervently he could not doubt her. "Mr. Curtis and I met only in public. There is no shame in that."

Relief coursed through him. But Miss Pankhurst wasn't finished.

"No shame at all," she agreed. "But I have been your companion this last year. If I were to claim knowledge of secret meetings, some lasting overnight, I would be believed."

She might at that. Worth chilled at the thought. Charlotte certainly saw the danger, for she was turning white.

Lydia giggled, turning all eyes to her.

"Miss Pankhurst, you are so funny," she said, green eyes bright. "But attempted blackmail? No, no, you simply don't have it in you. As the sister of a man steeped in the art, perhaps I could give you a lesson." She rose and went to sit beside the woman, for all as if she was intent on having a good coz. Worth couldn't look away.

"In the first place," Lydia explained sweetly, "it is well known that Lord Worthington spends an inordinate amount of time at home, and Charlotte is his nearly constant companion. Surely he would have noticed if his sister was entertaining, particularly a man he is known to abhor. Likewise, he would have noticed if Charlotte was gone for any length of time."

"Quite right," Worth said. He wanted to grin at her flawless logic, but he was afraid of spoiling the effort. And he couldn't wait to see what else she said as Miss Pankhurst's face turned an ugly shade of red.

"Then there is your failure to deliver an ultimatum," Lydia continued with a shake of her head that set her ringlets to bouncing. "A good blackmailer demands payment that is not out of reach. You demanded nothing."

"Much like the last threatening note," Worth realized. "I wonder, if we compared the handwriting, would yours be a match?"

"Very close," Charlotte put in, blinking as if suddenly coming into the light. "I should have recognized it from her journal entries."

Miss Pankhurst's tiny mouth worked, but she kept her head high.

Lydia nodded. "I suspect the earlier notes you mentioned may have come from someone on Mr. Curtis's staff, but I wonder how much Miss Pankhurst knows about peat."

"Or a brick in the night," Worth mused.

Miss Pankhurst sniffed. "Oh, come now. I wasn't anywhere near the Royal Institution that night."

Worth met Lydia's gaze. "Or in the garden when I explained to Charlotte what had happened. But someone told you."

"Curtis," Charlotte grumbled. "The weasel."

Lydia turned once more to their traitorous colleague. "It seems you have much to atone for, Miss Pankhurst. What was your aim with this latest attempt at blackmail? A reference from Charlotte so you can continue your games in some other family? Certainly you wouldn't earn Lord Worthington's regard. That is what you hoped in the beginning, wasn't it, before you succumbed to Mr. Curtis's lures? Like Miss Janssen, like myself, you fancied yourself in love, and you thought you could endear yourself to him."

Miss Janssen flamed and dropped her gaze. Miss Pankhurst glared at Lydia.

"You are a wicked girl," she pronounced. "I knew the moment you came into this house you would be trouble. What gentleman can resist those flaxen curls, those big innocent eyes? Well, I am on to you, miss. You may think you've won, but Lord Worthington is clever. He saw through you once, and he will again."

Once he had disregarded Lydia, not realizing the gem he held. Worse, he had judged her on the word of another. What slim evidence. He knew the danger of relying on the word of one person. Each contributor to a project brought a bias, however unrealized, to the work. That's why experiments had to be replicated, results validated. He'd had such poor evidence of his own abilities that he had easily believed he had been wrong again. The fault hadn't lain with Lydia. It had always been inside him.

And what evidence did he have now?

His own skills had not much improved. He had missed Miss Pankhurst's perfidy entirely. He hadn't noticed that both she and Miss Janssen had set their caps at him, though he supposed that was to his credit. At least he wasn't vain. But he hadn't realized that Curtis was digging away at the edges of his work, like a rat trying to find its way into a storeroom.

Still, now he understood Lydia better. Forced to compete on the marriage mart, she had done so with goodwill and charm. She had never set out to harm anyone. Since she had joined their team, she had worked beside him, never puffing herself up, always seeking answers. She had been kind and helpful to Charlotte, Miss Janssen, and even Miss Pankhurst, despite that lady's ongoing efforts to discredit her. She had attempted a reconciliation with Curtis, thinking only to advance their studies.

He may have a ways to go when it came to seeing true intentions, but he would be an idiot not to love a woman like that.

"Once more you are in error, Miss Pankhurst," he said, and they all looked at him, surprise evident in raised brows, open mouths. "Miss Villers has proven herself nothing but a godsend—to this work and to my life."

Lydia blushed, dropping her gaze to her hands. Miss Pankhurst's hands balled at her sides.

"You have no power over us," Worth told her. "Depart, and tell John Curtis, if he deigns to see you again, that he will have no part in our triumph. You'll both have to do your own work for once."

Miss Pankhurst rose, lips trembling. "My lord, you wouldn't be so unkind as to turn me away."

"If he doesn't," Charlotte said, crossing her arms over her chest and scowling in a neat imitation of Worth's bodyguard, "I will. Shall I have Mr. Bateman escort you out?"

The red that had inflamed Miss Pankhurst's cheeks fled with her bravado. "No need," she said, lowering her gaze. "I'll go."

She hurried from the room.

"You might want to follow her," Lydia advised Charlotte. "She may cause more trouble on the way out."

"And count the silver," Miss Janssen put in.

Charlotte rose and went after her former companion.

Miss Janssen sighed. "Such doings! Who would have thought her so devious?"

Lydia smiled at Worth. "Not everyone can see the wolf inside the fleece. It helps to have been raised with one."

Her brother's reputation had made it all too easy for him to believe the worst of her. Society had believed the worst as well. Though he and Lydia had had no time to discuss his proposal last night, he had begun to question the reason for her refusal. Indeed, he had ample evidence she felt strongly for him: the way she had reacted to his kiss, the look in her eyes when he'd bandaged her hand, her own admission that she had cared a year ago and still did.

So, why refuse him?

Did she doubt him as much as he'd doubted her? He'd given her ample evidence, not the least of which was his summary dismissal last year and his treatment of her when she first began working with his team. Miss Pankhurst wasn't the only one who had much to atone for.

They had weeks to prepare the balloon for the demonstration to the prince. The task was staggering. But his most important work would be to find a way to prove to Lydia once and for all that he loved her.

# CHAPTER TWENTY-ONE

Lydia stood with Charlotte on one side and Miss Janssen on the other as His Royal Highness and his retinue approached the balloon in the Green Park two weeks later. It had been a mad rush to repair everything and make ready for the demonstration.

Worth and Bateman had retrieved the balloon and set it up in the rear garden on the laboratory side. Once Charlotte and Worth had assured Miss Janssen her position was safe, she had set about rebuilding the wicker basket with a will. Charlotte had worked on expanding the brazier to accommodate a longer heating period, while Lydia took over management of the envelope.

"A poor use of your talents," Worth had said in apology. "But you have the most experience working closely on that task."

"And years spent on embroidery," Lydia had reminded him with a laugh. "Don't worry, Worth. I'm glad to be of use."

He'd given her a look, as if he'd longed to say more, but there had been no time for apologies or commiserations. After their adventure, it was clear the balloon required more lift, which meant not only a larger fire, but a bigger envelope.

Charlotte convinced the manufacturer to weave a large enough piece to add another panel, this time a vivid blue.

"Alas, they had no more of the scarlet," Worth had told Lydia when it had been delivered.

"I like it," Lydia had said, running a hand down the soft fabric. "It adds dash."

Worth had laughed.

She could grow to love that sound. A shame she could not convince herself he returned her love. The knowledge was a constant ache against their growing list of accomplishments.

Still, she had persevered, until everything was exactly as Worth had decreed. They had moved all the components to the Green Park near the top of Constitution Hill and reassembled them here only yesterday afternoon. Miss Janssen had helped Lydia spread the scarlet silk with its bold blue stripe across the green grass like a carpet. Through the trees that lined the distant edges of the sloping park, the red brick towers of St. James's Palace stood proud. No more proud than Worth as the envelope began to inflate. He and Bateman had stayed through the night to see the inflation completed.

Now the balloon stood tall, straining at the moorings, as a cavalcade headed their direction. Leading the way was a white-lacquered landau, hood pulled back and golden appointments gleaming, drawn by two perfectly matched white horses. Yeoman guards in their red and black uniforms marched on either side, pikes at the ready. Since the assassination of the prime minister, they appeared to be taking no chance with their illustrious liege. Other fine carriages followed. They all drew up a little way from the balloon.

Miss Janssen clutched Lydia's arm. "That's the prince!"

Indeed it was. Corpulent and slow-moving, His Royal Highness descended from the landau, navy tailored coat with a high collar framing the jowls of his face. Other men began appearing from the other carriages, and Lydia recognized several members of the Privy Council along with Julian Mayes, with whom her brother had worked on occasion on matters of utmost secrecy.

But it was the fellow hovering at the prince's elbow who gave her pause.

"What is Mr. Curtis doing here?" Charlotte demanded as that gentleman murmured something to the prince.

"Leeches always find something to cling to," Bateman predicted, tipping the last of the coal into the brazier with a puff of black dust.

Miss Janssen released Lydia. "I did not know leeches came in pairs."

Lydia followed her gaze. There, among the more than five dozen people staring at the balloon stood Miss Pankhurst, dressed in dainty ruffled muslin with a lace-edged parasol over her head, its tall point glinting in the sun. She looked entirely frivolous.

Lydia did not. She had dressed her best for the occasion, in a gown of fine muslin striped in lavender and white and sprigged with clusters of violets. Enid had flattered her curls into a bun behind her head and covered it with a narrow hat of purple velvet with a white ostrich plume in the lavender satin band. She rather thought she looked like someone to be reckoned with. She could only hope their audience, including Miss Pankhurst, would agree.

Worth, in a black coat and dun trousers, consulted his new chronometer, then snapped shut the gold case and stepped forward to address the group.

"Your Highness, ladies and gentlemen, thank you for joining us today. With His Highness's kind encouragement, we have been working to advance the science of ballooning."

"Distance and weight," John Curtis put in a few feet away from the prince and his guards. "I saw them as key from the beginning."

Charlotte glared.

"Ingenious," the prince said, gaze going to the balloon.

Charlotte nudged Lydia, and all three ladies dipped curtseys. The prince inclined his ponderous head before turning to Curtis. "And you're certain it's safe? I've read of some nasty explosions in France."

"In *France*," Curtis said with a curl of his lip. "I can assure His Highness that no English balloon under my leadership will ever explode."

"An excellent promise," Worth said. "Remind me to come see the balloon built under your leadership." He turned to the prince. "Your Highness, the balloons that exploded were filled with hydrogen. We used hot air only."

"English air," Curtis qualified.

Worth ignored him. "With your kind permission, I would like to make known the members of my team."

Once more the prince inclined his head. "Delighted."

Worth nodded toward their group. Lydia, Charlotte, and Miss Janssen stood taller. So did Bateman.

"You will remember my sister, Miss Worthington. She worked tirelessly to ensure the fire would warm the air to fill the envelope. Miss Janssen wove our fine basket, capable of carrying no less than three hundred pounds aloft for hours."

His Highness looked impressed. Mr. Curtis shifted. Lydia could only hope he was squirming like the worm he was.

"To the side, there, is Mr. Matthew Bateman," Worth continued. "He provided invaluable service to support all our efforts."

The prince squinted at Bateman, then brightened. "I say, I know the fellow. The Beast of Birmingham, what? I've seen him fight." He raised his voice. "Well done, Beast. The fellow deserved what he got."

Bateman grimaced and managed a bow.

"And finally," Worth said, "I give you the woman who is the heart of all we do. She helped construct the envelope you see before you and devised a way to more efficiently heat the fuel. Miss Lydia Villers."

Everyone was staring at her. Lydia felt as if she was as light as the balloon and as ready to soar.

"Ah, Miss Villers," Curtis said. "Yes. She and I met to discuss the balloon. I'm glad to hear she passed on my recommendations."

Before Lydia could respond, Worth drew himself up. "Miss Villers's contributions started long before she spoke to Mr. Curtis. Indeed, our work spans far beyond his expertise. We set out to improve each component: fuel, envelope, container, and control. Everything we have accomplished has been carefully documented, and my paper on the subject will be published in the next issue of *Philosophical Transactions*."

That set Charlotte to grinning. Lydia too. *Take that, Curtis!* She had never been prouder of Worth. And it seemed that, against all odds, he was proud of her too. Perhaps they had a chance for a future together after all.

Worth caught Lydia's eye and smiled. The color in her cheeks, the light in her eyes, her radiant smile, all said she was proud of what they'd done. Together, they had fulfilled all his dreams.

He thought he saw Curtis flinch at the news that Worth was publishing about the effort. For once, Worth's contributions would be noted as his own, and Charlotte and the others would be given their due.

But the weasel recovered and nodded. "Excellent. My work has been published there many times. Glad to have you join in, Worthington."

He refused to let the man's interference rattle him.

"As for today," Worth continued to the rest of his audience, "I will enter the container, which my associate Mr. Bateman has filled with bags of hay approximating one hundred and forty pounds. You may verify the weight if you like."

His friend Julian was smiling. Nice to have someone in his camp besides his team. Several of the ministers nearest the prince exchanged glances, but His Royal Highness waved a white-gloved hand. "No need, Worthington. I trust your word."

"Ah, but natural philosophy requires a witness, Your Highness," Curtis advised him. "If you would allow me?"

The prince nodded him forward.

Worth held himself still as the fellow approached. But Curtis wasn't done with his insults. He turned and held out a hand. "Miss Pankhurst, would you assist me? I believe all these fine gentlemen will recognize you as a disinterested party."

"Rubbish," Bateman muttered.

Charlotte shushed him.

"An honor, sir," Miss Pankhurst said in her high-pitched voice. Twirling her ridiculous pointed parasol that was far too large and long for her diminutive stature, she minced over to the balloon within inches of Worth as if he were no more than another of the trees that edged the park. She peered over the rim of the basket. "I see seven bags." Moving around the basket, one hand on the ropes, she reached in and poked each with her parasol. "They appear to be rather densely packed. You would have to estimate the weight, Mr. Curtis. You are much more well versed in such matters." She tittered appreciatively.

Curtis's patronizing smile should have warned the woman he had no real interest in her. "Of course, my dear. With bags of this sort, I would estimate a stone a piece, for a total of one hundred and forty pounds. And I believe you weigh upward of eight stone, my lord."

"One hundred fifty-seven and three-quarter pounds in the clothing I am currently wearing," Worth said, but he addressed the prince and the crowd instead of his rival. "Verified this morning on the scale at Berry Brothers and

Rudd, before witnesses."

"Excellent," said the prince, rubbing his meaty hands together. "That would make the weight of the container nearly three hundred pounds."

"Did the calculation all by himself, did he?" Bateman muttered. This time Charlotte elbowed him into silence.

"Precisely," Mr. Curtis said, though there was nothing precise about the prince's statement. "That should give Your Highness a good sense of the capability of ballooning, at least as far as Lord Worthington has been able to advance it."

"An idea of the capability of *this* balloon," Worth corrected him. "We believe the components scalable. A larger envelope and basket, a more intense heat, and you should have greater scope for transportation."

The prince's gaze traveled over the balloon, and a frown gathered on his brow just as Worth noticed a shadow rippling across the crowd.

"Is it supposed to do that?" His Royal Highness asked.

Charlotte gasped, even as Worth spun to face the balloon. The envelope was beginning to sag, just as it had the day the peat had clogged the fire. Worth's gaze darted to the brazier, which glowed as red as it should.

"What have you done?" Mr. Curtis cried, starting around the balloon for Miss Pankhurst's side.

Miss Pankhurst merely widened her eyes, all innocence, as the weight of the envelope began to collapse. But from the tip of her parasol hung a piece of scarlet silk. Worth's stomach dropped faster than the envelope.

"She's popped it!" Lydia cried.

Beyond them, the crowd began scattering amid gasps of dismay. They were so intent on escape they buffeted the yeoman guards back from their place beside the prince. Curtis left Miss Pankhurst and ran off to one side. Worth had other concerns. He turned and grabbed Lydia's hand. She took hold of Charlotte, who took hold of Miss Janssen, and together they pulled away from the balloon. His Royal Highness stood, more stunned than defiant Worth thought, as the warm silk descended toward him.

"Look out!" Bateman launched himself across the space. He hit the prince midsection, wrapped his arms about the fellow, and dragged him away from the danger.

The envelope thudded as it struck the ground where the prince had stood, then began puddling on the grass, the air hissing out like an angry snake.

The yeoman guard surrounded Bateman, pikes lowered and gazes fierce. He released the prince and held up his hands.

"He assaulted my person," the prince declared, tugging on his coat with hands that shook. "I'll see him hang."

Charlotte started forward. Worth caught her arm. "Don't, Charlotte. You'll only make matters worse."

Lydia stepped around both of them. "Allow me."

Charlotte frowned, but Miss Janssen patted her arm with a smile as if she had complete confidence.

So did Worth. "I would trust no one more than you, Lydia."

Her smile was his reward. She gathered her skirts and hurried toward the group.

# CHAPTER TWENTY-TWO

Of all the titled and wealthy gentlemen in London, the one Beau had never quite managed an introduction to was the prince. That fact did not deter Lydia now. Worth had said he believed in her, had extolled her virtues to some of the most important men in the Empire. Their balloon may lie gasping on the grass, but constructing it had taught her there was nothing she could not do if she set her mind to it.

"Oh, Your Highness!" she cried as she approached, making her eyes as wide as possible. "I am so thankful you are unharmed. Hundreds of pounds of silk and hot air falling toward your head, and you stood so manfully, so heroically. What an example to your adoring subjects!"

The prince put his nose in the air. "One must always try to rise above."

She refused to smile at the pun. "No doubt our prince's bravery is what inspired you, Mr. Bateman," she continued, turning to Worth's bodyguard, who was once more regarding her warily within the wall of pikes. "Only a man who has braved the boxing square and triumphed could truly appreciate what His Highness was doing. The Beast of Birmingham, saving the life of the prince."

Bateman's jaw hardened, but the prince eyed him. "Saving my life, eh? Yes, that's what you were about, wasn't it? Always thought you were a gentleman, despite what the papers said about that last fight."

Bateman must have decided to play along, for he lowered his hands to sketch a bow. "Thank you, Your Highness."

"Well?" the prince demanded, gaze spearing around to his guard. "Lower your weapons. This man is no danger to me."

"None at all," Lydia said blithely, making sure to hide her relief.

The prince was already embroidering the incident. "What an adventure. Staring death in the face, together with the Beast of Birmingham. Remarkable. Amazing! Never fear, sir. You shall have your reward. I promise you that. A shame we don't have any dukedoms lying about." He chuckled at his own wit.

One of his ministers, a tall fellow with sharply shaped sideburns, ventured closer. "Surely not a title, Your Highness. Only think how uncomfortable this fellow would feel with such a sudden and unmerited elevation."

Now Bateman was eyeing him.

"Unmerited?" The prince drew himself up, bulk bristling. "Unmerited, sirrah? This fellow saved my life. I will see him honored."

Lydia drew back, leaving them to argue over the appropriate manner of that honor. Charlotte, Worth, and Miss Janssen joined her.

"Thank you," Charlotte said, reaching out to squeeze her hand. "I couldn't have done half so well."

"*Jah*," Miss Janssen agreed. "Neither could I. I have heard the prince can be temperamental. You did well."

"It's all in the eyes," Lydia said, fluttering her lashes.

"It is considerably more than your lovely eyes," Worth said, and her flutter turned to a blink of surprise. "Your abilities to navigate Society with all its vagaries is an asset to this team. Forgive me for ever thinking otherwise."

Lydia blushed, dropping her chin. Her gaze landed on the sea of scarlet, its once proud stripe now rumpled. "Oh,

Worth! The envelope. Can it be saved?"

"Mr. Curtis doesn't appear to think so," Charlotte said. "Look."

The arrogant scientist stood on the other side of the collapsed envelope, fingers clenching and unclenching at his sides.

"Satisfied with your effort?" Worth called across the space.

Mr. Curtis's head jerked up, and his hair fell to one side like a curtain, revealing his reddening bald spot. "I can't imagine what you mean. I had the highest hopes for this experiment. It was your dalliance that destroyed it."

His dalliance. *His* dalliance? Worth had had enough. He started around the balloon, only vaguely aware of Lydia, Charlotte, and Miss Janssen scurrying in his wake. His indignation must have shown on his face, for Curtis retreated before him until Worth cornered him under one of the trees at the edge of the park.

"I have never dallied with any woman," Worth spit out as the natural philosopher he had once admired huddled against the bark. "You, on the other hand, attempted to convince my sister, my associate, and the woman I love that you were utterly devoted when you are devoted to only one thing—your ability to advance."

Curtis drew himself up, tugging down on his coat with elaborate self-importance, as if he was well aware of the audience behind Worth. "Nonsense. If I showed interest in any of your ladies it was merely as a colleague, sharing matters of joint interest."

"Stealing our work, you mean," Charlotte said around Worth's shoulder. "We are on to you, sir. I wouldn't be surprised if you sent those threatening letters and threw that brick at Worth."

Curtis spread his hands. "My dear Miss Worthington, I have no idea what you mean."

"Don't you?" Worth challenged. "You have done all you could to discredit my work, claim it as your own. Have you no ideas of your own left, man? Is that why you've tried to prevent me from discovering what you couldn't?"

The red climbed in Curtis's face. "You have no idea how hard it is to make a mark. Everything you had was given to you. And you would have squandered it without my guidance."

Could the man be any more insulting? Charlotte took equal umbrage.

"Yet look what he accomplished without you," she stormed. "This balloon, these advancements. And once again, you attempt to claim credit. You disgust me, sir."

Curtis rounded on her. "And you, madam, what have you done except ride on your brother's coattails? Yes, I sent those notes. If I wasn't to be helped, I certainly refused to be hindered or worse, to have my accomplishments claimed as his in spite."

"Spite," Worth said. "Yes, you'd know something about that, wouldn't you? Pure spite must have motivated you to seize a brick and hurl it at my head. But even then, you miscalculated."

Curtis looked as if he wanted to say more, but he pasted on a smile as Julian strolled up with a nod that included them all.

"Gentlemen, ladies. A very interesting demonstration. His Royal Highness would like to know when the balloon can be repaired."

"As quickly as possible," Curtis assured him. "I'll take charge of the matter myself."

Not today. Worth had retreated without protest before. He hadn't trusted his own insights. But he knew what was right now.

"There has been a misunderstanding," Worth told Julian.

"Mr. Curtis has had and will have no part in this effort. I introduced my team. We have faced adversity at every turn, but we will continue to triumph without any aid from Mr. Curtis."

"Now, really," Curtis started.

Charlotte stepped between Worth and him. By Curtis's grimace, she'd also stepped on the fellow's foot.

"Do go on, Worth," she said sweetly.

Lydia beamed as if she knew Charlotte sounded remarkably like her.

"To answer your question," Worth told Julian, who appeared to be trying to hide a smile, "we will need to assess the damage before we can tell whether the envelope can be salvaged, and how long that will take. I will send word as soon as possible."

Curtis leaned around Charlotte. "I would be happy to explain the mechanisms involved to His Royal Highness."

Julian waved a hand. "Thank you, Mr. Curtis, but I don't think that will be necessary. In fact, it is safe to say your services are no longer required. I will convey your regrets to His Highness. And I believe I will have a word with Sir Humphry. It may be time you retired from the Royal Institution." With a bow, he strode off.

"My dear sir," Curtis sputtered, jerking away from Charlotte to hurry after him. "You are mistaken. Allow me to explain myself."

"An interesting turn of events," Charlotte murmured to Worth. "You know Mr. Mayes better than I do. Can he do what he claimed, see Curtis blackballed?"

"I am one hundred percent certain of it," Worth said with a smile after his friend. "Curtis's days of basking in other people's glory are over."

Lydia wiggled her fingers in goodbye. Miss Janssen went to far as to spit after Curtis.

"Well," Charlotte said brightly. "How lovely."

He couldn't argue. For the first time in a long time, he

felt clean, clear, weightless, almost like his balloon.

The envelope of which was rippling in the breeze as it stretched across the grass.

The demonstration aborted, the drama done, most of the crowds had left. The prince was heading for his coach. His yeoman guard had surrounded someone else. Worth could just make out a flash of white among the red and black.

Bateman wandered back to join them.

"Will you be a duke, then?" Miss Janssen asked, eyeing him consideringly.

Bateman snorted. "No. Prinny is known for his enthusiasm, but his ministers will prevent him from doing anything that might embarrass them. I'll be lucky if I see a silver plate for my trouble, much less a fancy title."

"Still, it was very brave of you, Beast," Charlotte said, and he colored.

"I'm prouder of what I did after," he said, nodding to where the guard was marching for St. James's. "I let the guards know who caused the balloon to fall on the prince."

Miss Janssen gasped, while Lydia tilted her head this way and that as if trying to see through the phalanx of pikes.

"Is that Miss Pankhurst?" she asked.

Bateman nodded. "On her way to be questioned. Attempting to kill the monarch is high treason."

"Oh, Beast," Charlotte said, and there was something adoring in the way she said it.

Worth turned to Bateman, who was nearly as red as the fallen silk. "Nicely done. Can you see this bundled up and returned to the house?"

"Of course," his bodyguard said. Then he frowned. "What will you be doing?"

"Rectifying another matter," Worth assured him. He turned to Lydia. She was still watching the retreating guard, her eyes bright and smile winsome. His heart started beating faster.

"You've said little since I confronted Curtis," he told her.

"Why?"

She turned her gaze to his, the green as welcoming as the soft grass of the park. "You said Mr. Curtis attempted to convince your sister, your associate, and the woman you love. All your associates have vied for your attention. Miss Janssen says you do not love her. You clearly have no love for Miss Pankhurst."

Worth smiled. "Your logic is flawless. There is only one woman I have ever loved. To my shame, I sent her away once, but I never stopped loving her."

"Me?" The word came out a squeak.

"You," Worth assured her as the park, their eager audience, and his beloved balloon faded from his mind. Amazing how one woman brought such clarity.

"I offered for you the night we were stranded in the balloon," he said, "and you refused me. Unlike Mr. Curtis, I am not as persuasive as I should be."

He went down on one knee as she gazed at him in wonder. "Allow me to try once more to convince you. I love you, Lydia. I adore your enthusiasm, your clever mind, your willingness to work at a goal even when things seem hopeless. You help me rise above my foibles and faults. You give me insights I never thought possible. Together, I believe we can make our lives better, the world better. Will you do me the honor of marrying me?"

Lydia clasped her hands together to keep them from trembling. Charlotte, Miss Janssen, and Bateman were all watching, and she thought at least one had ceased breathing, waiting for Lydia's answer. Below her, Worth gazed up, smile tender, sweet. She wouldn't make him wait another second, not even for a new chronometer.

"Yes," she said. "Yes, always and forever."

Worth surged to his feet and wrapped her in his arms. In

his kiss was the answer to every question she had ever had, every dream she had dared to dream. They had taken a year to come back to each other, but it was nothing compared to all the years to come, together.

"I love you," she said when he raised his head. "I always will."

His gaze did not leave her face, as if he could not get enough of her. "Charlotte," he said. "I need your help."

His sister stepped closer, smile bright and tears in her eyes. "Anything, Worth. And congratulations to you both. I couldn't be happier."

Bateman and Miss Janssen echoed her congratulations.

"You saw Lady Lilith's wedding," Worth said, arms still about Lydia. "All the furbelows and gewgaws and fuss."

Charlotte glanced at Lydia, smile turning to dismay. "I did. I know it must have seemed ostentatious, Worth, but it was the kind of wedding most women want."

"So I surmised," he said. "I intend to surpass it."

Charlotte stared at him.

Oh, the darling man. Lydia giggled. "Don't worry, Charlotte. It doesn't have to be elaborate. I'd be content to marry your brother in a barn."

"Nonsense," Worth said. "I want all of London to know how happy I am with my bride. Book Westminster. Ask the prince to loan us his chef. Buy every flower from the sellers in Covent Garden. Invite everyone."

Now Charlotte was laughing along with Lydia. "I'll do my best. It might take a few months."

"A fortnight," Worth declared. "I'll wait no longer."

A fortnight? Well, she didn't want to wait longer either. What would Beau say when he returned from his honeymoon and discovered she was Lady Worthington?

*Lady Worthington.* She would never have thought it possible.

Charlotte shook her head. "And I suspect I must make arrangements for a honeymoon trip as well."

"No," Lydia answered before Worth could. "That I will plan. I think we'll travel in the Alps."

Worth stuck out his lower lip thoughtfully.

"In our balloon," Lydia concluded. "You'll need to know whether it can survive colder temperatures, greater heights."

He threw back his head and laughed.

Lydia hugged him close. Truly, it didn't matter where or when they married or took their wedding trip. She had vied for a viscount and given him her heart a year ago, and now she knew she held his heart as well. The future would be as bright and expansive as a scarlet balloon. And she would make sure it never deflated.

# CHAPTER TWENTY-THREE

A fortnight later, Meredith stood in Hyde Park among a crowd of people. It seemed everyone in London had turned out for the wedding of Viscount Worthington and Lydia Villers. The bride's brother Beau and his wife had even returned from their honeymoon early to attend. Most of the guests had accompanied them here, where their balloon waited, approved and lauded by the prince. The only person who looked the least uncomfortable was Mr. Bateman, and Meredith could only suppose the slumped shoulders came from humility. It had been in all the papers that he was to be knighted by the prince for his valor.

Now Lydia blew kisses to friends and family, while Worth looked so pleased he might have lifted the balloon from sheer joy alone. Men threw top hats in the air and ladies waved lace-edged handkerchiefs as the jaunty scarlet balloon, now boasting both a blue and a white stripe, rose into the sky. The pair planned to land near Ipswich before boarding a ship for Belgium.

Below the basket, playing out the rope with Mr. Bateman, Julian kept his gaze on the balloon. He had stood up with Lord Worthington as best man and had taken his duties so seriously he hadn't done more than shoot a smile in Meredith's direction. Much as she delighted in his smiles, she could not help wishing for more.

Meredith sighed as she turned away. Her arms always felt

empty without Fortune in them. She hadn't dared bring the cat to the park for fear of losing her. Meredith rather thought her house would feel empty without Lydia's smiling presence.

"Miss Thorn."

Meredith glanced back to see who had called. Charlotte Worthington strolled up, carriage serene, grey silk skirts brushing the gravel of the path.

"Miss Worthington," Meredith acknowledged. "Congratulations. I understand from Lydia that you made most of the wedding arrangements. Well done."

"I was happy to help," Charlotte assured her, tucking a stray auburn hair back under her feathered hat. "And I'm glad you could attend. May I beg a moment of your time to discuss business?"

Interesting. Lydia had said Lord Worthington intended to continue his studies on their return. Perhaps his sister wished to locate another lady to assist.

"It would be my pleasure," Meredith said.

Charlotte nodded toward the path, and the two commenced strolling toward the Serpentine.

"I cannot forget how you brought Lydia to us," the viscount's sister murmured, gaze on the greenery they passed. "You are an excellent advocate for your clients. How would a lady go about becoming one?"

Meredith faltered, but she made herself keep walking, mind busy. She had once considered approaching Charlotte about helping her find her future. But Charlotte was not her usual sort of client. She had no need to work for a living, and she'd seemed more than content lately with her role in her brother's work.

"I generally choose my clients based on an interview," she allowed. "I then place them according to needs I become aware of from time to time. I take it you know someone who'd like a position."

"Yes," Charlotte said. She drew in a breath. "Me."

"Indeed." Meredith paused as they drew near the water, trying to gather her thoughts. "May I ask why?"

Charlotte picked up a stone and tossed it into the Serpentine, sending ripples widening in every direction. "I am an oddity, Miss Thorn. I was raised to be a lady of Society, but I find I have little interest in it, and even less in the marriage mart. I would rather be useful, purposeful. And I find my purpose waning."

"You no longer wish to pursue natural philosophy?" Meredith asked.

"I have found it quite stimulating," Charlotte admitted, "but in truth I did what I thought Worth needed. We were both young when our parents passed. We learned to rely on each other."

The summer breeze tugged at Meredith's curls. "And will he support you in this decision? Some families react poorly when a lady chooses a direction they cannot appreciate."

Charlotte addressed the view instead of Meredith. "I haven't told Worth yet. But I don't require his support, at least not financially. My mother left me a small inheritance."

"So you have no need to work for a living," Meredith confirmed.

"Only the need for something new, some place new," Charlotte agreed, turning. "Worth and Lydia deserve a home together, without my interference."

Meredith had seen a few ladies who had grown bored with their lot. "A nice holiday in the Lakes District won't suffice?" she queried.

Charlotte made a face. "I don't do well in peace and quiet. I need challenges, worthwhile pursuits. Something to take my mind off…other matters."

Other matters? What was her potential client not saying? Charlotte's gaze had gone back the way they had come. Most of the crowd was dispersing. The two most prominent that remained were Mr. Bateman and Julian. Charlotte sighed. And all became clear.

Normally, she had one other requirement for her clients: that Fortune approve of them. Fortune was fond of Charlotte Worthington. And she had already approved of the gentleman Meredith had in mind.

"I may have an opportunity," Meredith said, and Charlotte turned to give her full attention. "It might require patience and hard work, but it is quite suitable for a lady like yourself."

"Do tell," Charlotte said, grey eyes bright.

"A low-born gentleman will shortly be elevated for services to the crown," Meredith said. "He will need guidance, lessons in etiquette, if he is to succeed in his new estate."

Charlotte nodded. "An etiquette teacher. I could be persuaded to try that for a while. Perhaps by the time the gentleman is sufficiently prepared, I'll know what to do next."

Meredith smiled. "You might at that. It will take me a few days to make the arrangements. Stop by on Tuesday next, and I will introduce you to your knight in shining armor."

"I cannot thank you enough," Charlotte said, just as Julian began heading in their direction. As if she were guilty of some indiscretion, she blushed. "I should go."

Meredith wished her well and watched as she hurried past Julian, who tipped his top hat to her. Dressed in a bottle green coat that made his hair appear all the more gold, he drew up beside her and sketched a bow. "Ready?"

Meredith blinked. "Ready? For what?"

"Didn't Cowls tell you? I sent word this morning. Ices at Gunter's, and then home to change for dinner with Carrolton and Yvette. And tomorrow evening, I have tickets for the two of us to the theatre." He paused as she stared at him, and his look turned wary. "Unless you're otherwise engaged, of course."

"No, no," Meredith managed. "Not at all." She wished

again Fortune could be with her. That thick fur would hide the trembling of her hands. "Julian, are you certain you wish to make such a public spectacle?"

"In public, with my friends, and with yours," he assured her, smile so warm her doubts fluttered away like startled moths. "I want no more misunderstandings as to my feelings for you."

He took her hands. "I realize my behavior has been suspect, Meredith. But if I have been guilty of anything, it is selfishly keeping you to myself. I am honored by your company and delighted to let others see how much I admire you. Let them try to chastise us for our love. I have only one question."

Heart full, Meredith gazed up into his dear face. "Ask it."

His eyes twinkled. "What's your favorite ice?"

Meredith tossed her head. "That, sir, you will shortly discover. And I look forward to the many treats to come."

Dear Reader

Thank you for choosing Lydia and Worth's story. Lydia had a bumpy road to finding true love, but I knew she could do it. If you missed her introduction to the Fortune's Brides series, look for *Never Borrow a Baronet*. Likewise, you can find Meredith and Julian's Christmas proposal in the novella, "Always Kiss at Christmas," in *A Yuletide Regency* anthology.

If you enjoyed this book, there are several things you could do now:

Sign up for a free email alert at **http://eepurl.com/baqwVT** with exclusive bonus content so you'll be the first to know whenever a new book is out or on sale.

Post a review on a bookseller or reader site to help others find the book.

Discover my many other books on my website at **www.reginascott.com.**

Turn the page for a sneak peek of the fifth book in the series, *Never Kneel to a Knight,* in which Charlotte Worthington must come to terms with her past as she counsels a certain former boxer and his passel of little sisters on how to navigate the waters of Society. In doing so, she just may discover that she will risk all for one knight of love.

Blessings!

*Regina Scott*

Sneak Peek
# NEVER KNEEL TO A KNIGHT
Book 5 in the Fortune's Brides Series by Regina Scott

*London, England, June 1812*

Charlotte Worthington peered out of the hired coach as it came to a stop on a narrow lane beyond Covent Garden. The houses were respectable—one room front and back on three levels, with an attic above for one or two servants. But the red brick facades with their white-framed windows were grimed with soot, and the stone stoop wanted sweeping.

"A knight of the realm lives here?" she asked.

Miss Thorn, seated across from her, gathered her cat Fortune close as she prepared to alight. Very likely she wasn't as nervous as Charlotte. She owned the employment agency, after all, and had arranged positions for other ladies of quality. Not a strand of her raven hair was out of place where it showed under a hat the exact shade of lavender as her eyes, and her lavender-striped day dress had nary a crease.

"His elevation is scheduled for the next fortnight," she explained, voice as cool and competent as her look. "This is his family home. He recently returned to it."

Perhaps he had been stationed in India or the Caribbean and was only now taking up the honor he had earned in service to the kingdom. She pictured a white-haired military fellow, still fit and trim, but perhaps wounded at one point in battle. Helping him navigate the intricacies of Society would be a worthwhile pursuit.

She certainly needed one. Ever since her father had died ten years ago when she was fourteen, her life had revolved around her older brother, Frederick, Viscount Worthington. She had lived in his home, gone through the requirement of a few London Seasons, then retired to run his house and help him with his scientific endeavors. Now Worth was married, and Charlotte was feeling extremely *de trop*. She admired his bride Lydia too much to wish to confuse the servants with two mistresses in the same house. And then there was Beast.

No, she would not think of Beast. As much as she admired him, he could have no place in her life. She was only glad Miss Thorn and dear Fortune had been willing to find her a respectable occupation to fill her time and augment her small inheritance.

Etiquette teacher to the newly elevated.

The title rang of nobility. She would be helping someone achieve a dream, encouraging them to grow. Worth had always served that role with her. Now she would pass that along to others.

Her head was high as they swept up to the door.

A blond girl of about ten answered Miss Thorn's knock, her pinafore wrinkled over her gingham dress. Wide brown eyes gazed at them, unblinking.

"We already gave," she announced, pointed chin in the

air.

"How commendable," Miss Thorn said, catching the door before the girl could close it on them. "But we're here to see your brother."

"Petunia?" A woman a little younger than Charlotte glided out of the doorway on the right. She had brown hair pulled back from a heart-shaped face and the same wide brown eyes. Her day dress of madras cotton betrayed a buxom figure. Petunia's older sister, most likely. Did that mean she was the daughter of Charlotte's intended pupil?

Seeing Miss Thorn and Charlotte, she hurried forward.

"Petunia, what have I told you about opening the door to strangers?" she scolded. She pointed to the curving stairs behind her, and Petunia traipsed up them obediently enough. As her sister turned her back on the girl, however, Petunia stopped on the landing to watch, hands bracing the polished wood balusters.

"May I help you?" the older sister asked, all polite inquiry now.

"I am Miss Thorn of the Fortune Employment Agency," Charlotte's companion said, "come to see the master of the house about a position." Fortune's tail swept back and forth as if to confirm the matter.

The young lady glanced between Miss Thorn and Charlotte, frown gathering. "I manage this household. We have no positions open, and certainly nothing for a lady."

"But you do have three young ladies and their brother who require tutoring in deportment," Miss Thorn said.

Three young ladies? All her pupil's sisters, by the sound of it. He must be unmarried, or she and Miss Thorn would have been presented to his wife.

The young lady in the doorway drew herself up. "I have done my best to school my sisters in deportment. Who told you we needed assistance?"

"Why your brother himself," Miss Thorn said.

Fortune stood in her arms and leveled her gaze on the

lady in the doorway. She blinked, Fortune blinked. She smiled.

"Your pet is lovely," she murmured, raising a hand, then hesitating. "May I?"

"Of course," Miss Thorn said.

Slowly, gently, she stroked a hand down the silky grey fur. Fortune stretched against the touch, mouth turning up for all the world as if she was smiling. The young lady's answering smile spoke of beauty within and without.

"If you could point me in your brother's direction," Miss Thorn said, "we can move forward."

As if mesmerized by the cat, the young lady stepped out of the doorway and let them in.

"Please wait in the sitting room, miss," she said to Charlotte with a nod to the room she'd excited. She turned for the stairs, where Petunia had disappeared now, and led Miss Thorn and Fortune upward.

Charlotte wandered into the sitting room. It was neat and clean, but well lived in. The tapestry-covered sofa had hills in places and valleys in others. The wooden arms of the two chairs opposite it were chipped, the wounds pale against the walnut. The rose-patterned wallpaper was fading to pink and mint. On the oak mantel over the hearth stood several miniatures in simple wood frames. She had just picked up one of a blond lady with a weary smile and Petunia's brown eyes when she heard a noise behind her.

"Oh!"

Turning, she found another young lady framed in the doorway. She looked about the age to make her debut. Like her younger sister and the woman in the miniature, she had sunny blond hair and liberally lashed brown eyes, and her figure was nearly as curvaceous as her sister's in her muslin day dress.

"Tuny said someone was here to help Matty become a knight," she said, sashaying into the room with far more confidence than Charlotte had had at that age. "But I never expected a lady."

Matty? Matthew, perhaps? A strong, proper name that touched her heart. And Tuny was clearly short for Petunia.

"I would be delighted to be of service to you and your brother," Charlotte told her. "After he's knighted, you may find yourself in higher circles."

Her eyes narrowed as if she doubted that, and Charlotte had an odd feeling they'd met before. But that was impossible. She'd never been to this part of London, and she hadn't associated with the ladies making their debuts in years.

"Higher circles?" she queried, the breathlessness of the question belying the skepticism in her gaze.

"She's bamming you, Daisy." Petunia squeezed past her sister into the room. "They want something from Matty, just like everyone else since his name was in the paper. Ask them why they really came to see us."

Daisy cocked her head. "Do you even know my brother?"

It was on the tip of her tongue to deny it, but something stopped her. She did know one man—one powerful, wonderful man Fate had decreed was forever beyond her reach. He had been highly featured in the papers lately. When one saved the life of the Prince Regent, one became something of a celebrity. And he tended to narrow his eyes on occasion, eyes the same shade of brown as Daisy's.

Her stomach collided with her lungs, pushing the breath from her body. Somehow, she managed to speak anyway.

"There's been a mistake," she said, hurrying past the girls. "A dreadful mistake. Miss Thorn!"

"See?" Petunia said as she and her sister followed Charlotte out into the entry hall. "I told you she was up to something."

Neither the oldest sister nor Miss Thorn answered Charlotte's call. She couldn't go through with this. She'd started down this path not only to give her brother and his bride space, but to distance herself from Bateman, otherwise known as the Beast of Birmingham. She had to stop Miss Thorn from agreeing to an alliance. Charlotte lifted her skirts and began climbing.

The soon-to-be Sir Matthew Bateman eyed the woman who'd been brought up to see him. Ivy had been highly apologetic.

"I'm terribly sorry, Matty," she'd said, shifting from foot to foot and setting her skirts to rustling. "I know you asked us for some peace and quiet this morning. I'll just leave you to it and get back to helping Anna with the baking."

He'd thanked his sister and watched as another woman entered the room. It wasn't as if Ivy had interrupted anything important. He'd been standing in the dining room, back to the scarred wood table, looking out at the rear garden, which seemed to consist mostly of scraggly weeds. Well, why was he surprised? The space was barely a dozen feet square. He had no need for a gardener. And what did his sisters know about raising plants, for all their mother had named them after the things?

Besides, why did he care that it didn't look like a proper garden? Until recently, he'd been proud to earn his living, providing a home, clothing, and food for his sisters. All this lazing about was eating at his brain, what hadn't been pounded out during his boxing days.

But that wasn't why he was curt to his visitor. He'd met Miss Thorn before and knew exactly what she could do to cut up a man's peace.

"Not interested," he said, crossing his arms over his chest. The coat pulled at his shoulders. Most of the second-hand coats he'd been able to purchase did. They weren't cut for a fellow of his size and activities. Very likely now that he was being awarded an hereditary knighthood he'd be expected to bespeak a proper coat from a proper tailor.

All because Prinny wanted to be generous.

"You haven't heard my proposal," Miss Thorn pointed out.

The cat in her arms regarded him with eyes like copper pennies. He'd far rather converse with the cat than her mistress. Cats were sensible things, useful. His sisters had wanted a cat for years. Did knights own pets?

"Don't need to hear your proposal," Matthew told the woman. "We don't need any fancy ladies in this house."

"Ah, then you are prepared for your knighting ceremony."

His gut tightened as if prepared to deflect a blow. "It's one day. I'll survive."

"And your sisters?" she inquired politely. "How well will they survive the change?"

Matthew lowered his arms. "What do my sisters have to do with this?"

"They will find themselves moving in different circles," she said primly. "With the right teacher, they could make advantageous marriages."

He'd seen enough of the upper classes to know that not all marriages were as advantageous as they seemed, but then, the aristocracy weren't the only ones to marry poorly. If he had any say in the matter, Ivy, Daisy, and Petunia would marry fine men who would love and respect them, not like the father none of them had mourned when he'd died as drunk as he'd lived. His sisters were smart and pretty and capable. Why shouldn't they marry a wealthy banker or even a lord like Viscount Worthington?

"So, you've brought me such a teacher, have you?" he asked the raven-haired woman in lavender before him. "Ivy seems a bit old for a governess."

"I prefer to think of my client as an etiquette teacher," she said. "A lady of breeding and taste who has herself been presented at court and survived more than one London Season."

Matthew narrowed his eyes. "If she's that much of a lady,

why does she need a position?"

She ran a hand back along her pet's fur, and the cat closed her eyes contentedly. "Her brother recently married, and she feels uncomfortable staying any longer in his home."

He could understand that. Their mother had died shortly after Tuny had been born, when Matthew was already out of the house and working as a carrier for the local inn, fighting prize matches on the side to earn extra money. Their father had married again, claiming the need for someone to watch over for his daughters, but their stepmother had turned Matthew's sisters, particularly Ivy, into her personal servants. It had been worse after his father had died, with the woman threatening them with the poor house if they failed to do her least bidding.

As soon as he'd won his first sizeable purse, he'd moved to London and brought them with him. Ivy had raised their sisters, taking over the running of the household when he'd begun working as a bodyguard for Lord Worthington a year ago.

"We don't have a spare bed," he warned Miss Thorn. "She'd have to stay elsewhere."

"She'll be staying with me for a time," Miss Thorn said. "I would expect a fair wage and transportation back to my establishment each day she's helping you, say Tuesdays, Thursdays, and Saturdays, for several hours."

That wouldn't be so bad. His sisters might gain the advantage, and he might learn a few things to keep from embarrassing himself when presented to the prince. And if he did this service for a lady, he might forget the one lady he could never have.

"All right," he agreed. "She can start tomorrow."

"No!"

Matthew blinked, turning to stare at the beauty in the doorway. That thick auburn hair with its fiery highlights, the flashing grey eyes, the lithe figure, supple as a sapling. Once more his gut clenched.

"Miss…Miss Worthington?" he stammered.

She rushed into the room, so unlike her usually poised and graceful self that he knew something terrible had happened. He strode to meet her.

"What is it?" he demanded, taking her hands. "Is it your brother? Has there been another threatening letter?"

"No, no." She pulled away, gathering her dignity like a queenly robe. Drawing an audible breath through her nose, she raised her head and met his gaze, hers now cool, emotionless.

"There's been a mistake," she said firmly. "I'm sorry we troubled you."

Matthew glanced between her and Miss Thorn, realization dawning and bringing horror with it. "*You're* the impoverished lady I'll be helping?"

Her delicate chin hardened until he would have been afraid to face her across the boxing square. "Scarcely impoverished, sir. Nor are you the white-haired general I was promised."

Miss Thorn gathered her cat closer, smile still pleasant. "I never claimed Miss Worthington was impoverished, and I certainly never commented on the color of Mr. Bateman's hair. I see no reason to protest, unless you can give me good reason, Miss Worthington."

She opened her mouth, closed it again, then bit her lip. Such a pretty lip too, pink and warm looking. Matthew snapped his gaze to her face. Were those tears in her eyes? What had he done that was so terrible? How could he make it up to her?

"I have worked with Mr. Bateman in the past," she said. "I do not believe continued connection to be appropriate."

Now, there was a facer. Still, what did he expect? The prince might want to honor him, but most men looking at him would see the Beast of Birmingham, a boxer so brutal he had permanently maimed a man in a fight. The latest round of press in the papers had only brought the sordid story up anew.

"I concur," he said, voice and body heavy.

Miss Thorn sailed for the door. "A pity. The negotiations are concluded. I have accepted your offer of employment for Miss Worthington's time. She will start tomorrow at eleven. No need to thank me. The results will speak for themselves."

Learn more at
*www.reginascott.com/neverkneeltoaknight.html*

# OTHER BOOKS BY REGINA SCOTT

## FORTUNE'S BRIDES SERIES
Never Doubt a Duke
Never Borrow a Baronet
Never Envy an Earl

## UNCOMMON COURTSHIPS SERIES
The Unflappable Miss Fairchild
The Incomparable Miss Compton
The Irredeemable Miss Renfield
The Unwilling Miss Watkin
An Uncommon Christmas

## LADY EMILY CAPERS
Secrets and Sensibilities
Art and Artifice
Ballrooms and Blackmail
Eloquence and Espionage
Love and Larceny

## MARVELOUS MUNROES SERIES
My True Love Gave to Me
Catch of the Season
The Marquis' Kiss
Sweeter Than Candy

## SPY MATCHMAKER SERIES
The Husband Mission
The June Bride Conspiracy
The Heiress Objective

Perfection

And other books for Love Inspired Historical and
Timeless Regency collections.

# ABOUT THE AUTHOR

Regina Scott started writing novels in the third grade. Thankfully for literature as we know it, she didn't sell her first novel until she learned a bit more about writing. Since her first book was published, her stories have traveled the globe, with translations in many languages including Dutch, German, Italian, and Portuguese. She now has more than forty published works of warm, witty romance.

She has spent many years dealing with scientists and science, working as a communications specialist and then scientist at a major national laboratory, though she never had Lydia's winning ways to recommend her. Her critique partner and dear friend Kristy J. Manhattan, who she met through her scientific work, helped her come up with the idea for Fortune's Brides. Kristy is an avid fan of cats, supporting spay and neuter clinics and pet rescue groups. If Fortune resembles any cat you know, credit Kristy.

Regina Scott and her husband of 30 years reside in the Puget Sound area of Washington State on the way to Mt. Rainier. She has dressed as a Regency dandy, driven four-in-hand, learned to fence, and sailed on a tall ship, all in the name of research, of course. Learn more about her at her website at *www.reginascott.com*.

CPSIA information can be obtained
at www.ICGtesting.com
Printed in the USA
LVHW091707081019
633564LV00005B/817/P